Pucked Up

Pucked Up

New York Times Bestselling Author

HELENA HUNTING

Entangled Publishing, LLC
644 Shrewsbury Commons Ave., STE 181
Shrewsbury, PA 17361
rights@entangledpublishing.com

Amara is an imprint of Entangled Publishing, LLC.

Visit our website at www.entangledpublishing.com.

Edited by Jessica Royer Ocken
Cover art and design by Elizabeth Turner Stokes
Edges illustrated by Elizabeth Turner Stokes
Stock art by royalmix/pixelsquid, royalmix/Pixelsquid,
and Paisarn Praha/shutterstock
Interior design by Britt Marczak

ISBN 978-1-64937-864-4 (Paperback)

Manufactured in the United States of America

First Edition January 2025

10 9 8 7 6 5 4 3 2 1

AMARA
an imprint of Entangled Publishing LLC

To my family, thank you for having my back, for being my cheerleaders and for letting me foster this dream. I love you.

Pucked Up is a hilarious and sexy stand-alone hockey romance. However, the story includes elements that might not be suitable for all readers including the loss of a parent in childhood, the use of edibles, and sex on the page—*several* pages. Readers who may be sensitive to these elements, please take note.

1

Make Better Choices

-MILLER-

"Whoever said shots were a good idea was wrong," I mumble as I attempt to put one foot in front of the other, passing the line of people waiting to get into the exclusive club we're leaving. "I need my bed." And several bottles of water. And probably a painkiller to ward off the headache already knocking at my temples.

Lance, my teammate puts a hand on my shoulder, his grin as sloppy me. "Your car's at my place, Butterson. Come back with us."

"I can get it in the morning."

"Just get in the limo, man." Lance looks to Randy, another teammate and one of my closest childhood friends, for backup.

"The trainer'll be at Lance's at ten-thirty, remember?" Randy says, in far better condition than me. "You can roll out of bed and right into the pool."

"Then I don't have to call you fifty times to get your ass up,"

Lance adds.

"Come back with us, Buck!"

One of Lance's new friends uses the nickname I've answered to since I was a kid. My real name is Miller. I wasn't named after beer. Buck Butterson has a nicer ring than Miller Butterson—one too many "ers".

The three women Lance has convinced to come back to his place are fixing each other's hair and messing with each other's makeup while I debate my options.

Lance smiles—all horny bastard—and pats me on the back. "Come on, man, you'll be away for a couple weeks. Last chance to party it up."

I mumble something even I can't understand and lean on the limo because the whole world feels like a Tilt-A-Whirl.

I wait while everyone files into the limo.

Lance holds on to the door frame, and leans down. "Whose lap am I sitting on?" He throws himself into the limo.

The girls squeal, and laughter follows.

Randy claps me on the shoulder. "Don't worry, Miller. I always have your back."

"Appreciate it," I mutter.

Randy is one of the few people who uses my real name, aside from my dad. Growing up in Chicago, he lived down the street from me. We've played hockey together since we learned how to skate. We ended up on different teams when we made the pros.

Five years later, we're on the same team. Being offseason, it took him all of two weeks to move back to the city. It's good to have him here. We've stayed tight over the years; if anyone can help me deflect excited bunnies, it's him.

Randy gets into the limo and sits between two of the women. This leaves the bench seat wide open for me. I slide in and stretch out, taking up the entire thing.

Lance already has his arm around one of them, and her friend in the middle seems like she's not sure what to do. When she makes a move to sit with me, Lance hugs her to his side and whispers something in her ear. Her eyes widen, but she stays where she is.

Going home in a cab by myself would've been the smarter move. Then I wouldn't be in a situation where I might have to make chit-chat with one of Lance's friends. It can get awkward. Especially since I'm not on the market like Lance and Randy are.

I should've said no to going out tonight. But Lance is persuasive, and he's right, I'm out of town for a couple weeks starting tomorrow.

I close my eyes and lean against the armrest. I'm tired. And hungry. I need pizza.

I root around in my pocket for my phone. I have messages: a couple of texts and a voice memo from my sister, Violet, and a few more from my girlfriend, Sunny. Well, I want her to be my girlfriend. I'm flying out to see her tomorrow, and hoping to make it all official.

I've been doing everything I can to move things in the girlfriend direction for the last few months, but she's not easily charmed. It doesn't help that her brother, Alex Waters, is the captain of my team, and he's not my biggest fan. He's also engaged to my sister.

It's a complicated situation. Last season I was traded to Chicago —for reasons. I may have made a bad choice that involved my former coach's niece and a viral photo. I've learned my lesson. Unfortunately, that kind of shit tends to haunt my ass.

And then I met Sunny. The second I laid eyes on her I knew

I was screwed. She's sweet, genuine, fun. And my teammate's sister. She should have been completely off-limits. But then Waters is dating my sister, so why can't I date his?

I try to read my text messages, but my vision is blurry, and the words all jumble together—even worse than usual. Fucking shots. I can't use the text-to-speech because the music's too loud. Plus my sister has no filter. At all. She's liable to say something embarrassing.

"I'm hungry. Anyone else hungry?" I yell over the music.

Lance is too busy sucking face, but Randy raises his hand. The girls on either side of him shrug. The one stuck in the middle of everything looks like she'd rather be anywhere but here.

I pull up Siri and ask her to call my favorite pizza joint. Someone turns the music down which helps immensely.

"Is the address five-two-one or two-five-one?" I ask Randy when they get to that part of the ordering process.

"Five-two-one."

"You're sure it's not two-five-one?"

Lance takes a break from making out to say, "You've been at my house a million times."

I flip him the bird. "I'm dyslexic and drunk, but thanks for being an asshole about it." I give the pizza guy the right address. Then I end the call and slip my phone back into my pocket.

Ten minutes later, we pull into Lance's driveway. We stumble into the house.

"Let's hit the hot tub," Lance suggests.

"I'll stay here until the pizza arrives, yeah?"

"If you want," Lance guides the women through the house.

"You good, man?" Randy asks.

I give him a thumbs up and he follows the rest of them

through the sliding door, to the back deck. I get comfy on the couch and wait for the pizza. When it arrives, I make a half-hearted attempt to let the rest of them know, but honestly, I don't want to risk going out there and witnessing a hot tub orgy, which wouldn't be a surprise when it comes to Lance. Or Randy.

I want to call Sunny, but need carbs to absorb some of the alcohol before I do that. I devour half the box, drink two bottles of water, then drag my ass upstairs to one of the spare bedrooms. Kicking the door closed, I pull my shirt over my head, drop my pants and boxers, and fall face down on the mattress. I'm half-asleep when I remember I still have voice memos and I want to at least leave Sunny one before I pass out.

I wish she lived closer. Canada isn't that far from Chicago, but it's enough distance that it makes this whole dating thing that much harder.

Calling her is a bad idea. I'm still half-drunk, and she's probably asleep, but my logic filter is on the fritz, so I feel around for my pants and dig the phone out of my pocket. The battery is at nine percent. It's enough for a quick call. It'll probably go to voicemail anyway.

As predicted, it rings four times, and I get her message. I smile as I listen.

"You've reached Sunshine Waters. I'm probably busy centering myself, or teaching a class, but when I'm done I'll give you a dingle. I hope your day is as beautiful as you!"

I end the call and try again. And again. Third time's the charm.

"Hello?" Her voice is sleep raspy. It's reminiscent of how she sounds when she comes. I've only had the pleasure of putting my hands on her so far, but she's worth the wait.

"Hey, sweets. Did I wake you?" Of course I woke her; I

called three times in the middle of the night.

"Miller?"

"I'm sorry. It's late isn't it?" I roll over onto my back and starfish. The rustle of sheets filters through the phone. I imagine what she might be wearing based on our late-night video chats. She's a baggy-shirt-and-shorts girl.

"What time is it?"

"Uh," I squint at the clock on the nightstand, as if that will make it easier to read the numbers. I'm better with analog than digital clocks. "Pretty early."

"In the morning?"

"Yeah."

"Is everything okay?"

"Yeah."

There's a long pause in which neither of us speaks. "Were you out with the boys tonight?"

"Yeah."

The softness in her voice is replaced by sharpness. "Who?"

"The usual. Randy and Lance. A few of the other guys showed up later."

"So you're drunk?"

Lance and shots always go hand in hand.

I shouldn't have called. I wish I had someone around to stop me from doing stupid shit all the time. Most of the time Lance isn't much help. He encourages bad decision-making.

"I had a few drinks. I wanted to hear your voice." I cringe. I can't decide if that sounds like a line, or the cheesy truth it is. "The whole time we were out all I could think about was getting home so I could see how your day was."

She makes a little noise, like maybe she's stretching or trying to get comfortable. "That's sweet, Miller."

I love that she uses my real name instead of my nickname.

"But don't you think it would be better to call when you're sober and it's not the middle of the night? You interrupted a nice dream."

"What kind of dream? Was it a sex dream?"

"I'm not telling you."

"It was, wasn't it?"

She hums, but doesn't confirm or deny it.

"I'll take care of you tomorrow when I see you."

"Don't get ahead of yourself." She sighs. "You should sleep off whatever you drank so you're not tired when you get here."

There's a knock on the door. Randy's voice is followed by a feminine giggle. I hold the phone against my chest and shout, "I'm sleeping!" I bring the phone back to my ear. "Sorry about that."

"Who's with you?"

"I'm at Lance's."

She inhales sharply. "Are you staying there overnight?"

"Natasha's coming in the morning."

"Who?"

"Our trainer. We're using Lance's pool for plyometrics. And my car's here, and I'm being responsible by not driving."

"Are there girls there now?"

"Lance invited some friends back. I'm in bed."

"How many friends?"

"A few. But I went straight to bed." A long silence follows. I shouldn't have called. Now she'll worry. "Sunny? You still there?"

"I'm here. I should go, though. It's late. I teach yoga first thing in the morning."

"You sure you don't want to tell me about your dream? I'll make notes for tomorrow."

That gets a half-hearted laugh. "You're impossible. You

should lock your door. 'Night, Miller."

My phone dies before I can answer. I don't have a charger handy, and I'm too tired to put clothes back on and look for one. So I close my eyes and pass fuck out.

2

Dickface

-Miller-

My head hurts, and my mouth tastes like ass. I try not to move, but I can hear horrible music coming from somewhere outside my room, and it's ruining my sleep. I crack a lid and cringe at the brightness coming through the curtains. The first thing I notice is that I'm not in my own bed. I'm at Lance's. I have a very vague recollection of a limo ride and eating pizza.

I lie in the bed that's not mine, trying to remember the end of my night. I reposition my pillow over my head to drown out the bad music.

I'm drifting off when there's a knock at the door. "Natasha will be here in twenty. Get your ass out of bed, Butterson," Randy calls.

I peek out from under the pillow and stare at the numbers on the clock, willing them to stop moving around so I can read them. It's after nine. My phone alarm should've gone off half an hour ago.

I lie there for another minute before I muster the energy to drag my sorry ass out of bed. Natasha has been our trainer since I was traded from Miami to Chicago. She's tough, but awesome. And if I'm late, she'll make me do sprints. I'm in no condition for those.

I check the nightstand for my phone, frowning when I come up empty. It's not on the floor either, so I sweep my hand across the comforter to see if I accidentally brought it to bed. I find it under the pillow. I hope I didn't drunk dial Sunny.

I bring my phone to the bathroom, pushing the button so I can key in my password and check my messages, but the screen stays blank. My battery must have died. I set it on the back of the toilet and flip up the seat. I'm hard, so relieving myself is impossible.

If my phone wasn't dead, I'd pull up a picture of Sunny (fully clothed) and take care of my problem. Instead, I'm forced to use my imagination. This morning sucks worse than usual. I pull up an image of her in my head and the memory of touching her. How sweet and soft she can be. The way she bites her lip and moans my name when I make her come with my fingers.

I brace my hand on the wall and let my shins rest against the cold porcelain as I let those memories wash over me. It doesn't take long to bring me to the edge. My knees buckle as the orgasm rolls through me and my phone shifts forward.

It bounces off the seat, and instead of landing on the floor, it falls straight into the bowl.

"Fuck! Fuck! Fuck!" I reach in and grab it which is beyond disgusting. Shaking it off, I grab the closest towel and wipe it clean. The battery's already dead, so I have no idea if I've ruined it or not.

And of course, there's another goddamn knock on my door. I quickly wash my hands and stalk across the room, holding the potentially ruined phone in a hand towel. I throw open the door.

"Dude, are you—" Randy stops mid-sentence.

There's a woman behind him. She looks vaguely familiar. She's sporting last night's makeup and wearing Randy's too-big shirt, and possibly nothing else. Her eyes drop below my waist.

"Oh my God!"

I'm naked and still half-hard. I cover my junk with the tiny towel. Randy covers her eyes with his hand.

She points in my direction even though she can't see me. "You have something on your—"

"Why don't you go downstairs and see what the girls are doing?"

"But—"

"I got it covered." He whispers something in her ear.

She takes off down the hall, yelling, "I saw Buck's dick, and it's huge!"

"Seriously, man?" Like I need this shit.

"You're the one answering your door like this." He motions to my lack of clothing. "The world isn't your locker room, Miller."

"My fucking phone fell in the toilet!" I hold out the hand towel with my phone still wrapped in it.

"Scrolling your socials on the shitter again?"

"Laugh it up, asshole. All my contacts are in there."

"Does it work?"

"The battery died, so I have no idea." He throws a pair of swim shorts at me.

"Put these on and bring it downstairs. I'll get a bag of rice. Hopefully it'll be working in a couple of hours."

I pull the suit on, and follow him downstairs. Randy doesn't look nearly as rough as I feel this morning.

Two women—the one who announced the size of my junk to the entire house, and another one I vaguely recognize from last night—are sitting at the breakfast bar with coffee. Another one lounges on the couch in the living room, clicking away on her phone. The girls at the breakfast bar stare at me, then drop their gazes to their cups, shoulders shaking.

"Showing off your jewels again, huh, Miller?" Natasha, our trainer, says from the other side of the kitchen, focused on the fruit she's throwing in the blender. She's in a mood, which means our workout will be extra painful today.

"Not on purpose."

She looks up as she hits the switch. I don't have time to cover my ears and it's like a bomb going off in my head.

Natasha's eyes bug out, and she barks out a laugh, dropping to the floor. I'm grateful the blender stops blending.

The room is filled with snickering. "What the shit? Is everyone high?"

"You said you were going to take care of it," one woman says to Randy.

He shrugs.

"Take care of what?" I'm totally confused.

"Go look in the mirror," Natasha says.

I drop my phone on the counter and step into the closest bathroom. On my forehead, in black marker, is a giant jizzing cock. It even has ball hairs. "Who did this?"

"It wasn't me," Randy says. "I can't even draw stickmen."

I pump a handful of soap into my palm and rub at my forehead, but the ink stays put. I stomp out of the bathroom and yell, "Get ready for an ass-kicking, Lance! If anyone took pictures I'm going to stick you in the balls."

Lance opens the sliding door leading out to the patio and the pool. "It'll wash off eventually."

"I have a flight tonight. They won't let me into Canada with a dick on my forehead."

"That's tonight?" Lance asks.

"Yeah, man. I told you that already." But he probably feels worse than I do today.

Natasha stops laughing long enough to ask, "Are you seeing Sunny?"

"Not if I can't get this off!" I point to my forehead.

"Who's Sunny?" one woman asks.

"Miller's girlfriend," Randy says.

"I thought his name was Buck."

"It's a nickname," I reply. "What is this? Permanent marker? How do I get rid of it?"

"Makeup remover might work," the one from the couch says.

"Do one of you have some of that handy?"

The two at the breakfast bar shake their heads. The quiet one on the couch perks up. "Oh! I have hand sanitizer!" She jumps up and runs off. A minute later she returns with three little bottles and points to the couch.

I take a seat.

"When you're done with the dick removal, drink this and come outside." Natasha sets a glass on the side table, along with two painkillers, and saunters out of the kitchen. Randy takes Dick Yeller and the other one at the breakfast bar outside with Natasha.

Natasha's used to this bullshit. Lance's pad is a revolving door of women and parties.

I stretch out on the couch so she doesn't have to strain to reach my forehead since she's tiny and I'm not. She sits beside me, crossing her legs.

"If you're going to rub a dick off my forehead, I should

know your name."

Her smile is muted by her pursed lips. "I'm Poppy. Lance is a real joker."

"Yup. That'd be him. Thanks for taking care of this."

"No problem." She rubs some stinky sanitizer into my skin. "Kristi's been following his career ever since he got drafted."

"Who?"

"The girl he was with last night."

"The one without the underwear?" I won't be the one to tell her Lance goes through girls like I go through food.

"That'd be Kristi. And I didn't sleep with Lance when she was done."

"Uh—"

"Sorry. I don't know why I told you that." She pours some of the sanitizer directly on my forehead. I can't see her face, but she sounds embarrassed.

"Lance is fun. He's not down for a relationship, you know?"

"Oh, I know. I went to grade school with him; then we moved away for a few years. He used to tease me all the time. Anyways, we were kids. He's different now. But then, so am I, I guess."

I've only known Lance since I was traded, so I don't know what he was like before he made the pros. He's a cocky bastard at the best of times now. "Does he know you know each other?"

"I don't think he remembers me. It'd be better if you didn't tell him. You guys are good friends, right?"

I can't decide if she's a stalker, a fan, or something else. She's got this look on her face, similar to the one I get when I'm not allowed to order chicken wings because I have to eat clean.

I give her a vague nod. "Now you need to tell me why you don't want him to know you know each other."

"No way." She wipes at my forehead more aggressively.

"This is on really good."

"I'm going to punch Lance in the dick."

"It's a pretty great drawing."

"So what's the history with him?"

"It's nothing. It's stupid."

"Was he, like, your first crush or something? Did you want to hold hands?"

She takes a break from scrubbing my skin, and I use the opportunity to look at her. Her entire face is red, and her lip is caught between her teeth. She's pretty, beautiful even, under the day-old makeup. She's exactly what Lance's type would be if he took a time out from the meaningless sex: petite with strawberry blond hair, freckles, and soft curves.

"He was! Holy shit." I can't believe I'm right. "How does he not remember you?"

"It wasn't like that. And it was ten years ago. He was two grades higher. I have an older sister. I tagged along to a high school party and there was, like, that game, you know? Seven Minutes in Heaven or whatever it's called?" She buries her face in her hands. "Oh my God. This is so embarrassing. I'm shutting up now."

I sit up, totally interested. This is like one of those terrible teen sitcoms, but real. I love that shit. "Did you fuck him?"

She drops her hands. "I was twelve!"

I cringe. "That would be incredibly wrong."

"Ya think?" She shoves my shoulder.

"So did he feel you up?"

"No!"

I nod my approval. "I didn't get to touch boobs until I was sixteen."

"Seriously?"

"Truth." I make a fist and tap over my heart twice.

"Wow. Well, I guess you've made up for that, haven't you?"

"Yeah. More than I needed to."

She pats the cushion, and I lie back down so she can finish rubbing the stupid dick off.

"So do they call you Buck because you walk around naked all the time?" she asks.

"Nope. I had bad teeth as a kid."

"Oh. That's mean."

"Kids are assholes. The nickname stuck, and after a while I didn't care anymore. My teeth are perfect now, but the ones in the front aren't real."

"What happened?"

"I got a puck in the face playing street hockey."

She sucks in a breath. "That must have hurt."

"Lots of things hurt. I would've had braces, but I have titanium implants, instead. They give you good drugs when they put those fuckers in. Anyway, the accident fixed my teeth, so I guess the pain was worth it."

"That's a lot of pain for a nice smile." She wipes my forehead one last time. "Okay. It looks like you're dick free."

I sit up. "Thanks for taking care of that."

"No problem."

I stand and extend a hand to help her up.

"You're a lot different than I thought you'd be."

"Is that good or bad?"

She smiles. "It's good. You're nice."

Lance yells for me to come outside. When Poppy doesn't make a move to follow me, I pause. "Aren't you coming?"

"I'll just wash all this stuff off my hands. I smell like a fruit salad."

"Okay. See you in a few." I grab the shake Natasha made, the bag of rice with my phone, and the charger and go outside, where Lance and Randy are already in the pool. I plug in the phone near the barbeque, check to see if it's working—it isn't—and down my shake.

Lance looks like he's having trouble keeping up. Randy seems to be doing okay, though. I jump in, dunking my head and rubbing my hands over my face to wash off the residual hand sanitizer and the artificial fruit smell.

"Took you long enough," Lance says through heavy breaths.

"No thanks to you, dickface."

"Shut up, both of you." Natasha blows her whistle. I hate that thing. "Miller, sprints in the shallow end."

Lance grins and gives me a thumbs up.

Natasha points to him. "You too, Lance Romance."

At least I'm not alone in hell this morning.

3

This Hole Gets Deeper

-MILLER-

After half an hour, I notice that Poppy hasn't come outside. Maybe she went back to sleep. I don't have time to ask questions; Natasha is on a rampage.

Plyometric workouts are intense on dry land, but in water and hungover, they're pretty much torture. We're on round three of cardio break when the doorbell rings.

I look to Lance, who's sitting on the edge of the pool, not doing what he's supposed to. "Who's that?"

"I invited a few people over." He nudges his new friend and asks her to let whoever it is in.

Lance doesn't invite "a few" people over. It's not how he works unless it's to get down and dirty, like last night. That these women are even still here is surprising. Usually he calls them a cab first thing in the morning.

"Where's your friend?" I ask Randy's friend.

She drags her eyes away from her phone and gives me a

funny look. "She went to answer the door."

"No. The other one." I motion to my forehead.

"Oh! Poppy? She wasn't feeling well. She took a cab home." She goes back to staring at her phone.

She seems like a questionable friend.

Natasha's already out of the pool, packing up her stuff. I'm sure we weren't finished, but it's clear she's given up. Lance's friend comes back with a couple of guys from my team and more women. I lift a hand in greeting, then grab the weights and bands we didn't get to use. Lance gets off his ass, not to help, but to greet his company.

"Sorry about today." I fold everything up the way Natasha likes it and pass it over so she can pack it in her duffle bag.

"You were fine; the other two were the problem. These home sessions don't work."

"It would've been fine if Lance had sent his company home."

"Yeah, well, he didn't, so I'm done." Natasha grabs her bag.

For some odd reason, I get the feeling there's more going on between her and Lance than I realized. She's been his trainer for two years, so she knows what a dick he can be. Hitting on women is a compulsion, and Natasha isn't exempt. It's understandable. She's super fit—even I can admit it's hot that she could kick my ass. I don't think she's the kind of woman who would fall for Lance's crap. You never know, though. People do stupid things when sex is involved.

"You're gone for a couple of weeks after this, right?" she asks me.

"Yeah. I fly to Toronto tonight. I think my flight's at nine." I need to check that when my phone works again.

Her eyes light up. "You excited to see Sunny?"

"Why are you so interested in my sex life?"

"It's your lack of sex life I'm interested in. Is she still holding out?" Natasha knows more about my personal life than most people.

When I don't answer, she gives me a knowing smile. "After you visit Sunny, you do that camp thing, right?"

"Yeah. Randy's meeting me in Toronto, and we're road tripping together."

"You'll have fun. It's not the usual hockey camp deal, is it?"

"I wanted to change it up this year, and it's close to Sunny." That I managed to get Randy to come was a serious feat. I sold the whole "camping experience" we had when we were kids. He has a few friends up that way, having played for Toronto during his first year.

"Smart. You coming back after that? Or do you have more stuff planned?"

"I have ideas for another project, but it's local, and I'll need Vi's help."

"How is Violet, anyway?"

"Annoying." Being the team trainer, Natasha's met her a few times.

"It's amazing she deals with you at all."

"I don't know what you're talking about. I'm awesome." I give her a cheeky grin. "Vi's good. She and Waters got engaged."

"I heard. You don't sound very happy about that."

"It's whatever. They haven't been together that long. Like, six months, maybe?"

"When you know, you know."

The first night I met Sunny, I knew she was different. Maybe it's the same for Vi and Alex. "I guess. She's a big girl, and she can make her own decisions, but if he fucks her over again, I'll break his face."

"I'm sure he'd do the same if you screwed Sunny over."

"That won't happen."

Natasha gives me a one-armed hug and waves to Randy, who's floating on his back in the pool. She doesn't so much as look at Lance as she walks past him to cut through the house, and he's too busy socializing to notice.

I fish my phone out of the bag of rice. It's been plugged in this entire time, but the screen stays blank. I want to call Sunny, but I haven't memorized her number. It's a weekday, so she's probably teaching yoga or volunteering at the animal shelter, anyway.

I shove my phone back into the rice. I'm not sure how long it needs to dry out. I'll hit the phone store if I still have problems in a couple of hours. I don't like not being able to contact Sunny for this long. I rely on daily messages so she knows she's on my mind.

Lance ambles over as he scans the patio. "Where's Tash at?"

"She left."

"What? When?"

"A minute ago."

He jogs toward the house, his brows creased. I wonder what the deal is there. Sometimes I feel like all the flirting Natasha puts up with from Lance isn't just him being him. Lance digging on her would be all kinds of fucked up since she knows what he's like.

He returns a minute later, frown still firmly in place. "Did you find Natasha?"

"Nah. She was already gone by the time I got inside." A twitch under his eye is the only tell that I've hit a nerve as he glances around his backyard full of bikini-clad women and our teammates. "You've got willpower of steel resisting all this temptation."

I take off my sunglasses and pin him with a cold glare. "My balls could be so fucking blue they look like they've been handled by a Smurf, and I still wouldn't do that to Sunny."

He raises his hands. "I'm sorry, man. I shouldn't have said that. It can't be easy. She's all the way in Canada, and you're here. Long-distance relationships don't really work, you know?"

I drop my sunglasses back in place.

Realistically, for me and Sunny to work long-term, one of us will have to relocate. Since my job is always subject to change, Sunny would need to go where I am, and she'd need a job that's easy to do anywhere. It's something I've already considered. It's what my other project is about.

Lance leaves me to greet more guests as they continue to arrive.

The pool is full of people, so I drop down in one of the lounge chairs on the patio while I wait for my phone to come back to life.

"Oh my God! You're Buck Butterson! But your real name is Miller, right?"

A curvy brunette is standing right in front of me, and her friend looks horrified. I'm shocked she knows my real name.

"I'm sorry. I don't mean to—God, I can't—you're amazing. I love you. I mean, you're an awesome player. Chicago won after you got traded! And that was bogus on Miami's part. You didn't do a damn thing wrong. The media can suck it. Anyway, you were outstanding during the finals. I'm so sorry. I don't think I can stop myself."

I smile. She seems like a real fan—the kind who gets genuinely excited about the game.

"It's cool." I extend a hand.

She grabs it and squeezes, shaking harder than necessary. "Jessabelle." Her cheeks go a vibrant shade of red. "But my friends call me Jellie."

"Like peanut butter and jelly?"

"But with an -ie on the end. Is that weird? It probably is. Is it okay for me to call you Miller? I know you go by Buck, but if it's okay—"

"It's cool. You're cool. Take a breath."

"Wow. Great. Awesome. You're so blond. You're like a real-life Ken doll, but your hair's not plastic. Who's the girl who always posts stuff about you being a yeti?" She glances at my arms. "You don't have that much hair."

Fucking Vi and her comments on my social media posts. "I only turn on the yeti moon." When all I get is a blank look, I say, "My sister thinks it's hilarious to post that stuff."

She nods like she understands. "She's funny, right? Do you think I could get a picture with you?"

"Yeah. Sure." I don't consider her outfit—she's in a pair of short shorts and a bikini top—or that I'm only wearing swim shorts.

She hands her phone to her friend. Then she drops down in my lap and wraps herself around me. Before I can stop her, Jellie's friend starts snapping pics.

"Whoa! Hold up!" I raise my hands in the air so I'm not touching her anywhere. Well, except for where she's touching me with all her bare skin, which is a lot of places. "You can't post those."

Her friend stops clicking away and once again looks like she's about to sink into the cement. I move Jellie off of me, touching as little of her as possible. "I have a girlfriend. My lap isn't your chair."

"Oh! Oh shit. I thought that was a rumor. I mean, God. You've never had a girlfriend, and I thought maybe since there weren't any pictures in the last few weeks you were done..." she trails off.

"We're not done."

"Not even after last night?"

What would she know about last night? "I was out with the guys."

She gets this weird look on her face. She shakes her head. "I'm sorry. I just…you're an awesome player." She snatches the phone from her friend and starts deleting pictures, or that's what I assume she's doing. I don't want to be a creepy asshole and stand over her shoulder to make sure she deletes them all.

"It's cool. I just don't want problems. You know?"

"Sure. Right. Of course."

I let her friend take another, far less problematic picture of us standing next to each other, somewhat awkwardly, while smiling. "Well, if you ever break up and you're looking for someone to make you feel better, you can always hit me up on social."

She holds up the phone so I can see her profile. Below is a picture of her sitting in Lance's lap. Up until this moment I liked her in a player-to-fan way. Now she's just another bunny making chairs out of us.

4

It's Not What It Looks Like

-SUNNY-

"Have a wonderful weekend!" I smile as my final morning yogis roll up their mats and leave the studio.

I'm in a particularly good mood today. Miller is coming to see me. And my parents are away with friends for the entire weekend, so we'll have the house all to ourselves. Well, almost all to ourselves. Titan and Andy, our family dogs who are really my dogs, have been keeping me company.

I pack up my things and head out to my car. I check my phone, hoping that Miller has responded to my text from first thing this morning. I have a very vague memory of talking to him in the middle of the night, but it's foggy. I'm disappointed to see he still hasn't messaged, but he probably had training this morning, and knows I'm teaching, so I'm sure he'll get back to me soon.

I have messages from my older brother, Alex. He's the captain of The Rage, Chicago's hockey team, and Miller's teammate.

Alex: *Are you okay?*
Message when you see this, please.
I will bury him in a very deep grave.

My throat tightens. Memories from the middle of the night phone call pop like bubbles in my brain. Miller stayed at Lance's last night. And Randy was there. They're always going to bars and picking up women. My brother used to be like that. Well, the bar part, not really the picking up women part. He's a closet nerd-jock and his favorite game to play aside from hockey is Scrabble.

But Miller used to be a certifiable player. He was traded to Chicago in the middle of last season because his actions got him into trouble. That's not the version of Miller I know, though.

My Miller is sweet and thoughtful. He messages every day. We talk all the time. He's altruistic and kind. He volunteers at hockey camps in the summer and loves snuggles. Unfortunately, social media paints him in a different less flattering light.

And I'm very, very nervous to find out what new pictures have appeared to make Alex want to break his kneecaps.

I avoid the messages from my brother and call my best friend instead. She's equally wary about Miller, but she won't threaten to maim him. I also need to check in on her because she's supposed to go camping with her long-time boyfriend and they've been having issues. Well, they've had issues for a while, but they've gotten worse recently.

Lily answers on the second ring. "Hey, bestie, how's my favorite person in the world today?"

"Okay. Good. Okay." My voice is terribly pitchy.

"Uh oh, what happened?"

"I don't know," I whisper. "But Alex sent me these this morning."

I send her a screenshot of his messages.

"Shit." She sighs. "Do you want me to look for you?"

"No. Yes. No. I don't know. Miller's supposed to be here later today. Maybe I should wait." My fingers are at my lips. I curl them so I don't give into the urge to chew my nails. "How are things with you?"

"Same as usual. Are you sure you want to wait?"

"That doesn't sound good."

"You're deflecting," Lily says gently.

I swallow thickly. "I just don't want to give you more reasons to join Alex's Don't Date Miller Club."

"I just think the way social media portrays him leaves a lot to be desired." She blows out a breath. "Oh my...what the sweet fu—"

"What? Did you look? What did you see?" My stomach twists.

"Oh, Sunny. Shit." She brightens her tone. "Look, maybe you should come camping with me and Benji and Rach and XXX. Charles and Frankie might even come. It'll be like old times. But more fun because we don't have to get Alex to buy us coolers. I could really use you as backup. Benji has been... really difficult lately."

"But Miller's coming," I say weakly, unwilling to address the problem.

"Yeah. I know. We're not leaving until Sunday, so if he does come, you'll still get to see him. And you might really want to come," she chokes out. "And honestly, Sunny, I mean it, I could really use you there."

"It's that bad?" I whisper. "Whatever is out there and Benji."

"Yeah. Both are that bad."

"I'm going to look."

"I can come over in an hour. It's my lunch break. We can look together."

I go to social media and type in Miller's name.

What I see makes my stomach feel like it's trying to turn itself inside out.

It's not what it looks like.

It's not what it looks like.

It's not what it looks like.

But what if it is?

"Okay. I'll come camping with you." I hope I can keep it together long enough to make it home.

"I'm sorry, Sunny."

"Me, too."

I want to believe it's not what it looks like, but then why haven't I heard from him at all today?

5

About to Hit the Bottom

-MILLER-

I'm manning the burgers on the BBQ. It's the safest place to hang out. Randy hands me my phone. "You need to check this."

"Is it working again?"

He drops the device in my palm. "Yeah, it's good to go. You've got a shitton of messages. You might want to check your flight details."

"Good call." Usually I can count on Amber, my Personal Assistant to send me a million messages—most of them audio—so I don't mix up important things. But since she's away on some portaging trip in the middle of nowhere for the next two weeks, I'm trying to be responsible for myself.

I don't like the look on his face as I pass him the flipper and key in my code. A lot of the messages are from Sunny. Some are from Violet. And there are voice memos.

"I'll be back in a bit."

"Take your time. I've got this. 'Sides, I need a break. It's like mating season in the pool."

I pat him on the back, bypass the kitchen, and head for the stairs. I hit the spare bedroom on the second floor and lock myself in.

I start with the voice memos. They don't require reading so they're easiest to deal with. The first message is from Vi. I can still hear her screaming when I hold the phone away from my ear. She's loud when she's angry.

"You're a fucking asshole! What the shit is wrong with you? Do you have any idea how much shit you're in? Alex is going to rip your balls off, not that it matters since they're the size of raisins, and your dick can only be seen by a microscope. You better call me as soon as you get this. You're fucked. Get ready for the ass-kicking of a century, you yeti bastard!"

I have no idea why I'm in so much trouble, but I figure it's in my best interest to listen to the memos before I call her. The time stamp on that one is from early this morning.

The next message is from Sunny. I can't understand most of it because it's garbled. The only words I make out are *pictures* and *bunnies*.

Shit. This can't be good. It has to be a misunderstanding. God knows there've been enough of them in the past few months. I can't seem to stop messing things up with her, no matter how hard I try. That's been the biggest roadblock to progress with Sunny. People post pictures all the time. Sometimes they don't even ask before they snap their shots.

There are two voice memos from my PA, but they can wait. This drama needs to be taken care of first. I flip to the text messages. These are way more of a challenge to go through. I've always been a slow reader. But the dyslexia gets the better of me when I'm stressed, and right now I'm super stressed.

I have an endless number of texts from Vi and Sunny, but

one is from Waters. He normally doesn't message me. His is easy to read:

Alex: *YOU'RE FUCKING DEAD, ASSHOLE.*

The ones from Violet and Sunny are more difficult with all the autocorrect and shortforms.

I bring up the text-to-speech app and listen as it takes the butchered English and turns it into Violet ranting. It's much easier to understand, even with all the inaccurately corrected words.

Violet: *Why the fork would you let someone draw a dock on your face?*

Duck

Fork

Goddammit Dick Fucking DICK, not duck. Autocorrect can suck my clot.

Clit. Asshole

The next set of messages came several hours later. The first one has twenty or so angry face emoticons attached to it.

Violet: *Seriously?!!!!!! You're naked! Who is that girl?*

The question is followed by several screenshotted pictures. The first is one of me sleeping. It wouldn't be a big deal if I wasn't obviously naked—my left ass cheek is visible—and if I didn't have a huge dick drawn on my forehead. Worse is that Lance's friend is giving the thumbs up and pretending to ride me from behind.

I'm seriously going to kick Lance's ass.

A few are from last night. They don't look nearly as bad—just me with the guys and a few fans taking selfies. But the one from today with the woman in her bikini sitting in my lap is damn incriminating.

Violet: *Where the hell are you?*

You better fucking call me.

I'm coming to your house.

Those last two were sent ten minutes ago.

Violet: *Why aren't you here? You have a flight to catch! I'm coming for you.*

My phone rings as I finish listening to her texts. It's Vi. Answering it is better than letting it go to voicemail.

"I'm at Lance's front door. Let me in."

"What? How did you know I was here?"

"Because I'm psychic, and social media is my oracle. Now let me in. You are seriously interfering with my weekly orgasm quota right now."

I have no interest in hearing more about that. I run down the stairs to the front door. Before I open it, I ask, "Is Waters with you?"

"Are you kidding? I left him at home. I'm not interested in reducing our sex life to conjugal visits. Besides, he's too pretty for prison."

"That's more than I needed—"

"I don't care what you need. I need Alex to not be pissed off. I can see you through the damn door. Open it."

Violet is a small person. Maybe five-four in heels, but she's got an enormous personality to make up for her lack of size. I have a feeling I'm in for the verbal beatdown of a lifetime.

"Should we shave your body hair so they can make wigs for the elderly?" she asks as soon as the door opens.

"What are you talking about?"

"After Alex kills you, you can donate your fur to charity. And maybe some of your more viable organs. I'm pretty sure everything but your liver is good."

"This isn't funny, Vi."

"I think the brain surgeons would love to take a peek inside your head—you know, for science, so they can learn more about what happens when yetis and humans mate."

I'm really not that fuzzy. She just knows it's a weak spot for me. I'm about to close the door in her face. She drops the sarcasm. "What the hell were you thinking?"

I step outside and close it behind me. "I didn't do anything wrong."

"You didn't do anything wrong? Are you serious? Did you happen to see the pictures I sent you today? Those aren't even the worst ones. What's wrong with you? And why haven't you been answering your phone? Do you know how suspect that makes you look? Also, why aren't you at the airport right now, catching your damn flight?"

"It's not until nine, and it's only, like, two in the afternoon. I've got lots of time."

"It's five, not two. And your flight leaves in an hour. You missed it."

"But I checked—"

"Apparently not. Seriously, Buck. Isn't this why you have a PA? Even your agent called me this morning when no one could get in touch with you."

"Amber's on vacation."

"And she also knows how bad you are with dates. I can't imagine her not putting an alarm on your phone, or calling or something."

"My phone was giving me problems. I thought I had it all sorted out. I guess I got the times mixed up."

Violet rubs her forehead. The giant, marble-sized diamond on her ring finger sparkles in the sun. It's enormous. She expels a breath and looks up at the sky. She's wearing sunglasses, so I can't see her eyes. She swallows a few times.

When she speaks, it's quiet and too calm. "I know flipping numbers is a thing for you, but it's *Sunny*. You should be on top of this." She takes off the sunglasses.

Her eyes have that watery thing going on. It makes me nervous. I can deal with Violet's sarcasm and anger, but when she gets emotional, I don't know how to manage her other than to give her ice cream.

"You know, if you're not interested in that relationship, you better man up and deal with it instead of blowing her off. I won't have you fucking up my sex life because she's not interested in your tiny dick."

"My dick isn't tiny."

She's back to being pissed, thankfully. "Who fucking cares? That's not the point. Why are you here anyway? Lance is a douche."

"He's not—"

A song about peacocks starts playing from her back pocket.

"Hold on." She answers it. "Yes, he's still here." She looks me over and twirls her finger in the air. "Turn around."

I do what I'm told.

"He's shirtless, and I don't see any nail marks or hickeys." There's a pause. I can hear Waters' muffled voice. Judging from his tone, he's not very happy. "No. Absolutely not. That's where I draw the line, Alex. I'm not interested in requiring therapy." She purses her lips and glares at me. "Are you going to Hulk out?... Are you sure?... Fine." She passes me the phone. "Alex wants to talk to you."

My phone buzzes with new messages. I need to call Sunny. More than that, I need to reschedule my flight and get my ass to the airport. But I bring Vi's phone to my ear.

"Butterson, if you give me one of your bullshit excuses, I'm going to break your knees."

Violet is making hand gestures. I can't listen to Waters' heavy breathing and the buzz of my phone and watch her at the same time.

"If you break my knees, you'll be out for the season," I say. "I'll get Violet to do it."

Violet's not very strong, so that's not much of a threat. I don't share this with Waters, though. He's already pissed off enough. I make a noise of disbelief instead. Turns out that's almost as bad as saying what I'm thinking.

"You think this is funny, Butterson? My sister is bawling her eyes out over fucking media snapshots of you and all your damn puck bunnies—"

"I was asleep. I didn't know they drew a dick on my face until this morning. And that girl dropped into my lap and started taking pictures. I didn't do anything wrong."

He exhales like Darth Vader. When he speaks again, it's much more softly. "This is your last chance, Butterson. If you don't fix this mess, I'm going to schedule a meeting with the manager to tell him you're a cancer to the team."

It pisses me off that Waters, of all people, drops threats like this. He knows better than anyone how the media misconstrues things. "That's not fair."

"What's not fair is you playing my sister and thinking you can get away with it."

"Kind of like you played mine."

"Don't even start with me. You have no idea what it's like to make sacrifices for someone else. Put Violet back on the phone."

"Your boyfriend's an asshole," I mutter, passing the device back to her.

"Fiancé," she corrects, flipping me off. She turns away while she has a back and forth with Waters.

I pull up my email and search for something from Amber. She forwarded the one with my flight details last night. I open it and stare at the numbers and letters swimming together on the tiny screen. Under the flight times in her message is my entire monthly calendar. Everything is color-coded so I know what it means without having to read it. Practice is highlighted in red (there aren't any this month because we're offseason), workouts in blue, free days in pink, travel days in purple, and time with Sunny is a red heart.

My flight is at six, not nine.

Amber also sent a voice memo:

"Just a reminder that you fly to Toronto this evening at six. Your tickets are attached in the email. I also picked up a few of the items on the list of things you felt might make good gifts for Sunny. Those are packed in your carry-on bag. Your luggage for the camp has been sent ahead of you. I can confirm it's already there."

Damn, she's good. And she's not even finished.

"An SUV has been rented for you," her message continues. "There's an email with the reservation. You'll pick it up at the airport in Toronto. Sunny's address and the directions to the camp will be pre-programmed into the GPS system. I hope you're managing without me. Call if you need anything. I should have phone reception between today and tomorrow, but I'm unsure after that. You can always call Violet; she has all the information. So does your dad, but remember he and Skye are on a cruise for the next two weeks.

"This message will self-destruct in thirty seconds. Kidding! You'll be fine, Miller. Good luck with Sunny."

I should've known I'd mess this up.

Even with my bags already packed, there's no way I can make this flight.

"Come on, let's go." Violet grabs my wrist and pulls me toward an old-school Torino. It's Waters' car. I've only seen him drive it a couple times.

"I have my car, and I need my wallet."

"Leave your car here. You need to rebook your flight, and you don't need to be distracted with driving. It's too much for your yeti mind to handle."

"Can you give the damn yeti jokes a rest, please? I feel shitty enough without the insults, today, thanks."

As I turn to go back into the house, the door opens. "Hey, man! There you are! I thought you'd taken off already." Randy glances behind me at Violet. "Hey, how's it going, Vi?"

"Hi, Randy." She makes this sound, like she's choking on something. Here we go. It happens every time she sees him. She can't get past his name. And she thinks *I'm* immature.

I look over my shoulder; her whole body is shaking. She balls her hands into fists and pulls them up like she's morphing into a tiny MMA fighter. Then she thrusts her hips, not once or twice, but three times. When she's done, her face is blotchy, and she pretends to be mortified.

"Get your wallet. I'll be in the car." She spins around and almost trips on her way down the front steps.

"Bye, Violet," Randy calls after her.

She waves over her shoulder. "Bye, Ran—"

She stops, turns again, and gets back into a half squat. Her face is all pinched and weird-looking. She cups her hands like she's holding a pair of melons. "Balls! Randy Balls!" she yells.

"You do know my last name is Ballistic, right?" He's smiling.

"You'll always be horny nut sac to me!"

Then she runs the rest of the way to the car and slinks down in the front seat. It'd be way funnier if I wasn't in shit.

"She's a little out there, huh?"

"Uh yeah. You get used to it. Eventually. I have to go; I missed my flight." I brush past him, back into the house.

"I thought it wasn't until nine."

"I got it wrong."

"I'm sorry, Miller."

"Yeah. Me, too. I'll check in when I get to Toronto. You'll have to send me your flight details so I know when to pick you up from the airport for camp."

"You got it. Don't worry about it now. We'll get it handled." He pats me on the shoulder. "I'll tell Lance you had to bail."

"Thanks." Randy is good people.

I run up to the spare room and grab my clothes from last night, along with my wallet.

Once I'm in the car, Violet revs the engine and books it back to my house. If Waters knew how she was driving his ride, he'd shit a brick. Not that I care to tell him. That would mean talking to him.

While Violet drives like a maniac, I call the airline and rebook my flight. This flight doesn't leave until nine thirty-eight. It should leave me plenty of time to make sure I have all my crap organized.

I call Sunny, but her phone goes directly to voicemail. I leave a message explaining that Amber's on vacation, and I mixed up the flight times, but that I'll be in Toronto by about eleven and at her house around midnight. Hopefully she'll let me in.

"I'm coming up with you." Violet shoulders her purse and gets out of the car.

"I'll only be a few minutes."

"Like hell. Plus there's no air in that stupid car, and it's hotter than a nut sac in a cup."

"That's disgusting."

"I know. You're welcome."

We leave the car parked in front of my building. Violet stops at the front desk to ask about the bag Amber apparently sent. They've had it since yesterday morning. She asks Travis, the front desk guy, to throw it in the back of the Torino.

I thank him and follow Vi to the elevators. She checks her messages as we head for the penthouse floor. "Great. Now Sunny isn't answering my texts. I hope you haven't screwed this up permanently."

She crosses her arms. She's pissed. Really pissed. Probably the angriest she's ever been with me. I send Sunny a message, but I get nothing back.

Once we're in my condo, I grab the bag I packed two days ago at Amber's insistence from my closet. Inside the front pocket are my passport and travel documents, including printed directions from the airport to Sunny's parents' house in Guelph. There are also directions to the camp, which is farther north.

Since it's an international flight, I can't mess around. It's already six. I'm not taking any chances. With my luck, there'll be a fifty-car pileup on the freeway.

When I come out of my bedroom, Violet's standing in the middle of my living room, frowning at her phone.

"I'm ready."

She looks up and arches a brow. "Oh, really?"

"I told you it would only take a minute."

"You don't think you should clean yourself up? Maybe take a quick shower? Put a shirt on? Or does your chest hair count as clothing in your mind?"

I drop the bag on the floor. "Look, I get you're pissed at me. No one is more pissed than I am, but seriously, I already know I'm a fucking idiot. Okay?" I stomp back in the direction of the bathroom.

"You're not an idiot."

I run a hand through my hair. It feels gross. "I know I fucked up. It's clearly what I do best. I need your help, and that includes not making me feel worse than I already do.

"I'm sorry, I'll be less of a sarcastic jerk. Grab a quick shower and we'll be on our way."

Fifteen minutes later I'm showered, dressed and refreshed. If I had enough time, I'd do a full-body trim, but it's a process. I throw my trimmer and a couple of razors in a bag so I can handle that situation later.

I check out the bag of gifts for Sunny on our way to the airport. It's half an hour from my condo without traffic, and the roads are clear, so we make good time. Amber did a great job picking things from the list I gave her. Everything is holistic and organic cotton, and no animals were harmed in their making.

Violet pulls up to the curb and gets out to give me a hug. "I'm always on your side. You know that right?"

"Yeah."

"Just remember that Alex will always be on Sunny's. So if you can't figure out what you want, you need to stop chasing her like she's some bunny you want to catch."

"She's not a bunny."

"Exactly." She sighs. "If you want to have a relationship, you have to make compromises."

"Gotcha." I don't really, but it's seven, and I don't want to be late for my flight.

"Message when you get there."

"Will do."

As I head for the check-in desk, I wonder what compromises she's made for him, and what Sunny will have to give up to be with me. If she still wants to.

6

I Wish I Had a Crystal Ball

-Sunny-

I listen to Miller's voicemail at least fifteen times. I don't know what to do or how to feel. My mom thinks he can do no wrong. My bestie hates his online presence and his constant appearance in pictures with other girls, although to be fair, he's in just as many pictures with random guys and his teammates. But she also doesn't love that he's frequently out with his single hockey friends. But what is he supposed to do? I live here and he lives in Chicago. I don't expect him to stay home and pine for me. I don't stay home and pine for him.

Except tonight I am pining.

And worrying.

And wondering what the heck I'm doing.

My brother has messaged me relentlessly today, promising if Miller really fucked this up for good this time he'd take matters into his own hand. I don't know what that means, but Alex used to get in a lot of on-ice fights, so I can guess.

Everything is a mess.

And yet.

He called to tell me he was coming.

But all those pictures still exist.

So much gets taken out of context.

I know this because of my brother. He used to look like a giant playboy. He was the biggest player in the league. There are countless pictures of him making out with women scattered all over the internet and he didn't have a problem with it. Our dad wasn't impressed and my mom was living in a time warp where the phrase "boys will be boys" seemed to explain away his behavior.

Until Violet came along and rocked his world. And all the things he let people believe, all the things *I* believed turned out to be untrue. Yes he'd kissed all those random women, but that was as far as it ever went.

So I have to believe that these pictures of Miller with smiling, happy bunnies are just him being kind to fans. And a little oblivious to how it looks to *me*.

But I do something I shouldn't. I read the comments. And I look up the girl in the picture. And then the other girl in the *other* picture. Which was not my best choice, but I made it and regretted it instantly.

I've been a blubbering, anxious, crying mess ever since.

I haven't even been able to call Miller back.

Every time I try I start panicking again.

Because what if he's coming here to tell me something I don't want to hear?

What if this time what I want to believe *isn't* the truth?

What if all these feelings I've developed for him over the past few months aren't reciprocated?

What if he breaks my heart?

No amount of deep breathing helps.

I wish I had a crystal ball so I know what's coming for me when he finally gets here.

7

Let Me Make It Up to You

-MILLER-

I do not miss my flight on the second attempt, but it's two-thirty in the morning by the time I make it to Sunny's. There was construction on the highway, and the GPS cut out while I was on a detour. I accidentally put the wrong address back into it and went forty kilometers in the wrong direction by the time I noticed. The open field of cows indicated I'd missed a turn.

I grab my duffle from the front seat. I'm exhausted, but I still have to deal with the fallout from today. The pictures from last night and today don't look good, especially taken out of context. I don't have much of a relationship track record and proving I can handle a real one is turning out to be a real uphill battle.

The motion sensor kicks in as I get out of the car, flooding the driveway with light. Sunny's tiny eco car is parked in front of my rented SUV.

I shoulder my bag, lock up my rental, and hit the doorbell. Anxious barking accompanies the clip of nails on the stairs. Titus, a Papillon, and Andromeda—Andy for short—are Sunny's dogs. They're both rescues with serious anxiety issues. Titus likes to lick people's toes, and Sunny doesn't seem to mind. It's weird.

Andy's a Dane, so I can see him through the curtain covering the front window. He paces back and forth, whining. I have treats in the car for him. I run back to the SUV and grab the bag with all the gifts. Fishing out the gourmet dog biscuits, I slip one through the mail slot. Andy snarfs it down and then pokes his nose back through, looking for more.

When Sunny still hasn't come down a minute later, I pull up her contact and speech to text her.

"I'm at your front door."

I must not enunciate properly because *front door* is autocorrected to *foghorn*. I hit the doorbell a second time, erase the message, wait for Andy to stop barking, and try again. I can't dictate for shit when I'm tired. This time front door comes up looking mostly right. There aren't any red lines, so I press send.

I get a message back almost instantly.

Sunny Sunshine: *WTH? Y r U at frat dorm?*

I read the text and frown, then hit the text-to-speech function so I can listen to it, because it's half random letters instead of words. The posh British woman in my phone reads the words *frat dorm* back to me instead of *front door*. That's what I get for not listening before I send something.

Sunny Sunshine: *Sry. Autocorrect. Front Door. Please let me in.*

Short and to the point works better.

I crouch down and open the mail slot. Andy stops pacing

and sticks his nose through the hole. "Hey, buddy. Can you go get Sunny for me and bring her down here? Go get Sunny. Go get 'er. Go on." He runs to the stairs and looks back at me. "Good boy. Go get her for me. I got more treats if you bring Sunny."

He turns toward the stairs and barks a few times, then runs back to the door and sticks his nose up to the mail slot.

"You have to get her." With a little more coaxing he finally runs up the stairs. He comes up and down twice more without her, so I ring the doorbell and knock.

Sunny calls out, "For doody's sake! I'm coming. Stop it, Andy! I'm answering the door."

I grin. Sunny doesn't swear. It's fucking adorable.

The light in the front foyer turns on, and the door swings open. Andy rushes me, jumping up so his paws are on my shoulders and his nose is level with mine. I don't turn away when he licks my face.

"How's my buddy?" I scratch behind his ears. "Good boy. You're a good boy." I reach into my back pocket and pull out a treat. He gets into position. I set the treat on the end of his nose. He adjusts his stance but waits until I give him the go-ahead. Then he flips it up, catching it in his mouth.

Sunny stands behind him, one hand propped on her hip, looking unimpressed. Titus hides behind her ankles. There's a good chance he'll pee on the floor.

Sunny's sandy blond hair is lighter than the last time I saw her, with streaks so pale they're almost white. It's pulled up into a messy ponytail. She's wearing a pair of loose shorts and a T-shirt with a unicorn galloping out of a forest. I'm nine thousand percent sure she's not wearing a bra, but I'm smart enough not to stare at her chest.

Her soft, usually pouty lips are mashed into a line. Her eyes are puffy. Her sun-freckled cheeks are blotchy and red.

She's been crying. It's my fault.

"It's too late for Andy to have treats."

"I'm sorry." I shift from one foot to the other.

She crosses her arms. "You're not forgiven."

"It was just a couple of cookies." Andy sits on my foot and nudges my pocket with his nose. There's another biscuit in there, and he knows it.

"I don't care about the dog treats!"

"Right. Of course. I'm sorry I missed my flight. I got the time wrong. I thought I was supposed to fly at nine, not six. My phone fell in the toilet, so I couldn't check to make sure. We had to put it in a bag of rice for most of the day to dry it out. The rice worked, though, so that's good, right?" I get silence, so I tack on, "Amber's on vacation, and you know how I am with dates and stuff."

Her jaw tics. Nothing I've said is making this better. If anything, she looks angrier since I started talking.

"Andy, inside." She has to say it twice more and snap her fingers before he obeys. For a second, I think this means she's going to let me in, but she widens her stance and bars my way with her arm across the jamb.

Sweet talking won't get me out of this. I should've had one of the gifts Amber picked up in my hands. Like the basket of organic treats still in my rental. Instead, I have myself and my mouth to fix the problem.

"You think I'm upset because you're a few hours late?"

"Well, I—it's not... I try to be on time. Amber's away." I'm not helping my case.

She throws her hands up in the air. "Your PA being away is not an excuse, Miller, and it doesn't explain the bunnies hanging all over you, snapping their selfies today!"

In the past when I've dealt with a jealous woman, I say a few nice things and smooth it all over. Orgasms work well. Lots of them. But I need a different strategy because Sunny isn't in this for the sex. Instead of digging myself out of this hole, I say something stupid, proving words definitely aren't my forte.

"You know how the fans are."

"The fans? The *fans*? What fan draws a penis on your forehead? You were naked! And there was some bunny in that bed with you! It's all over social media! Who is she? Were you with her?" Her eyes well with more tears.

I feel like the biggest asshole in the world. "I was passed out. I didn't even know she was in there with me."

"Who took the picture? What if that had been a tattoo? It would've been permanent." She's been watching a lot of reality tattoos show on TV lately, otherwise this wouldn't make much sense.

"I don't think I would've slept through a tattoo. Especially not on my face." It's out of my mouth before I can consider how unhelpful it is.

"Ugh!"

I slide my arm in before she can shut the door.

Sunny's a yoga instructor; she's stronger than she looks. It's a lot of pressure on my forearm.

"Sweets, come on. Things get taken out of context. I was hanging with Lance and Randy. He invited some friends over."

She makes a disgusted sound.

"They're not bad guys; Lance just likes parties. He invited a bunch of people by, and you know how that goes. You invite a few people who invite a few more people... I can't control what he does."

"Oh, right! Of course that explains why a naked bunny ended up in your lap."

"No one was naked, Sunny."

"Pretty darn close!" She holds her phone up in front of my face. It's the picture of the girl sitting in my lap. There really isn't much to her outfit: a minimalist bikini top and a pair of equally minimalist shorts. My shirtlessness doesn't help.

She turns the phone around and swipes angrily across the screen, then holds it back up for me to see. "And last time I checked, *this* counts as being naked."

It's the picture of me, asleep in bed with that stupid dick on my forehead. I'm definitely naked there.

"I wasn't conscious."

"Because you passed out drunk. Want to know how I know?" She doesn't wait for an answer. "You called me last night. Do you even remember that?"

"I remember calling you." My voice rises at the end.

She arches a brow. "No, you don't."

"Yes, I do. I told you I wanted to hear your voice." I always want to hear her voice. At least I do when she's not pissed off at me.

"There was more to the conversation than that."

"I've been on the road all day. Can I come in so we can talk about this? I rebooked my flight so I could get here tonight. You haven't answered any of my calls. There are two sides to every story. You haven't even heard mine yet. Please."

She takes several deep breaths. "There are three sides to every story."

"What do you mean?"

"There's your version, the other person's, and then there's the truth, which is somewhere in the middle of the two."

She's right. But in the case of the dick picture, my version is missing the whole part where the event took place, being asleep and all.

"Are you willing to hear my side?" I give her my best I'm-sorry face.

Eventually she steps away from the door and lets me in, locking it behind her.

Sunny still lives with her parents. She's only twenty, and she's in school. She's already completed a diploma in general arts and science, and she has her yoga certification. Last year she started a Public Relations program. She's great with people and animals and all sorts of stuff, so whatever she decides to do, I'm sure she'll be awesome.

Thankfully her parents, Robbie and Daisy, are out of town for the weekend, so I don't have to deal with them. It's not that I don't like them. I do. They're cool for parents, but they're the only ones I've ever met on purpose. Her mom, Daisy, likes to be involved in everything, so her not being here means I can focus on making things better with Sunny without any interference.

I glance around the front foyer. The Waters' house is dated. Most of the furniture is new, but the curtains are poufy, and there are an exceptional number of knickknacks. None of the colors belong together. Vi calls it a boxing match between a bohemian and a southern belle. I'm not sure what that means, but it's an assault on the senses.

I set my bag by the front door. Sunny'll let me stay the night. She's too sweet to make me leave. I think it might be the Canadian in her. The question is, where will I be sleeping?

Sunny motions for me to follow her into the living room. She drops into one of the uncomfortable pink floral wingback chairs.

I sit in the middle of the couch and pat the cushion beside me. "Come on, Sunny Sunshine. Talk to me."

She tucks her feet under her. "I can do that from here."

I keep patting the cushion, and she keeps glaring. Eventually I abandon the couch and go to her, kneeling so we're at eye level. "I know you're mad, and I don't blame you, Sunny, but you know how things look through social media. Think about all the pictures of your brother floating around out there."

She twists her hands and sighs. "It's not the same, and you know it. All that stuff about Alex is garbage, and all the stuff about you is true."

"Used to be true. That's not how it is anymore."

Up until the last few months, the pictures that appeared on the hockey fan sites and gossip columns had been just what they seemed. My unfortunate reputation has been well-earned. I tried to protect Sunny from it—but she looked up my history after her friend Lily, who hates me, told her she should be careful about dating me.

Sunny wasn't all that concerned at first. She's a free spirit. She liked my aura, and that was enough for her. Then reality smacked her in the face like an unwashed dick. And the pictures in the media keep happening, but not because I'm being unfaithful—I just don't want to be rude to my fans.

I need to convince Sunny I'm not full of shit.

Sunny sighs. "How do I know you weren't joining the Kilometer-High Club in the airplane bathroom with some bunny?"

"I didn't even use the bathroom on the plane. They're disgusting. I go before I get on."

"You were supposed to be here hours ago, even with your missed flight. How do I know you actually missed the flight in the first place?"

"You can ask Violet. She dropped me off at the airport."

She crosses her arms. "How do I know she wouldn't lie for you?"

"There's no way Vi would lie for me, especially about something like that."

She gives me an incredulous look. "You forgot you were coming to see me!"

"I got the flight times wrong."

Her cute little chin starts to tremble. I've seen this happen before. Not with Sunny, but with Vi. She's going to cry. Up until now, I haven't seen tears, and I'm not sure how to deal with them. With Vi I usually get her a dairy treat, and we play violent video games until her lactose intolerance gives her stomach cramps and she makes me leave. But Sunny isn't Vi.

"I want to trust you, Miller, but you make it so hard."

I sigh and drop my head to her knee. Her skin is soft and warm, and it smells like her name. Her whole body tenses. After a few seconds she runs her fingers through my hair. I totally get why dogs love to be scratched behind their ears. I forget there's a question and rub my cheek on her leg.

Her fingers curl at the crown of my head, and she lifts me by my hair. Her normally soft green eyes are hard.

"What am I supposed to believe, Miller?"

"We'd been drinking, and Lance scheduled a workout at his place in the morning. I was being responsible by staying put. I'm trying here, Sunny. It's been a long time since I've done the relationship thing, and it's a lot different than it was in high school, you know?"

"You're just figuring that out now?" She twirls her hair around her finger.

"Well, yeah. I've been doing my own thing for the past five years—"

"You mean playing the field."

"There's a learning curve. I really like you. I want to see if we can make this work. I'm asking you to be patient."

"I have been patient. And tolerant. Put yourself in my sandals, Miller."

"My feet are way too big for your sandals." Why can't I be serious when the situation calls for it?

"How am I supposed to believe what you say when all the pictures of you out there make it look like the exact opposite?" She holds up her phone and scrolls through the posts of girls hugging me. There are a few new ones from the bar last night that I don't remember.

"Shit. Okay. That looks way worse than it is. I promise I'm only using my hand when I'm horny."

She looks confused, or maybe disturbed, so I keep going, hoping to clarify. "Last week I considered using a bag of marshmallows that I'd left in the sun because they're soft and warm, but I figured it'd be a messy clean up and fuckin' weird, so I went with lotion instead. Technically that means it's not just my hand, but if I don't use lotion I chafe, especially during the regular season when I'm always wearing a cup and all my gear. Is that too much detail?"

Sunny covers her mouth with her palm. I hope she doesn't puke.

"It's too much detail. It's all the time I'm spending with Vi. Her lack of filter is rubbing off."

A laugh bubbles up, and Sunny's shoulders start to shake. "You know, that explains a lot."

"Vi's a bad influence."

"No, she's not. And that's not what I'm talking about. When Alex was a teenager, I used to wonder why he went through so much lotion, and so many pairs of socks."

I don't know why she's bringing up her brother. "What do socks have to do with anything?"

"He used them when he..." She gestures below my waist

and makes a whacking-off motion. "You know, to contain the explosion."

Her cheeks go pink, and she looks away.

"He blew his load in a sock?"

Her nose scrunches up in this cute way, similar to her reaction when I suggested we go for wings and beer, before I knew she didn't eat animals.

"Man, he must have gone through an awful lot of socks." Sometimes in high school when Barbie Claremont wore her white sundress that didn't fit the dress code, I'd have to take a time out during second period so I could manage the rest of the morning. And that was after I'd already taken care of my morning problem in the shower.

"He went barefoot a lot. His sneakers smelled awful."

"I bet. It's kind of genius, eh?" It would cut down on the use of tissues, that's for sure. "Wait. How do you know about Waters' masturbating habits?"

"I used to do his laundry because he always helped me with homework and stuff. But I stopped after I discovered his mountain of crusty socks."

"Fair. We should probably talk about something else, yeah?" I'm not even sure how we got on this topic in the first place.

"Probably." Sunny brushes the hair she's twirling between her fingers across her lips.

I lean closer until my chest is pressed against her knees and our faces are only inches apart. I'd love to kiss her, but she still looks uncertain, and I don't want to push.

I twirl a lock of her hair around my finger until it fans out like a paintbrush and rub them over my own lips.

Sunny laughs. It's a soft, breathy giggle. Cute. Sweet. A little uncomfortable, even. "What are you doing?"

"I don't know. What are you doing?"

Her gaze shifts past me. "Thinking."

"About what?" I drop her hair and run my fingertip along the contour of her bottom lip. She has fantastic lips. I haven't had them on mine in more than two weeks.

"About how I'm not sure what you want from me."

I drop my hand and hold onto the armrests instead. "You still think I'm trying to play you?"

"You're always talking the talk."

"You think so, eh? Well, why don't we look at the facts?" I drop that bit of Canadian in there to make her smile. She does, but it's gone almost as quickly as it appears.

"There you go again! You're doing it right now."

"Doing what?"

"Saying *eh*, being all cute."

"You think I'm cute?"

She pushes at my chest with her toe. Annoyed. "You have the biggest ego in the world."

I grab her ankle and run my hand up the outside of her calf. Her legs are amazing—long, toned, and sun-kissed. I want my hands and my mouth on every last inch of skin, starting at her ankle and ending at her mouth. I want to make her smile and gasp and sigh.

"Your brother has the biggest ego," I tell her. "It's at least ten times the size of mine."

"He does not."

"Fine. My ego is bigger. Let's get back to the facts. How long have I been calling you?"

"Since you came to Toronto."

"How many times have I come to Guelph to see you?"

"This is the third."

"How many times have I tried to get in your pants?"

Sunny taps her lip. "You mean for sex?"

I release her leg and hold onto the arms of the chair again. My knees hurt from kneeling for so long, but I'm making a point. "Yeah, I mean for sex."

She looks down, her eyes on my chin rather than my face. "Never."

"That's right. Never. So you tell me, Sunny. What do you think I'm here for?"

She peeks up, her expression sweet like those maple candies I steal from my sister all the time. "Just me?"

"Not *just* you. *You.* I'm here because I want to be with you, and no other reason."

I've only ever dealt with this once before, way back at the beginning of college when crushes crushed a kid. This is different; the feelings are bigger. Deeper. I care about her. I don't want to be without her.

"Come on, Sunny Sunshine. You know how much I like you. I'm trying hard not to screw it up."

She exhales slowly, finally letting her guard down. She parts her legs, and they slide along either side of me. It gives me the access I've been waiting for since I walked in her door. I don't move into the space yet, though.

Instead, I run my hand up the outside of her bare calf again. Stopping behind her knee, I stroke with my thumb before I reverse the movement, kneading all the way to her ankle. Sunny's a big fan of the leg massage. On the way back up, I follow her shin bone with my thumbs. All her muscles are tight. Sitting back on my heels, I get a glimpse of pale blue cotton through the small gap between her shorts and her inner thigh.

Panties are panties: frilly, frill-less, plain, fancy, lacy, cotton, satin. But for some reason, I want to know what style

Sunny's wearing. Will they be regular bikini briefs? Boy shorts? Cheekies? I want her to parade around in them, and then I want to get her naked and keep her that way for hours. Show her exactly how I feel about her. Make her feel good.

I rub up and down the back of her calf until she starts to sigh and shift. Her head drops against the back of the chair, and her eyes flutter shut. Her toes curl against my forearm, and her lips part.

"You're real tight. That feel good?" I go up higher, avoiding the ticklish spot on her knee.

"I taught three classes and then ran eight kilometers with this new greyhound we got at the shelter."

"You must be tired."

She cracks one lid. "Probably not as tired as you."

"I caused you all kinds of stress today." I might as well acknowledge it.

"I'm over it."

"You sure about that?"

She traces one of the ugly flowers on the arm of the chair. "I'm mostly over it."

"Anything I can do to help you get totally over it?"

"I don't know."

"You don't know, or you don't want to tell me?"

I spread my fingers wide, covering the tops of her thighs. When I'm a few inches from the hem of her shorts, I graze her inner thighs with my thumbs. It's a sensitive spot, holding the promise of something way more fun, like Sunny's soft sweetness and her little moans of excitement.

I lean down and kiss the inside of her knee. "I'm sorry I made today difficult."

"I know."

I keep my hands where they are, thumbs sweeping in slow

circles. Her skin is flushed, warm; her pulse is racing. Backing off, I rest my hands on her knees.

"I hate it when I upset you, Sunny Sunshine. I'm trying my best. I know it's not good enough, but maybe you can help me get better at it." She's had way more relationship experience than I have.

Sunny's knees press hard against my sides for a long moment. Her fingers flutter close to her hair, like she's about to do the twirl thing. I'm sure she wants to stay angry a little longer, but I'm wearing her down. I'm not sure what it is about me that makes her fold—because let's face it, I'm not prime boyfriend material—but whatever she sees, I want to be that for her. Be worthy of her.

She pushes her fingers through my hair. Her nails scratch my scalp. I love it when she does that. Then her fingers tighten and release, over and over. I love it when she does that, too.

If I was Titan or Andy, my tail would be thumping on the ground about now.

"Stop letting the bunnies take pictures."

"They're fans."

"Who have their hands all over you."

Her fingers tighten again so I smooth my hands up her legs and squeeze when I get to the hem of her shorts. I'm distracting again. It's not fair. She makes a good point. I wouldn't like it if it was the other way around. I don't always have control of where other people put their hands. I can only control what I do with mine.

"You're the only one who matters, Sunny."

Her uncertainty is obvious in the tightness of her jaw and the flex of her fingers. Some people avoid confrontation. I don't. This situation is the perfect catalyst for a sweet make-up session. One where I can show her the best way I know how that she's important. That she's the only one I want.

Sunny cups the back of my neck and yanks me forward. Our lips connect. Hers are soft and warm. It's a balm after two long weeks of nothing.

Kissing is an art. It's the most important part of foreplay. It's a precursor to everything else that's coming.

She tries to push her tongue past my lips, but I nip her with my teeth. She makes a frustrated, needy sound.

As soon as her lips part I slip my tongue inside, stroking slowly. She tastes like the cinnamon and clove toothpaste she uses. It reminds me of gingerbread cookies. That means she stopped to brush her teeth before she answered the door.

I cup her cheek in my palm and suck her tongue. It drives her wild when I do that.

Sunny groans and winds herself around me, hooking her feet at my waist, fingers twisting in my hair to keep me close.

I inch my palm up her thigh until the tip of my middle finger slips under the hem of her shorts. Sunny arches, chest pressing against mine. I ease my hand back down her thigh to her knee, staying away from all the most exciting places.

I love teasing her, getting her all excited, reminding her how good we can be together, when my stupidity doesn't get in the way.

"I hate it when the bunnies are all over you, and I hate being jealous," Sunny mumbles around my tongue.

I break the kiss. "You don't need to be jealous. You're the only one I want all over me."

Sunny's hands slide ease down my back. She palms my ass and shifts forward. It feels fucking incredible. She wiggles her fingers under my waistband. I'm commando. I firmly believe underwear is mostly useless. This time I feel the sharp bite of her nails when she grabs my ass.

I move the hand on her upper thigh to her waist, sliding up to her ribcage, my thumb two inches shy of the underside of her boob.

The less I touch where she wants me to, the more frantic she gets. She grabs the hem of my shirt and tries to remove it, but suck her bottom lip, in no rush to get naked. When she makes a frustrated noise, I lean back. She yanks my shirt over my head and tosses it on the floor, then sighs.

She runs her fingers through my hair, nails scratching lightly down my neck. When she reaches my shoulders she pauses, her eyes moving over my chest and down my abs.

"I wish it was summer all the time. You look so good without a shirt."

"I won't wear one while we're in the house."

"Or by the pool." Her fingertips drift down my arms.

"I won't even wear shorts, if that's what you want. I'll swing free all weekend, just for you."

"Just for me, eh?"

There's the cute Canadianism I like so much.

"Mmm. Just for you."

"That'd be fun, but the neighbors can see everything."

"Aren't they, like, ninety?"

"Yeah, but the old guy is shady. He watches me sunbathe with binoculars."

"Seriously?"

"Sometimes. He's harmless, though."

"I'm skinny dipping tomorrow."

Sunny laughs and runs her hands over my shoulders. "I think you want to get naked in front of me."

"Look at how excited you are about me being shirtless. I don't know if you can handle me naked, sweets."

She narrows her eyes.

Leaning in, I drop a kiss on the end of her nose, and another on her chin. "I'm fucking with you, Sunny. I think you can handle me fine."

She cups the back of my neck, drawing me in for another kiss. Our tongues meet and tangle, softness giving way to need as the kiss deepens and Sunny rolls her hips. I cup her ass and help out with some friction.

"Maybe we should go upstairs," she murmurs when I kiss a path down her neck.

"That's an idea."

Except it will take us out of the moment. Plus, there's something extra enticing about making out with her in one of these hideous chairs, in the middle of her family living room. All the curtains are drawn, giving us the privacy we need. I want to make her come right here. That way, every time I sit in this room, I'll have the memory of her soft moans and sweet taste.

I inch toward the top of her thigh. Sunny groans and her legs tighten on my hips.

"Let's go to my room."

"What do you want to do up there that we can't do here?" I nibble her collarbone and brush over her nipple with my thumb.

"Miller."

"Yes, sweets?" I slide a hand under her shirt, tickling along her ribs as I push her bra up until her breasts pop out the bottom. Her perfect nipples are visible through the sheer fabric. It's almost better than having an unobstructed view.

"Let's just go—"

The words die when I cover her nipple with my mouth.

"Oh, God." She wraps both arms around my head.

I cup one breast while I suck the other nipple. With my free hand, I feel my way into her shorts until I reach the edge of her panties. I don't go under, though. Instead I follow the elastic.

Here's the thing about foreplay: sometimes it's better with clothes on. There's something extra sexy about making a woman come fully dressed.

I palm her through the damp cotton, and she tries to lift her hips. It's a challenge considering her back is arched, and she's sitting in a chair.

I release her nipple. The pale pink shirt sticks to her skin. "You still want to go upstairs?"

Sunny blinks, her confusion cute. "What?"

"Upstairs? You want to go there?" Her panties are blue with a tiny white and dark blue polka dot pattern. I slide the tip of my finger under the elastic.

"Right now?" Her expression is incredulous.

"If you want."

"I'm good here."

"You sure are," I mutter as I drag a knuckle over soft, smooth skin. She's wet and hot, and I'm desperate to get my mouth on her, but one step at a time.

I unwrap her legs from around my waist and drape her leg over the arm of the chair, the other one I hook over my forearm. "You're so damn beautiful."

I push her panties to the side, exposing her to me.

"Know what I can't stop thinking about?"

"Hmm?" Her gaze is slow to lift from my fingers.

"The way you look when you come." I brush my knuckle over her clit.

Sunny's eyes close, and she bites her lip.

"And your sweet little moans when I find the right spot." I slip one finger inside, and she makes the sound I'm hoping for. "Just like that."

I add another finger, going deeper until her cheeks flush and her mouth drops open. She clutches my forearm.

"Holy—" she gasps. "Oh! I—*Miller.*" She draws out my name, eyes wide, her expression hot with need.

"Did I find the spot, sweets?"

She nods furiously, her grip tightening. "You always do." She digs her nails into my skin. "I'm right th—"

She contracts around my fingers, showing me what she was about to tell me. Sunny's eyes meet mine, wide with shock. She's always surprised when she comes, like it's unexpected.

Sunny grabs my shoulders, pulling me forward until our lips collide. Her tongue slides against mine as she moans. I feel like a fucking champion right now.

That is until she breaks the kiss, flops back in the chair, and mumbles, "I hate that you're so good at that."

There's bite to her words. Looks like she's not as over the social media stuff as she thinks. I remove my hand from inside her panties, adjust them, and lower her leg to the floor. "I can always pretend I don't know what I'm doing." I make a joke out of it, but there's a weight in my chest. I don't like it.

"I don't mean it the way you're taking it." Her hand curves around the back of my neck. "It's just that I come every time. What if I can't do the same for you? It's a lot of pressure, and I don't have nearly as much practice…"

"You're worried about not being able to get me off?" I sound confused because, well, I don't get it. Just looking at her jacks me up. Women aren't nearly as mechanically simple.

"Well, yeah. I mean that happens, right? Sometimes guys can't—"

"Blast the cannon?"

"Yeah."

"I guess. I mean, maybe if I whacked off, like, twenty times that day I might have a problem, but just looking at you gets me excited."

Her eyes dart down, and her hand moves from my chest to my waistband, palming me. "You're already hard."

"I got to watch you come on my fingers. Of course I'm hard."

"That turns you on?" I can't tell if she's surprised or curious. "Definitely."

She gives me a squeeze and whispers. "Fingering me made you this hard?"

Those words coming out of her mouth, combined with the feel of her hand on me, even through my shorts, reroutes my blood flow south of the waistband. "Touching you, the way you feel on my fingers, how soft you are, those sweet sounds you make, and being able to make you come like I did? All of that gets me hard."

"Oh. That's...wow." She gives me a little squeeze. "I make you really hard."

I grin. "You sure fucking do, Sunny Sunshine."

She goes for my zipper, and I put my hand over hers.

My balls already hate me. But I can't have her hand on me yet. I'll embarrass myself, so I use the only reasonable excuse I can. "I've been traveling all night. I'd like to get cleaned up first. Grab a shower. I'll be fast for you."

"I don't mind. You smell good to me." She makes another attempt.

I lace my fingers with hers. "Sunny, sweets, I appreciate your enthusiasm, and I share it, but a shower would be a good idea."

"You could shower after." She tips her head. "It probably won't take long, right?"

I can't stop the laugh this time. She's so fucking innocent. "I'd much rather you put your hand on me *after* I shower, not before. And to be honest, I'd feel better if it did take a long time—you know, instead of two minutes or less."

"Oh! Right. Of course. Longer is always better." Her grin is a front-row seat to a sunrise. It makes the near-embarrassment worth it. She adjusts her bra, then swings her legs over the edge of the chair, bouncing to her feet. She holds out her hand. "Come on!"

I rearrange myself so I'm not tenting my shorts and lace my fingers with hers.

I grab my bag from the front hallway on our way upstairs. Sunny's parents are smart when it comes to protecting their only daughter's virtue. To get to her bedroom, you have to pass the master suite. There's an office separating their rooms, and the spare room is at the other end of the hall. That's also where the staircase leading to the third floor is. Her brother had the room there growing up.

The two times I've stayed here previously I slept in the spare room. It's a minefield of squeaky spots to get to Sunny. I sure as hell tried. Also, Titan sleeps outside her door; he might be small, but he's loud. I had to pretend I forgot where the bathroom was when her mom came out to see why he was making so much noise.

I head for the spare room out of habit, but Sunny grabs my hand and leads me down the hall. "You can use my bathroom."

Sunny's room resembles a student apartment. She has a quilt made of concert T-shirts in place of a duvet. A desk takes up one corner to create an office-like space. It's separated with strings of beads hanging from the ceiling. Titan comes running through the room, making the beads jingle as he jumps up on her desk chair. It spins around as he sits there, tongue lolling.

The best part about Sunny's room is her bed. She has a king. It's the only mistake her parents made, from what I can see—that and leaving her alone this weekend so I could visit without supervision. If I had a daughter, she'd be sleeping in a single bed until she moved out. I want to get naked, roll around on her concert duvet, and test out her flexibility while we fuck our brains out on that huge bed.

But first, a shower.

8

I'll Be the First

-MILLER-

I drop my bags and follow Sunny into the bathroom. She opens the linen closet and hands me a towel, then gestures to the tub with the see-through curtain. "There's shampoo and soap and my loofah in there, if you want to use it."

"Awesome. Thanks."

"Do you need anything else?" She glances at my crotch.

I still have a hard-on. "I think I'm good."

"You don't need anything else?" She waits a few more seconds, eyes darting from my crotch to my face and back again.

"I think everything's covered."

"You're positive?" She takes a step toward the door; she doesn't look all that excited about leaving.

"I'll be out in, like, ten." I turn on the water, and Sunny backs out into her room, closing the door behind her.

I'd love to invite her to join me, but my blue balls are something else. If she gets naked and wet and puts her hand on me, I'm done for. Better to take care of this situation on my own. I won't need much recovery time. I'll probably be ready to go again as soon as I'm out of the shower.

Shoving my shorts down, I set my cock free. My balls aren't even hanging, they're so tight. I step under the hot spray and give myself a couple of test strokes. It's not even enjoyable, my balls are so achy. Also, my hands are still postseason rough, upping the sensitivity factor.

I grab the closest bottle and squirt some into my palm to help speed things along—not that I need much. The minty aroma fills the steamy space. It explains why Sunny's hair always smells like a mojito. I'm stroking away, and all of a sudden things start to get hot. I turn into the spray to wash it off, but it compounds the heat. My dick feels like it's on fire.

I bite my knuckle to keep from swearing. Even with the blue balls and the fire dick, I finish in less than two minutes.

Now that I've taken care of issue number one, I check out the state of my balls. The situation could be worse. For now I'll have to make do with a clean up. I use the pink razor in the shower since mine is in my bag. Using it means my balls have now vicariously touched Sunny's legs, and possibly her pussy. Yup. I can already feel the blood rushing back down below the waist. I hurry through the rest of the shower.

It isn't until I'm toweling off that I realize I left my clean clothes in my duffle bag, which is on the other side of the door. I peek my head out, expecting to find Sunny lying on her bed, waiting for me—in my head she was naked—but she's nowhere to be found. She doesn't respond when I call her name.

I cross over to my bag and drop the towel as I hunt for a pair of shorts. The floor creaks as I find what I'm looking for.

"I brought you a giant penis." Sunny stands in the hall holding a bottle in each hand. "I mean a drink, since you already have one of those." She points in the direction of my crotch with the beer bottle.

"You think my thunder stick is gigantic?"

"Thunder stick?"

"Is lightning rod of pleasure better?"

She sets the drinks down on the nightstand and sits on the edge of the bed. "You're ridiculous."

I turn to the side and fumble around, trying to get my foot in the leg without flashing her again. I'm hoping the shower intermission doesn't backfire on me and they come off again soon.

Her eyes drop to my waist as I tuck myself into the shorts. "You're not hard anymore."

"Dicks are like balloons, they deflate."

She cocks an eyebrow. "Did you make it deflate?"

Lying is pointless. "Yeah."

She crosses her arms. "I wanted to make it deflate."

I walk over and stroke her cheek. "You can deflate my dick any damn time you want. You don't even have to ask."

She rolls her eyes, but leans into the touch. "Was the shower an excuse to deflate?"

"That and I always feel gross after flying." Violet's the one who made it a problem after she mentioned that I'm breathing recycled air, and it's full of people's skin particles and shit floating around in the confined space.

"So you—" She gestures to my crotch, making the whacking-off motion. She's generous in the way she holds her hand in a "C" shape, so it looks like I have a beer can for a dick.

"I did."

"I hope you cleaned my shower after you spanked your monkey in it." She sits on her bed and shifts toward the middle.

"Spank my—did you—" I follow after her. "I think you've

been talking to Violet too much."

"I have an older brother, remember? His skating friends were always here, being gross. I went to my first party before I was legal to vote. I might not have the personal experience you do, but I've heard it all. Oh, and those boys in figure skating are way worse than the ones who play hockey."

"Really?" Waters figure skated for a lot of years before he went to professional hockey. Almost every professional hockey player does a year of figure skating. It helps develop skills on the ice.

"Well, yeah, there are girls in figure skating. Those boys were always trying to get with them. Everyone was dating everyone else. Except Alex. He didn't date anyone because he was too busy." She cocks her head to the side. "I bet the girls loved you when you were in figure skating. Those spandex outfits don't hide anything."

"I didn't have to wear any spandex. I just took the lessons. I didn't do the performance stuff."

"Probably better that way. You would've terrified the ladies with your sword of lust."

"I like that one." I straddle her legs and lie on top of her, bracing my weight on my forearms, like a plank, and settle my head on her chest.

"What are you doing?"

"Cuddling with you. I like the snuggles."

We lie there for a while, not saying anything, existing. When it's me and her, and there isn't any bunny BS to get in the way, things are easy. We don't have to fill silence with meaningless conversation.

From my spot on her chest, I have a close-up view of her nipple through her bra and shirt. It's right there, so I do the logical thing and circle it with a fingertip. Then I go over it with my knuckle like it's a tiny speedbump and my finger is a miniature car. In my head I make the accompanying sound effects.

"Miller?" Her voice is breathy.

"Sweets?"

"Can you lift your head for a second?"

I don't want to, but I do because she asked. Sunny arches up, pulling her shirt and that horrible sports bra over her head. And just like that she's topless. And I'm hard again. Faint tan lines highlight her breasts.

"I thought maybe we could pick up where we left off."

"That's a great idea." I shift so I'm on my side next to her, one of my legs between hers.

With guys, all the foreplay is nice but unnecessary. We're happy with a hand grab and some stroking. Women are different. They need more than physical contact. It's psychological. It's always better when there's a lead up. I've seen some cool documentaries on the topic. It's like research. Porn is probably the worst possible thing a guy can watch to get pointers on what gets a woman off. Pounding away like a jackhammer won't do it. There has to be connection.

I kiss her neck and rest my hand on her waist, inching my way up until I'm almost palming the swell. Leaning to the side, I prop myself up on an elbow and go back to circling her nipple with a fingertip while I kiss my way across her jaw.

Sunny curves her hand around the back of my neck and pulls my mouth to hers. We make out for a while, and every time things start to heat up, I change my approach. Her little hums and moans turn desperate, so I nibble along her throat and over her collarbone until I reach her breast. When her hands go into my hair and she arches her back, I lick her nipple.

"Miller." It's more groan than word.

"You want more of that?" I ask.

"Please," she whispers.

"Like this?" I cover her nipple with my mouth, sucking softly.

"Exactly like that."

While I give her nipple attention, I ease a hand down her toned stomach and palm her through her shorts.

"What're you doing?" Sunny asks.

I stop sucking her nipple so I can answer. "Uh...touching you? Do you want me to stop?" I can't see why she would considering she's been rubbing herself on my thigh since I started with the nipple love, but it's better to ask than assume.

"Yes. No. Wha—I don't, but you already did that."

"I'm happy to do it again."

"But I already came, and you haven't."

I lift my head and meet her gaze. "It doesn't have to be a one-for-one thing, Sunny. I'll make you come as many times as you want, unless you have a thing against multiple orgasms." It's supposed to be a joke, but when she doesn't answer right away I move my hand to her stomach. "Sunny?"

Her eyes dart to the ceiling. "I've never had more than one."

"Seriously? But can't you have a bunch in a row?" If I were a woman I'd get myself off all the time, every hour of every day, probably. It's a good thing guys can't have that many in a row. Otherwise we'd never get anything done.

Sunny shrugs. "I've never tried to have another one. Usually my wrist is sore after the first one since it takes so long."

"It didn't take long for me to get you off downstairs."

She bites her lip. "It didn't."

"You cool with it if I try again?"

"Okay. If you want, but don't worry if you can't make it happen."

"Oh, I'll make it happen." I fold back on my knees and hook my fingers into the waistband of her shorts. "Can I take these off?"

At her nod, I drag them over her hips and down her legs. I take a moment to appreciate her panties. They're cotton, with little flowers on them. Pretty and sweet, just like Sunny. And they lead to the one place I want to bury my face in more than anything else in this world.

"Can these go, too?" I ask, fingering the waistband.

She lifts her hips, pulls them down, and tosses them over the edge of the bed, along with her shorts.

"Sunny Sunshine." I let out a low whistle as my gaze roves over her curves. "You naked is a sight to behold."

Her cheeks flush and she bites her lip, then sighs as I run my hands up the outside of her thighs. I stretch out over her, skin to skin—apart from the barrier of my shorts—as I settle between her parted thighs. Starting at her lips, I kiss my way down her body, stopping at her nipples before moving on. Halfway down her stomach, she grabs me by the hair. "What are you doing?"

"I'm going to make you come again, remember?"

"But—I—you—down?"

She seems flustered, so I explain, in case my actions aren't clear enough. "I wasn't planning on using my fingers this time."

"Oh. You want to—"

"Go down on you."

"With your mouth?"

"That's generally how it's done, unless you know another way I'm unfamiliar with."

"Uhhhhhhh…" She draws it out.

"Unless you don't want me to."

"It's not that," she whispers.

"Awesome. I can't wait to taste you, sweetness." I kiss the

spot below her navel again, but her fingers tighten in my hair.

"Miller."

I bring my gaze back to hers.

"I have to tell you something."

"Sure. Fire away."

Her blond hair is fanned out over the pillow and her cheeks are flushed. "It's nice that you want to try to make me come with your mouth, but that's never happened before. So don't, like, sprain your tongue trying or anything."

Hear those tires screeching? That's my brain backing up. "Whoa. Wait. What?" I must have heard that wrong. "Do you mean no one's ever made you come with their mouth, or no one's ever gone down on you before?"

"Well..." There she goes, twirling her hair around her finger. "I mean, until you no one had made me come, ever."

"What the fuck? You never had an orgasm until me?" Inside my head there's a stadium cheering for me.

Sunny stares at my forehead. "I've had orgasms."

I need more information. "So what do you mean it's never happened before? No one's ever eaten your cookie?"

"No. I mean, yes. I mean—God, I shouldn't have said anything."

I'm embarrassing her. I want to ask more questions about how the hell she managed to have a long-term boyfriend in high school—that's the information Violet passed on to me from Waters—and never managed to have an orgasm. But I don't want her to feel bad about it. I do want to find the guy and smack him upside the head—and possibly thank him at the same time. His inadequacy means I get to experience all these beautiful firsts with Sunny.

I plant an elbow on either side of her ribs and hover over her so we're face to face. "Yes or no questions only, okay?"

"Okay."

"You've had orgasms?"

"Yes."

"On your own?" I'm clarifying. Also, it's sexy as fuck to think about her touching herself.

"Yes."

"With your fingers?"

"Yes."

"Anything else?"

Her cheeks flame. "That's not a yes or no question."

That's definitely a yes. "We'll come back to that one later. Has anyone else ever gotten you off?" She's already told me the answer to this question. I'm making one hundred percent certain I heard her correctly.

"No."

"Never?"

"Miller." She clamps her legs against my sides.

I lean down and kiss the side of her jaw. I also shift my hips, rubbing up on her. "But you've had sex before?"

She ducks her head so the top is tucked under my chin and her nose is at my throat. I like that she's shy about this stuff.

"Sunny?"

Her head moves up and down.

"Is that a yes?" When she bites my collarbone, I press my hips into hers. "You do realize I'm on a mission now, right?"

She releases my skin from her teeth. "What kind of mission?"

"An orgasm mission. I'll make you see stars with my tongue."

"You can give it a shot." She says this like she expects it not to happen.

It's on like Donkey Kong now. "It'll happen, sweets."

I make my way down her body with my mouth, taking a detour across her right hip to her navel. Her muscles tighten as I kiss along that sensitive place between the top of her thigh and her pelvis. As nervous as she is, her legs part farther, giving me the go-ahead to make good on my promise.

Hooking a palm behind her knee, I kiss the inside of her thigh. I pause at her sharp inhalation, taking in all her long limbs and soft curves.

This is about more than the orgasm; it's about Sunny and her absolute lack of them. And I want to be the one who changes that.

I take things slow, starting at her knee and kissing a path along the inside of her thigh. I pay special attention to her moans and the way her hips shift to help me gauge what she likes. After a few minutes of teasing, I move over an inch and nibble the skin at the juncture between her thigh. Her clit is peeking out, all swollen and looking to be licked, so I do.

"Oh my God." Sunny's legs clamp around my head.

"Too much?" I prop myself up on my elbows and put a palm on the inside of her thighs.

"Yes. No. I'm not sure."

"Should I try that again?"

"Okay." She nods vigorously. "Please."

I keep my eyes on her as I kiss her clit. She doesn't try to vice-grip my head with her thighs this time, so I press my tongue flat against her and lick up, real slow. Her brow furrows and her mouth drops.

"You tell me if it's too much, okay?"

"It's not too much. It's incrawsome."

"Is that good?"

"Sorry." She sucks in a deep breath. "I meant to say awesome or incredible, but it came out as one word."

"I like it." I drop my head, alternating soft strokes of my tongue with gentle suction, taking my cues based on how much she wants to decapitate me with her thighs. My forearms are getting a serious workout from holding them open.

Her toes curl at my ribs, telling me that she's getting close. I suck her clit as I slip two fingers inside her.

"How's that feel, Sunny Sunshine?" I curl my fingers.

"Gooooood." Her eyes roll up.

I do it again. "Just good?"

"So good?"

"You tell me when it's amazing." I watch her as I curl my fingers and suck harder.

"Oh...that's—" She throws her head back, and a needy whimper escapes.

"How's that now?"

"Amazing."

"If I keep it up, you think you'll come?"

Her nod is frantic. One hand fists my hair, the other grips the sheets. All of a sudden her eyes pop open and her mouth drops. Her shock as her whole body tenses is the best damn thing I've ever seen.

"Ride it out, sweets."

She keeps her eyes on me while she does just that. I give her one more courtesy finger curl, in case of residual orgasm shocks. She shudders, then melts into the bed as I kiss my way up her body. I sweep a few strands of damp hair away from her face and wait for her to open her eyes.

"Hi."

She gives me a dopey smile. "Hi."

"Was that fun?"

Sunny nods. "So fun."

"How you feeling?" I ask, grinning at her sated expression.

"So relaxed. It's so much better when it's someone else doing all the work."

I laugh. "Right?"

"Your mouth is made of awesome."

"You think so?"

"Totally made of awesome." She wraps her arms around my neck and her legs around my waist. My cock is nestled right where my mouth was a minute ago. I'm so damn hard right now. My balls are back to being achy.

Sunny sucks on my bottom lip before she slips her tongue inside my mouth. Breaking away, she asks, "Is that what I taste like?"

"Mm-hmm."

She sucks my top lip this time. "Do you like that? The way I taste?"

God, I love how sweetly curious she is.

"I love the way you taste. I'll go down on you whenever you want."

"Really?"

"Definitely."

"Like, if I asked you to do it again right now, you would?"

"You want me to, and I will."

"You're serious." She looks baffled.

"For fucking right I'm serious." I make a move to head back down, but she tightens her legs around my waist.

"You can eat me again later."

"Oh, I plan to."

She ends the conversation with her tongue in my mouth again.

Eventually her hands start to wander. She pushes my shorts over my hips. The waistband gets caught on the head, but we manage to wrestle it free.

As soon as I'm naked, we line everything up so we're playing slip 'n' slide with my cock. She's so wet and hot and soft. I want her, want to show her how good we can be.

But I don't want to push her, either. "We don't have to have sex."

I'd love to have hot, sweaty sex with Sunny, but I'd settle for slip 'n' sliding my way to the land of Jizztopia.

For a long moment we stare at each other, not moving. I study her face the same way I would the offense when I'm figuring out the next play. There's a flash of uncertainty. That's all I need. Just a hint that she's not sure she wants this, so I back off.

Sunny's legs wrap tighter around my waist and her nails dig into the back of my neck again. Shifting so my weight is on my left arm, I pick up a lock of her hair and twist it around my fingers, brushing it along her neck. "I'm not pushing for anything from you, Sunny. I know I keep messing things up. I don't want to risk you feeling bad about your decisions when it comes to being with me."

There's nothing tentative about the way she shifts her pelvis so my cock slides low. There's no hesitation when she turns her cheek and bites the fleshy part of my palm before she kisses it.

"I'm the only person you're seeing?"

"It's been me and my hand—and yours, when I see you."

"Me, too." She smiles, but it turns pensive almost immediately. "Well, mostly."

I tense, because what the fuck does that mean?

Her eyes go wide, possibly at my expression. "I mean, it's just been me, but sometimes I use…helpers."

"Helpers?" I have no idea what she's talking about. It makes me think of little elves running around down there, rubbing her clit for her.

"Mmm... I have this little vibrating thing called a bullet, but it's still just me touching myself. I'll stop talking now so we can have sex."

She pulls me back down to her mouth. We're slipping and sliding until it gets to the point where we're both moaning, and I'm at risk of blowing my load all over her stomach if I don't get in there soon. I glance down at the floor where my pants lie in a heap, wondering how I'm going to get to my wallet. Which is when I realize, I don't have a condom.

9

Some Things I Didn't Need to Know

-MILLER-

"Shit." I bury my face in her neck.

I haven't been carrying condoms because I haven't had a reason to use them. And in my rush to get to the airport I didn't think to grab them from my nightstand drawer.

"What's wrong?" Sunny runs her foot up the outside of my leg, shifting things around. I go lower, away from the safety of her clit and closer to hot heaven.

"I didn't come prepared." If my dick were a person, he would grow arms and legs and kick the shit out of me. I can't believe I didn't pack the most important damn item of them all. And I'm supposed to be a top-tier boy scout.

"Prepared?" She runs a hand through my hair and tilts her head back, giving me access to her neck. Her other hand curves over my ass.

I kiss along her throat to her lips. "I didn't bring condoms."

"Oh."

Her obvious disappointment makes me feel better and worse. We can't go without protection. Even if she's on the pill. I need a personal assistant to help manage my life, and even that isn't entirely successful. I'm not ready to add a mini human to the equation.

"Oh! Wait! Alex always used to keep some in his bedroom. I'll go check!" She unhooks her legs and pushes on my chest. I fold back on my knees and hope like hell the condom gods have my back. Sunny rolls out from under me and bounces off the edge of the bed. She stops at the door. "Don't go anywhere. I'll be right back."

I lie on my side, my hard-on hovering a few inches off the bed, suspended in mid-air. "I'll be right here, in this exact position, when you get back."

She bites her lip and looks me over, then turns and runs down the hall, her pert ass jiggling. As I lie on her bed, waiting for her to return, I wonder how she knows about her brother's stash of condoms. Maybe she snooped in his room. I can't imagine Waters offering up that information willingly. He's far too protective of Sunny to help her out in the prophylactic department. If he knew she was about to use them with me, he'd probably end me.

Sunny returns a minute later wearing only a huge smile as she jumps on the bed. "Jackpot!" She drops a pile of condoms on the comforter.

We can have multiple rounds tonight. Morning sex could be an option—along with afternoon, mid-afternoon, early evening, and late-night sex. I pick up one of the gold squares and flip it over. It's not a regular, run-of-the-mill condom. It's one of the XLs.

"These came from your brother's room?"

"Yeah!"

"Did you bring his entire stash?"

"Nope. There's loads more if we need them!" She's bouncing, and her boobs jiggle with the movement. It's distracting. "He used to have a couple of boxes in there, back before he moved to Chicago. I figured I'd take a chance and see if there were any left, and this is what I found. I guess he probably doesn't need them anymore, so they're all ours."

I ignore the last part. I don't want to think about what he and my sister get up to since I've already witnessed the tail end of fuckery—literally—in the team locker room after he got ejected from a game for fighting. No amount of brain scouring will get rid of walking in on that. The only good part about that night was meeting Sunny.

I sift through the pile, flipping them over as I go. So far they're all XLs. "You think he used these?"

Sunny nods.

"You're sure he didn't get them for promo or something?" I've never checked out Waters' junk on purpose, but we all walk around the locker room and air our shit out after it's been cramped in a cup. Except Randy. He's weird about shit like that. Waters doesn't look like he should need these. I'm way bigger than he is when I'm hanging low. But then I'm a shower, not a grower.

"I have no idea. All I know is he keeps them in his closet."

"Why would he need all of these if he wasn't planning on using them?"

She waves off the comment. "I don't think he usually has this many. His friend Reid gave these to him as a joke for his twenty-fifth birthday."

"Huh. Well, I guess we lucked out. It looks like you found the mother lode." Now I know way too much about Waters' business end. I sift through the pile and finally find the right kind.

"I checked the expiration date. They're all good for, like, two more years." She's doing that thing with her hair again.

I hold up the green foil square. "This is perfect. I'll thank your brother the next time I see him."

Sunny's eyes go wide. "You better not! He'll castrate you."

I slip an arm around her waist, and condoms crinkle under us as I roll over on top of her. "You don't think he'd be cool with us being safe?"

"Alex would like to think he's done a great job acting as my guard dog since high school."

"You're right. I won't thank him. We'll keep his secret stash between us." I drop a kiss on her chin and another on her lips.

Now that we have protection, I want to take my time with Sunny. Being the provider of the first big "O" is one hell of an ego boost already. But if I can make her come during sex…I'm the White Knight in the land of Orgasmia. I want to be the one who makes her feel good, who takes care of her.

We make out until Sunny claws her way down my back and starts jabbing her nails into my ass. I fold back on my knees, but Sunny grabs the foil packet before I can.

"I want to do it," she declares.

"It's all you, sweets."

She's gorgeous, cheeks flushed, hair a golden riot, eyes heavy-lidded. My cock twitches as she strokes me slowly. She tears open the wrapper, inspects it to make sure she has it the right way around, then rolls it over the head.

Her tongue peeks out, and she glances up. "Is this okay?"

"It's perfect. You're perfect." I help her roll it down the rest of the way.

Sunny folds her legs underneath her and raises her knees, one hand gripping my erection, the other one smooths up my chest. I bend to meet her lips.

"You're all ready for me," she whispers against my lips.

"I sure am."

She lays down on the bed and I stretch out over her, settling between her thighs. She rubs the head of my cock over her clit, then moves me lower. I cup her cheek and keep my eyes on her as I ease inside.

A soft sigh falls from her lips. I can't focus on any one sensation without being sidetracked by another. The visual and physical stimulation has me on overload.

Sunny's fingers sweep up my back, the lightness of her touch causes my muscles to jump. When she reaches my shoulder she makes a circle, then draws a line up my neck, following the edge of my jaw all the way to my chin.

Even though she's underneath me, she's the one in control. I won't move until she tells me to. Being inside her, being this close to her, surrounded by her... "You feel incredible." My voice is low and gritty.

"So do you." Sunny's fingers drift over my lips, her eyes searching mine. Her smile is as soft as her touch. "Kiss me, please."

I drop my head. It's unhurried, gentle brushes of lips and warm sweeps of tongue. There's none of the earlier aggression when I wanted her worked up. A knot of guilt settles in my stomach. For a moment I worry that I don't deserve her, to have this piece of her. But then Sunny shifts under me, circling her hips, and I forget everything but the way she feels.

We move together, and I'm utterly captivated. I want every memory branded in my brain, the softness of her body, the warmth, the way she sighs and moans, her hands in my hair, nails biting my skin. We kiss and move and groan into each other's mouths as I change the angle and draw her left leg up higher so I can hit that sweet spot with every slow thrust.

She gasps, and her sweet moans get deeper, more primal. I push up on one arm, one hand curved against her cheek.

Sunny's fingertips rest under my bottom lip and her palm curls around my chin. It's intimate and dominating at the same time. And I fucking love it. Her eyes are locked on mine again, something like surprise making them flare.

She starts to tremble, her legs tightening around my hips, her left knee pulling higher. I hold it there, between my ribs and my biceps, helping to keep the angle for her.

"Oh God, Miller. I think—" The words are cut off by her ragged inhale. Her grip on my chin tightens as her mouth drops open, and she shakes her head like she doesn't believe it's happening.

"Just let go, sweets. Let me feel what I can do for you." I'm right there with her, unable to look away as the orgasm rolls through her. "So beautiful. Just stunning."

Something happens then, and it's unexplainable. It's like being body-checked by all the sensations I associate with orgasms: the tingle, the burn, the tightness, the expansion, and the final explosion—all of it happens at the same time. With it comes an emotional cocktail that I'm unprepared for. It's that high feeling again, but more extreme. I'm submerged *in* her. Like I'm inside her in more than just the literal sense.

When the orgasm finally subsides, I slide my arm under her and roll to the side, taking her with me.

"I don't even know what happened there," I mumble into her hair.

She makes a contented little noise. Her nose brushes my cheek and her lips move along my jaw.

When she reaches the corner of my mouth I turn my head and kiss her, going deep, holding her close. My cock kicks, like maybe he's fighting to get hard again and keep going. It's

"We're good. We got things sorted."

"Talked your way out of it, did you?" She doesn't sound all that surprised.

I think about all the ways I made Sunny come last night. "It always looks worse than it is. But yeah, I managed to smooth things over."

"So you found the box of condoms in the bag of gifts, then?"

"Box of condoms?"

"I got you two, in case you were extra busy."

"No shit. You're the best, Amber."

"Remember that when the bill for my birthday present comes in this year."

I don't think she's joking. "You're always saving my ass, so you deserve whatever you choose—as long as it's not a car."

"Well, there goes that plan." She sighs dramatically. "So I wanted to talk to you about the camp and some possible promotion opportunities."

"You know how I feel about that—"

"Hear me out before you say no."

I sigh, but let her try to sell it to me before I shut her down.

"I think it would be a good idea for you to let one of the local papers interview you."

"I don't do well in interviews."

"You don't do well in scripted interviews. You're fine when there aren't any lines to learn. It doesn't have to be a big thing, just a few questions about your role at the camp."

"It'll be a circus."

"It won't. It's small town out there, Miller. It's not like being in Chicago where everyone goes wild over you guys."

"Okay. I'll think about it. Oh, hey, Randy emailed me something about a car wash fundraiser out near the camp. I'm probably going to go with him if the timing works out."

"Do you know who's hosting it?" Amber asks.

"No. Some guy Randy knows from when he played for Toronto. Randy says he puts on a lot of events."

"What's the charity? Can you forward me any information?"

"It's for breast cancer. And sure, I've got an email I can flip you."

"Okay. Sounds good. I'll make sure it's on the up and up."

Any cancer fundraiser gets me, and Amber knows it; so does Vi. I lost my mom when I was three to a brain tumor. I don't have a lot of memories of her, but I try to give back where I can. "Okay. Yeah. And I'll check with Balls."

"Great. Don't forget you're picking him up from the airport, either. I'm sending you his flight details. You'll have time to connect with him before Sunday?"

"Yeah. Of course."

"Just checking. You might be busy blowing through all those condoms."

Amber has a sense of humor. She has to if she wants to work with guys like me. "Ha ha. I'll take a ten-minute break to deal with details."

"Have fun with Sunny."

"I plan to. Repeatedly. Enjoy the bears."

"Fuck you, Miller."

I get a dial tone and smile. Amber's an awesome PA.

Before I go looking for Sunny, I decide to get the trimmer out. I'll be off to camp soon enough, and mosquitoes have a tendency to get caught in my arm hair and bite the shit out of me if I don't take it down to a number three.

I'm not as hairy as Vi makes me out to be with her mythical fur-covered creature comparisons. Trimming is messy business, so I step out on the balcony overlooking the backyard. There's a lattice for privacy, but I don't want to flash the neighbors, so I leave my shorts on.

Resting my foot on the railing, I start on my left leg. I go over everything twice. My shorts are problematic, though. I peek around the lattice. I can see the edge of the pool. On the other side is the neighbor's patio. An old dude sits in a lounge chair, drinking iced tea and reading the paper in his bathrobe. There's a pair of binoculars on the table beside his drink. This has to be Sunny's neighbor. But he can't see me, so I'm safe to drop the shorts.

Moving on to my arms, I resume my mission. On the final pass with the trimmer, a strong gust of wind lifts the liberated hairs, and the cross-breeze from inside the house creates a cataclysmic weather system. A mini-tornado spins the fluff around in a circle. The tumbleweed of blond rises into the air, disappearing over the edge of the balcony.

There's some sputtering and clanging from the patio next door. "What is that?" A yippy dog barks in distress as the yelling continues. "Thor! You made me spill my tea!"

I turn off the trimmer and flatten myself against the sliding door. Shimmying over a couple of steps, I peek through the lattice. Sunny's neighbor has knocked over his chair and drink. His dog, Thor—which, incidentally, is tiny—chases after one of my fuzz tumbleweeds.

"Is everything okay?" Sunny calls out.

"Oh, hello, Sunshine. Thor's chasing fluffs."

"That's nice—Oh! Mr. Woodcock! It looks like you forgot to put on your pants again."

I take another peek through the lattice. Mr. Woodcock's robe has come undone, his saggy nuts and his wrinkled wiener hanging out. I hope my nuts never droop that low.

I slip back into the house and return to Sunny's room. I rinse off in the shower and throw on a pair of swim shorts. The condoms Amber was talking about are in my duffle. I tuck a couple into my back pocket, just in case.

I cut through the kitchen and pour myself a cup of coffee on my way to find Sunny.

I find her sitting in a lounge chair with her laptop. She's wearing a pale green bikini and a sheer white cover-up. Titan and Andy are sleeping at her feet. She's wearing headphones and concentrating on whatever she's reading, so she doesn't hear me.

She's so engrossed that she still hasn't noticed me standing behind her. Her hair is twisted up in a clip, but a few strands have fallen loose, and they sweep across her shoulders when the breeze picks up. I glance around the backyard, checking to see how visible we are to Mr. Woodcock. It seems protected. Only the second-floor windows of his house have a view of the pool.

I set my coffee on the side table, then move to the end of her lounger, gently running my finger up the bottom of her foot. Sunny screams and nearly tosses her laptop at me. Her high-pitched scream wakes up Andy and Titan, who both start barking.

"You scared the heck out of me, Miller!"

"You were deep in thought." I take the laptop from her and set it on the side table, then uncross her ankles and kneel at the end of the chair between them.

"What are you doing?"

"I'm saying good morning."

"It's almost noon."

"It's still morning." I run my hands up the outside of her legs and fit myself between them. "And I woke up to an empty bed." I kiss her collarbone and make a path with my lips all the way to her mouth.

"My ancient neighbors are probably watching."

"He flashed you. It's only fair I flash him back." I reach behind me and shove my shorts down past my ass, grabbing the condoms while I'm at it.

"You saw that?"

"If he's creeping on us, we might as well give him something to look at." I drop the condoms on the side table.

"We're outside." She bites her lip.

"You don't have to lose any clothes." I skim her thigh with gentle fingers. "You just have to be quiet."

She nabs a condom. "You're a bad influence."

11

I Should Have Planned This Better

-MILLER-

An hour later we're still hanging out by the pool. I have a bite mark on my shoulder from when Sunny came. She's extra relaxed.

"You should let me put some sunscreen on your back." I'm looking for an excuse to touch her again.

"Am I getting a burn?" She glances at her shoulder.

"You're okay for now." I pat the space between my legs.

She eases between them, her hands on my calves. Her shoulders are dotted with freckles from being out in the sun so much already. Sunny spent a few days last month volunteering at a community garden, planting flowers as part of a revitalization project. She's into stuff like that. It's one of the things we have in common.

"So I head out to that camp tomorrow," I tell her, smoothing lotion over her skin.

"I love that you do this."

"Thanks. It's fun." I make sure I get under the halter strap on her bikini.

"Anyway, maybe you'd want to visit while I'm there?" At her silence, I rush on. "You could come at the end if you're not into the whole hockey camp deal. You could even meet some of the kids if you wanted to, or not. They have cabins, so you wouldn't have to tent it. Then we could rent a cottage for a few days."

She's quiet for another moment. "That sounds fun. I wish you would've asked sooner." Sunny turns so she's mostly facing me.

Oh shit. I know this look. It's a bad one. "If getting time off work is a problem maybe I can take care of it—"

"Getting time off work isn't the issue, Miller."

"So it shouldn't be a problem, right? You can come, then. Unless you don't want to."

She twists her hair around her finger. "Lily asked me to go camping with her. She and her boyfriend have been having problems lately and he can be...not always the nicest. At first I wasn't going to go, because there was already a group, but then all that stuff happened, and she asked again, and I promised her yesterday I would."

Sunny isn't used to actual camping. I know this because she's grown up doing the cottage thing. It's big in Canada. People buy houses on lakes and drive through terrible traffic on the weekends so they can get hang out on a dock and have campfires.

"So go camping with her for a few days and then visit me."

"It's not really that simple. Chapleau is pretty far north and we're taking Benji's family's RV."

"You can't change your plans? You don't even really like camping."

"Their trailer has a bathroom. I can't back out on her, Miller. Benji has been really difficult lately. Honestly I'm worried about how she'll be able to deal with him if I'm not there."

This doesn't work with my plan. I should've asked before I came, but I didn't want to get ahead of myself, and now I'm screwed. Things start to wind back up for training soon. I have endorsement campaigns.

"What if I meet you there afterward? Can I drive to you?" Lily isn't my biggest fan, but camping with her might force her to at least talk to me.

"It's about eight hours by car."

"What about flying? Can I do that instead?"

"There isn't an airport nearby. We could plan another visit for a few weeks from now, before my fall semester starts," she says softly.

No way am I leaving it that long. I need to see more of Sunny, not less. "I'll drive out there after I'm done at the camp. We can spend a few days doing whatever. Then we can drive back together. I just need to know where it is."

I'll take whatever time I can get with Sunny, even if it means dealing with her not-so-friendly bestie. Those two are tight. I need to find a way to get her to like me.

"I can call you when I'm there and drop a pin in maps? It's pretty remote." She taps her lip with her finger.

"Is it even safe?"

"Benji's camped there before. Last year he went with a bunch of his friends. But Lily warned me that reception might not be the best out there."

Having no line of communication with Sunny isn't ideal. I was without a phone for less than twenty-four hours and look how that blew up in my face. Sunny alone with Lily for a week could undo the last twenty-four hours.

"So how will I let you know when I'm on my way?"

"We'll probably go into town for food and stuff every few days. There's one about half an hour away. Maybe we can touch base then? I'm sorry, Miller. I've been thinking about backing out since I woke up this morning, but I can't bail on Lily. She's my best friend." She brushes her hair over her lips.

It occurs to me that Sunny's directionally challenged. Driving out into the middle of the Canadian wilderness to go commune with nature is all well and good, as long as she has someone else to navigate. I have no clue how adept Lily is when it comes to this kind of thing.

"Does Alex know you're going?" This is one of those times where I actually wouldn't hate it if her older brother pulled the over-protective card.

"He knows. He thinks it's great. And Lily and Benji go camping all the time. She was in Girl Guides all the way to Pathfinders."

I have no idea what that is, but it sounds like it might be like the Canadian female equivalent of Boy Scouts for girls in Canada. "So it's the three of you? What if they get into a fight?"

"A couple of Benji's friends are coming, too. We all went to high school together."

"So there's a group of you going?" More than three people is good, especially if Benji is a problem.

"Yeah. I've known them all for years. If you did come after the camp you could get to know Lily better," Sunny says hopefully.

"She's definitely not my number one fan," I grumble.

"She's only met you once, and she doesn't know you apart from what she sees on social media. Maybe if you were more open about all the good things you do outside of hockey, and parties, and going to the bar, people would have something else to focus on besides the negative stuff."

I sigh and lean back in the chair. This conversation is on the road to becoming another fight. I don't want to spend what's left of my time with her arguing. "It's complicated, Sunny. If people know where I'm going to be, it floods programs with kids who don't need the support." As it is, I usually have a campaign set up to fund the highest-need families. I get Amber and my dad to go through the applications first and pick the top five. I find it too hard to choose on my own. And I make sure any promo stuff happens after the fact, so the camps are full for the following summer.

I wrap my arms around her waist and pull her against my chest. I need to work this from a different angle. Being a possessive boyfriend won't help. I need to be understanding. "I know you're being a good friend."

I need to make the most of the time we have left together and secure more sooner rather than later.

"September is coming fast," I continue. "You'll be back in school, and I'll be in training. Then the season starts, and I'll be traveling a lot. I want more than a couple of days here and there."

"I want that, too. I like being with you."

I kiss her shoulder. "So it's cool if I come out there and do the drive back with you? Maybe I can get Lily to warm up to me."

"That'd be nice. She's a great friend."

"Will I get to meet the people you're camping with before I leave?"

"That's the other thing I was meaning to tell you..."

This doesn't sound good.

"Lily is picking me up tomorrow morning."

"Morning? I thought we had the day together." Randy sent

me his flight details, I'm not picking him up until dinner.

"Lily said eight, but Benji is always late, so probably closer to nine or ten."

"Can't you leave in the afternoon?"

"It's a long drive. We need to be there before dark so we can set up camp; otherwise we'll all have to sleep in the trailer." Sunny's voice softens. "I'm sorry. I don't want this to ruin the rest of our time together."

I trace the edge of her jaw with a fingertip. I'm pulling out all the stops. "You don't have to explain. It's my fault."

"It was a misunderstanding."

"I'm sorry I was an idiot."

"You're not."

"Sometimes I am." I kiss the bottom of her chin and the tip of her nose, hovering over her lips. "You want to go inside?"

"Inside?"

"I feel like I should apologize."

"And we need to go inside for that?"

"I like to demonstrate how sorry I am with actions, not words."

"We should definitely go inside then."

12

Cookie Break

-MILLER-

Sunny and I spend the afternoon in bed, working up a serious appetite while I explore exactly how bendy she is. By the time we're done, she's had four orgasms, I've had two, and we've had sex in positions I'd never considered feasible.

"I'm starving." I'm still between her legs, enjoying the feel of Sunny's hands running up and down my back. The come-down from my orgasm lingers. It's an incredible feeling, even better than winning a hockey game.

"I don't think you need any more cookie today."

"I haven't even eaten—" I lift my head from her chest. She has the cutest look on her face, all wide-eyed and pleased with herself. "You being funny, Sunny Sunshine?"

She grins.

"I can always eat more cookie." I start kissing a path down her stomach, but she grabs my head in her hands.

"If you go down on me again, you'll either have a callus on

your tongue, or I'll have one on my cookie."

I laugh and kiss my way back up to her mouth. "I need to eat some real food anyway. Let's put clothes on and go out. I want to take you somewhere nice."

"Oooh! I know the perfect place. You'll love it!"

Sunny pushes on my chest and rolls out from under me, hopping to her feet.

Half an hour later we're dressed and in downtown Guelph. My idea of the perfect place to eat isn't the same as Sunny's. We're at a vegan restaurant. I'm not knocking the food. Plants are actually pretty tasty. I just know I'll be hungry again by the time we get back in the car. Still, she's excited, so I order half the menu and stuff my face with food that's never canoodled with a cow or even a fish.

I falsely believe that no one who works here can possibly watch hockey. They all have dreads and wear shoes made out of hemp. But I'm dead wrong about the hockey thing. The guy who seats us knows who I am, and he can't stop talking about how much he wishes I'd been traded to Toronto.

Sunny must come to this place often, because the wait staff knows her by name. She introduces me to a bunch of people, but she doesn't call me her boyfriend. She doesn't call me anything other than my name, but we sit on the same side of the table instead of across from each other, and she snuggles into my side. That says a lot more than a title.

• • •

Later, when we get back to her house, we watch a movie. Naked. Well, there isn't much watching after the first fifteen minutes, but it was fun while it lasted, and even more fun afterward. When Sunny falls asleep on the couch, I raid the fridge. I don't find much aside from healthy options and rice and almond milk.

I think I've hit the jackpot when I check the freezer and find it full of baked goods. Sadly, all the lids have those red circles with the line through them covering the face of a stick man eating the contents. There's also a pot leaf on there. It must be Sunny's dad's research. He works for a medical marijuana lab, perfecting strains. He's wildly intelligent. Apparently Sunny likes to help with the baking part of that. I call a local pizza shop and order myself a snack.

Sunny wakes up as I'm polishing off my midnight meal. A pile of cleaned-off chicken wing bones sits next to the Styrofoam container. Sunny stretches, and the blanket I've covered her with falls so her nipples peek out.

"What're you doing?"

"Staring at your boobs."

She blinks blearily, pulling the blanket up and leaning forward to inspect what's in my bowl. Her nose crinkles in that cute way that tells me she's grossed out. "Your bowl is an animal graveyard."

"It was delicious, though."

"You like a box of death for a snack?"

"It sounds way less appealing when you say it like that."

She stands, dropping the blanket on the floor. "I'm going to bed."

I drop the last bone in the bowl. "Hold on. I'm coming, too."

"You can't leave those there." She points to the death bowl. "Andy will eat them and be sick."

I rush to clean them up as she heads for the stairs.

Tonight's the last night we get to sleep together. Tomorrow morning she's leaving on that stupid road trip. I need to make sure I'm on her mind while we're apart. I don't try for sex again; I go for the snuggle instead. Sunny falls asleep wrapped around me, her warm cheek on my chest.

13

So Close

-Miller-

I wake up to terrible, humid breath in my face. I crack a lid to find Andy's nose an inch away from mine. "Hey, buddy. You need a mint." I roll over, but Sunny's side of the bed is already empty. It's only seven, but she's leaving in a couple of hours, so I drag myself out of bed, throwing off the heavy hands of sleep. I don't bother with boxers. My plan is to find her and use my morning wood to my advantage.

When I reach the stairs, I'm hit with the sweet smell of cinnamon. Sunny can bake, as evidenced by the treats in the freezer. Her cookies are the best. I snicker as I take the stairs down to the kitchen. Now that I've eaten her actual cookie, I have all kinds of dirty baked goods jokes. Unfortunately, it's another one of those things I can't share with the guys.

I find her in the kitchen. Her hair is still in the same braid from last night, except it's a mess. The sun streams in the window over the sink where she's rinsing fresh fruit, the light catching the fine blond flyaways, creating a halo. She's wearing shorts and a tank top, and she's braless.

She doesn't notice me right away, so I lean against the doorjamb to watch her. She hums along to the radio as she peels peaches. I wish she wasn't leaving this morning.

I move in behind her, wrapping an arm around her waist. She gasps, and at first I think it's out of surprise, but then I notice the fine line of blood welling across the pad of her index finger.

"Ah, shit, Sunny. I'm sorry." I shimmy us over to the sink, turn on the tap, and adjust the water temperature. When it's cold I put her hand under the stream. So much for a good morning surprise.

Sunny turns her head away, pressing her cheek into my chest. "Is it still bleeding?"

I put pressure below the gash, checking to see how bad it is. It's a clean cut, and it's not too deep, just a surface wound. Blood wells again so I move her hand back under the water. "It's not bad. It doesn't need stitches or anything." I kiss the top of her head.

She does this shuddery thing.

"You got bandages down here?"

"I think there might be some in the drawer." She flops her hand to the right.

"I'll get one, then?" I can't move until she stops leaning on me.

"I think I need to sit down." The words come out all drunk-sounding. Then Sunny slides down my body. I catch her under the arms before she hits the floor. It takes me a second to realize she's fainted.

The paper towels are a couple inches out of reach. To prevent her from falling over, I stand in front of her, bracing my thigh against her shoulder to hold her up. It isn't the best position, well, not for the situation, anyway. My dick is two inches from her face, and I'm naked.

She starts to come to as I snatch up the paper towels. Ripping off a couple of sheets, I start to crouch again, but she wraps her arms around my legs and face-butts me in the junk. I grunt, pain shooting up my spine and nailing me right in the back of the throat. Bile comes with it, as does the sensation that my balls are going to forever reside below my Adam's apple.

I drop to the floor in front of her, gritting my teeth. My vision blurs and then clears.

"Miller?" She's all breathy and confused.

I feel her palm on my cheek. Her piercing scream makes my ears hurt as much as my balls. Then she faints again.

I wipe at the damp spot on my cheek and check my fingers. There's a faint streak of red, almost dried already. I wet the paper towel and wipe my cheek until it comes clean. Then I wrap a clean paper towel around her finger and wait for her to come around a second time. My balls still really fucking hurt, but they'll be fine in a couple hours. A face-butt to the groin is nothing like a puck or a stick to the cup.

Her eyes flutter open.

"Hey."

She glances around. "Did I faint?"

"Twice."

"I don't handle the sight of blood well."

"I figured that out."

"Sorry."

"Aside from the face-butt to the balls, it's cool."

"The face-butt to what?"

"Nothing. Don't worry about it. I'll get you a bandage now, 'kay?"

At her nod, I stand and turn toward the cabinets she pointed to in the first place.

"You're naked."

"Yup." I open the drawer and rummage around, looking for a bandage. I move aside a ball of elastic bands and a million pens and pieces of scrap paper.

"Why?"

I glance over my shoulder. "I'm giving being a nudist a shot. What do you think?"

"Naked looks good on you."

She gives me a weak smile and sits cross-legged on the floor, showing me her lack of panties under her shorts.

"Not as good as it looks on you."

I find the bandages at the back of the drawer, along with some antibiotic cream that's two months out of date. It'll do.

I sit on the tile floor in front of her. My balls clench up, and my dick retreats, in an attempt to escape the cold tile. Sunny closes her eyes as I unwrap the paper towel and check the cut. It's stopped bleeding, so all I need to do is cover it up. I use two bandages instead of one, toss the bloody paper towels in the trash, and kiss the back of her hand. "All done."

She peeks up, her expression wary until she sees the bandage.

"How'd you ever manage to make it through a hockey game?"

Hockey players get roughed up all the time. Everyone who plays professional sports should expect a few stitches along the way, especially with skates in the mix. I've had at least five occasions I can think of where I've needed stitches, whether from skates, a fast-moving puck, or a stick to a place without much padding. Most of the time, if it isn't too bad, I get sewn up on the bench and get back in the game.

"I try not to look when people get into fights. I can handle it on TV, but in real life…" She pales.

The oven beeps, and she uses my shoulders to pull herself up. I stand along with her, gripping her at the waist when she falters.

"Why don't you let me get it?"

"I'm fine. I can do it myself." She's almost snippy.

I let go, and she face-plants into my chest. Wrapping an arm around her waist, I lift her onto the counter. "I can take a pan out of the oven, Sunny. Heating frozen food until it's edible is one of my specialties."

She makes a sound somewhere between a stifled laugh and an aggravated sigh.

"I'm not joking. I'm the best cook of frozen food in all of Chicago. I'd go as far as to say all of Illinois, but I don't want to seem like I have a big ego or anything."

"Miller."

"Sunny."

The oven beeps again. This time she lets go of my shoulders and motions toward it. I grab an apron off the counter and tie it around my waist for protection. Inside the oven is a huge pan of cinnamon buns, covered in pecans and bubbling around the edges. I put the mitts on and take them out, setting them on the granite counter.

"Where did you get these?"

"I made them."

"When?"

"This morning, while you were sleeping."

"Like, from scratch?"

"Yup."

"Dough and all?"

"I'm pretty sure that's what *scratch* means."

I stop ogling the buns and look over my shoulder. I'm almost one hundred percent sure that was sarcasm. She's still sitting on the counter, her feet and head dangling.

"I'm impressed." I search the cupboards for a couple of plates and rifle through the drawers until I find something to help remove them from the pan.

"They still need to be iced."

"I don't need icing."

I'm about to dig in when I hear the soft thud of her feet hitting the ground.

"You're impatient." She hip-checks me out of the way and grabs a serving tray.

I step aside and lean against the counter while she places the tray over the buns and then flips the whole thing upside down. Jiggling it around, she lifts the baking pan to reveal glistening, pecan-and-syrupy rolls. Fragrant steam wafts into the air. My mouth is watering, and I'm starving. My post-sex wings last night have already been burned off. I need to feed the beast.

I go to grab one, and Sunny smacks my hand. "They're too hot."

"I'll be fine."

"Let me put the icing on first so you don't burn off your tongue."

"I'm hungry."

"As hungry as you were last night?" She's looking at the bowl, not me.

"Is that an invitation or a request for a repeat?" I move closer until my chest meets her back. "Because I'm definitely interested in more of last night, and more of this morning."

"This morning?"

"Well, maybe not the fainting part, or you trying to dice off your fingertip, but this—" I gesture to the kitchen and kiss her shoulder. "What we're doing here, I like this. I've never done it before."

"Had someone faint on you?" She stirs the icing, but her breath hitches and a flush creeps up her neck.

"Woken up to someone I like making me breakfast."

"No one's ever made you breakfast?"

"Nope. Except for Skye, but that doesn't count since she's my stepmom, and everything she makes comes from a package."

Sunny turns around in my arms, her expression pensive. "What about when you were a kid? Didn't anyone make you breakfast before school and stuff?"

"Mostly I ate cereal in the morning, since it was just me and my dad." I stare at the cupboards, taking in the details. Memories of my mom are vague. Also, most of them aren't nice. She was so sick at the end. Just a shadow of a person. It's not something I talk about much. Up until now I've avoided it with Sunny.

Sunny runs a finger up my arm and over my shoulder until she reaches my jaw. She curls it around my chin and angles my head so I'm looking at her, not into space. "What happened to your mom?"

I twirl a lock of her hair between my fingers, considering how much I want to share. Fanning out the end, I brush it back and forth across my lips before I speak. "She had an inoperable brain tumor. She died when I was three."

Sunny strokes my cheek. Her affection doesn't feel like it's made of pity. "I'm so sorry."

I shrug. "I don't remember her much. She got headaches a lot. They thought they were migraines. Mostly I remember her being in the hospital. Then it was me and my dad for the most part. Even before she was gone it was my dad taking care of things."

"That must've been so hard."

"It was hardest on my dad. I was too young to get what was going on. I wasn't an easy kid. I had lots of energy. School was tough for me. I needed a lot of attention, and my dad worked long hours."

I leave out the hardest part to talk about: that none of Dad's attempted relationships worked out because of me. Single dads are only cool in movies. It was clear early on that school wasn't my thing. Between my struggle with dyslexia, losing my mom and my inability to sit still for five seconds, I lagged behind the other kids. One woman told my dad she didn't sign up for a kid like me. I never saw her again after that.

There weren't any other girlfriends until my junior year of high school—none that I ever met until my dad started dating Skye, Vi's mom, anyway. She was nice and fun to be around.

"Sidney raised you on his own?"

"Yeah, for the most part. I spent a lot of time at Randy's when I was growing up. His mom cooked and stuff, but it was different." Not that his situation was much easier. His dad played professional hockey and was gone a lot. His parents divorced when he was eleven.

Sunny's eyes go the kind of liquid I equate with sadness.

"Anyways, it's nice to have someone want to do things for me."

I don't want to talk about depressing shit. It reminds me that this thing me and Sunny have going is complicated. Before her, I never would've considered spending a weekend with the same woman. In the past, last night would've been followed by either more of the same come morning, or a quiet departure on the part of whoever shared my bed. No one ever went out of their way to make breakfast for me. It feels good—less like I'm an occasional convenience and more like I'm important beyond my ability to provide orgasms in bulk.

I reach for one of the cinnamon buns, done with talking. A puff of steam follows, and my fingers instantly heat to the point of being uncomfortable. Still, I want to end this conversation, and I'm hungry.

"Those are still too hot!" Sunny grabs it out of my hand.

I hold onto her wrist and try to pull it toward my mouth, but she drops it.

"That was a waste!" I debate eating it even though it's been on the floor.

"It was burning my fingers!"

"Let me see." The tips are pink and covered in cinnamon bun goo, so I suck each one into my mouth and finish cleaning them off with a kiss. "Better?"

"Better."

I push the bowl of icing out of the way and lift her onto the counter. "I know what we can do while we wait for those to cool." I part her legs with my palms and step between them, pulling her close to the edge. My erection sticks straight out under the apron. Sunny reaches around and pulls the tie, setting me free.

"You have the best ideas."

"I know, right?" I pull her tank over her head and palm her breasts.

She wraps her warm fingers around my erection. We make out, feeling each other up until Sunny lets go and shoves her shorts down her thighs. Everything goes from playful to frantic when she hooks her legs around my waist and pulls me in tight against her. Which is when I remember the condoms are upstairs, in the bedroom.

I drop my head into the crook of her neck as I slide through that heavenly, hot wetness. I've only had sex without a condom once. It was back in high school with the girl I thought I was in love with. The paranoia after the fact was almost worth how good it felt. *Almost*. The two weeks I spent terrified I'd gotten her pregnant ruined all the fun.

I groan as she swivels her hips. "We need to go upstairs."

"I like it here just fine," she says.

"The condoms are in your bedroom."

"I've been on the pill since I was sixteen." She's giving me permission to go bareback. It's hard to say no.

"It's not a hundred percent effective." It sounds more like a question than it does a statement.

"You can pull out at the end if you're worried."

I bite her shoulder and then along her neck. Sunny gasps and shifts her hips. I slide low. Really low.

We both startle when Andy and Titan start barking their heads off. It's only eight. Sunny's ride isn't supposed to be here yet.

"Sunshine? Sweetie? We're home."

Oh shit. The 'rents are back early.

14

Not the Surprise I Was Hoping For

-MILLER-

I'm naked. Sunny's naked, and we were about to fuck on her mother's counter.

I grab Sunny's tank from the floor, toss it to her, and wrap the apron around my waist. Then I bolt. My first thought is to go for the pantry, but then I'll be trapped in the kitchen. My rental is in the driveway. They know I'm here.

I bust it down the hall toward Robbie's office, skidding to a stop before I hit the living room. I can hear her parents, but I can't tell where they are. The stairs are too risky, being close to the front door.

My swim shorts are hanging on the line outside by the pool. If I can get to them, Sunny and I can avoid this being more of a shitstorm. I'm not sure the 'rents will be all that happy about my presence this early on a Sunday morning. Sunny might be an adult, but her parents are damn protective of her. I haven't dealt with a disapproving dad in some years.

I'm about to hit the sliding door when Daisy's voice filters down the hall. "It smells wonderful in here! Oh! Those look delicious."

She's in the kitchen. This is perfect. I can make it to the backyard without being seen.

"Whose car is in the driveway?" Robbie asks.

"Miller stopped by to visit." Sunny's voice has that high, reedy quality that comes with getting caught doing something she shouldn't have.

"Miller's here? That's great! I was afraid you weren't seeing him anymore!" Daisy replies, her enthusiasm appreciated on my part.

"Mom!"

"Well, it's been a few weeks. I know how Alex feels about all that stuff on social media. I was worried maybe you'd changed your mind."

I don't know what she's seen, but it can't be very flattering if Waters has mentioned it. I need to be more careful. And not just because it makes Sunny look bad. It makes me look bad, and it makes her parents less likely to like me.

"I haven't changed my mind."

"Well I'm pleasantly surprised. Where is he? I'd love to say hello."

"Yeah. Where is Miller? When did he get here exactly?" Robbie's usually calm voice has an edge to it.

"Um... Well... He, uh... He was visiting a couple of friends in Toronto, and he's got this camp thing he's volunteering at in Muskoka—did you know it's close to Alex's cottage?" She's stalling, trying to come up with a lie. Sunny's not an inherently good liar. She's too honest and sweet. I slip onto the patio, accidentally kicking Andy's favorite ball. He rushes past me, running after it. I don't have time to corral him. I need to be not naked. I yank my shorts off the line and shove my legs into them.

Across the yard I see a flash of white hair and what I'm sure are binoculars. I'd call Mr. Woodcock out, but I don't have time. I toss the apron over the line and cover the distance to the pool in two long strides, diving in.

I swim across to the other side. Andy drops the ball at the edge when my head pops out, barking excitedly. I snatch up the ball, toss it across the yard, and pull myself out.

"We'll play later, buddy. Come on, let's go see Sunny." Grabbing a towel from the back of the chair, I run it over my chest and wrap it around my waist. Andy trots behind me with that ball in his mouth, desperate for more attention.

I pop my head in the door leading to the kitchen. "Hey, sweets, you coming for a swim before you leave?" I fake surprise and almost choke on my tongue when I get a load of Sunny's mom. "Mr. and Mrs. Waters! How's it goin'?"

Daisy Waters is a fashion nightmare resurrected from the eighties. Her helmet-y hair keeps hairspray companies in business. Currently one side is flat, like maybe she fell asleep on the way home and crushed it. "I wasn't sure I would get a chance to see you."

I stay on the mat by the door, since I'm dripping water, and assess everyone's stance. I can't read Sunny's expression, but I assume she's stressed. I think her tank top might be on backwards. I'm worried about what I might have missed while I was getting my shorts.

"I guess it's a good thing our flight was changed!" Sunny's mom crosses over and gives me an affectionate hug. Her over-sprayed hair hits my wet cheek. "Don't stand by the door. Come on in, Miller! It's been a while! I'm so glad you came by. Are you hungry? You must be starving!" She squeezes my bicep.

"You must be the reason Sunny's making her cinnamon buns!"

"I've never had them before."

I let her slip her arm through mine. Daisy loves me, despite how much I keep fucking things up with Sunny.

"Well, you're in for a real treat."

Robbie's leaning against the doorjamb, eating one of Sunny's cinnamon buns. He's wearing a pair of plaid shorts and a tie-dye T-shirt with a band I've never heard of on it. He looks suspicious and not excited to see me. Sunny's poor lying skills probably aren't helping. "Sunny tells us you stopped by this morning."

I avoid answering the question directly so I don't have to lie outright. "I couldn't go to Muskoka without stopping by. I'm disappointed she's leaving this morning."

Robbie glances at Sunny. "Leave? Where are you going?"

Sunny twirls her hair around her finger. "Remember we talked about me going camping with Lily? Up in Chapleau?"

Daisy looks absolutely horrified. "Camping? You've never gone camping. And that's so far away. Will you even have cell phone reception? What about running water? Why wouldn't you use Alex's cottage? He's not there this week—at least I don't think he is. Even if he was I'm sure he'd be more than happy for you and Lily to come along. It has six bedrooms. There's plenty of room."

Robbie gives Daisy a look, but she's too busy being appalled by the idea of camping to catch it. "What about your shifts at the shelter?" he asks.

"Those are all covered, and my yoga classes, too. I've taken care of everything."

"But you don't camp." Daisy's stuck on this point.

"I do too camp."

"Spending one night in a tent in Alex's backyard at the

cottage doesn't count, Sunshine," Daisy says.

Sunny puts her hands on her hips. "I've camped with Lily before."

"Doesn't her aunt have a trailer on Lake Erie?"

Sunny huffs, annoyed. "Well, I would've camped if you'd let me go to Girl Guides, but Alex always had those hockey camps, and I never could!"

Robbie picks up another cinnamon bun and takes a bite. "These are fantastic."

"Thanks, Dad." Sunny looks at Daisy. "Lily says we're borrowing a camping van or something, and she has all the gear we'll need. It'll be great!" She sounds less enthusiastic about it than she did yesterday. Maybe she'll end up cutting it short.

"Is it just you and Lily going?" Daisy asks. "I don't know if I like that idea."

"There's a group of us." Sunny's hair twirling gets more and more aggressive until it's twisted all the way around her finger. She'd never make it as a professional poker player.

"Who else is coming with you?" Robbie's eyes shift in my direction as he takes a huge bite of bun. I want one.

The doorbell rings, cutting off Sunny's response. I check the clock on the wall—it's analog, which is easier to read. It's after nine. Shit. Lily's here, and my time with Sunny is almost up. I didn't even get to give her a good morning/see you soon orgasm.

Sunny skips around the counter and gazelles her way to the front door, throwing it open with a squeal. Her bestie throws her arms around her, and they do that weird overly affectionate hug thing girls do when they haven't seen each other in five minutes.

Lily has dark eyes and a short black bob that rests against the edge of her jaw. She's lean, and muscular thanks to years of figure skating.

Her smile widens when she sees Robbie, and then slides right off like her face when she sees me. She whispers something to Sunny, her eyes wide with surprise.

"Lily!" Daisy flails her arms like a cheerleader on hallucinogenics. Lily turns away from her huge hair and accepts the hug.

"Hi, Momma Two. How was your weekend away? Did you have fun?"

"Too much to talk about without embarrassing everyone!" Daisy winks.

I glance at Robbie. He gives me a smug smile and nabs another bun. I think he might have already been into his research today.

Two guys dressed in matching khaki shorts, threadbare shirts, open plaid button-downs, wool socks, and sandals appear in the doorway. They're clearly trying to join the beard brigade and failing. While there's hair on their chins and cheeks, it's patchy and ungroomed. They look like they picked their outfit from the Khaki and Plaid Depot.

Robbie gives me an eyebrow lift, grabs a fourth cinnamon bun, and nods in the direction of the door. "You better get over there, son."

Every fucking alarm bell in my head goes off.

"Oh! Kale, Benji! I didn't see you there!" Daisy's voice is high-pitched, and she gives Sunny an odd look.

But Sunny is busy exchanging wide-eyed looks with Lily and they're mouthing things at each other. The color from Sunny's face has drained, and Lily's is going red. I don't know what the hell is going on, but it seems bad.

I glance behind the guys, searching for more people, hopefully with an XY chromosome, but it's just these two guys.

"I thought Rachel and Nanda were coming?" Sunny wears a strained smile.

"Nanda has food poisoning and Rachel's staying back to take care of her and Kale didn't have plans, so I invited him along this morning," Benji says. "I hope that's cool."

This dude's name is Kale? Like the vegetable?

"What about Kait? Is she coming?" Sunny's pitch is dog whistle high now.

"We broke up last week." Kale shoves a hand in his pocket and his eyes slide to me.

"I'm so sorry, Kale. Time with friends is exactly what you need to get over a broken heart," Daisy wears the same expression as her daughter as she hugs him.

When he spots Sunny's dad, his eyes light up. "Hey! Robbie, how's it going? I was all bummed out thinking you wouldn't be back until later today and we'd miss you."

"Our flight was changed at the last minute." Robbie's eyes pass over me again.

Kale goes in for a man hug. Now I want to know about the friend dynamics here, based on how familiar this Kale guy is with her family. Or maybe it's been a long-ass time since they've seen him. Like since Sunny graduated high school three years ago.

I make sure I'm not leaking pool water all over Sunny's mom's floor before I cross the hardwood.

"Hey, Lily, how you doin'?" I open my arms like I'm looking for a hug.

Her eyes do this weird widening thing and her lips contort, as if she's fighting not to make a face. She leans forward and pats my back, straining her neck so almost none of her touches me. It'd be funny if I wasn't already offended.

I loop an arm around Sunny's waist from behind.

"Miller! You're all wet!"

"That makes one of us." I don't mean it the way it sounds, but everyone's eyes shoot in my direction. Sunny's cheeks go pink, Lily looks mortified, and Daisy looks stunned. Only Robbie's too engrossed in licking his fingers to notice. Kale looks annoyed.

I pretend I haven't said something inappropriate and offer my hand to Benji first. "You must be Lily's boyfriend. I'm Miller."

"Oh, I know who you are." He takes my hand and squeezes. "Benji."

I return the flex until he flinches. "You watch hockey?" This guy looks like hacky sack is more his speed.

"Sunshine watches a lot of hockey, so that means we all watch a lot of hockey," Lily says.

"When Toronto's out, I root for Chicago because of Sunshine." He winks at her. If he wasn't dating Lily, I'd want to punch him in the face.

"It's not like Alex had any choice in what city he plays for." Sunny laughs, but it sounds forced. "Oh! Kale, this is Miller. He plays with Alex."

If we hadn't been interrupted, I would have asked her to be my girlfriend this morning and made us official.

"Is Alex here this weekend?" Kale stretches up, like he's trying to see over my shoulder.

"Um, no. He's at home. Miller's sister is his fiancée," she explains.

Kale seems confused. "So, you came to Guelph…"

"To see Sunny."

He frowns as he connects the dots. Yeah, I need to know more about this situation.

Daisy breaks the awkward stare-down. "You don't have to

leave right away, do you? I'll put on some coffee, and herbal tea for you, Lily. Sunny made cinnamon buns!"

"They're delicious." Robbie pats his stomach.

"And they're vegan, of course," Sunny chimes in.

"I love your buns!" Kale winks at Sunny.

I get the distinct impression that Kale and Sunny might have some history, which would explain why she's so twitchy and why Kale is so familiar with her family. I hope I'm wrong.

"I'm looking forward to trying one. I've only eaten Sunny's cookies." I adjust the strap of her tank top.

Sunny flushes. Lily gives me a look. Daisy misses the innuendo and links arms with Lily, leading her into the kitchen.

"I could go for some cookies right now." Robbie saunters over to the fridge.

"I'll put on some dry clothes." I hook my pinkie with hers and kiss her cheek. "You seem nervous, sweets, everything okay?"

"Sunny, can we get your help?" Kale pokes his head around the corner.

"Yeah. Sure." She turns back to me and whispers. "There are wrappers all over my bedroom floor."

Shit. That's right. "I'll handle it."

"Okay. Don't take too long." At least she doesn't look any happier about this development than I do.

I head up the stairs, taking them two at a time. I need to clean up our mess and get all my shit out of Sunny's room before her parents make it upstairs.

15

This is the Opposite of Good

-SUNNY-

Miller disappears up the stairs. I have half a mind to follow him so I can explain that I had no idea Kale was coming until he showed up at the door. And someone—probably Kale—will say something that will tip Miller off as to how well Kale and I know each other. The only upside to this whole new nightmare is that Miller—who hasn't been excited about my camping trip since I told him about it—looks even less excited now.

Before I can make a move, Kale pokes his head around the corner, all freaking smiles, and wide eyes. "Hey Sunny Bunny, can we get your help?"

I spin around and pin him with a glare. "Do not call me that."

He raises his hands. It's his go-to move whenever he does something to irk me. Which happens often. "Sorry, old habits die hard."

I follow him into the kitchen, where my parents, Benji and

Lily are. My mom looks worried, my dad looks high and hungry, Benji and Kale look like they coordinated their outfits, and Lily looks apologetic. I need to pull her aside and find out what the heck is going on and how I'm supposed to deal with this new development.

"What can I do to help?" I ask brightly, channeling my inner someone-just-farted-in-yoga-smile-and-we're-going-to-pretend-it-doesn't-smell-like-rotten-eggs.

"A few of the cinnamon buns are light on icing," Kale replies helpfully.

Dad dunks his special freezer cookie into the remains of the icing, the bowl tucked protectively against his chest. "I think the cinnamon buns look great."

"There's no more icing," I tell Kale.

Andy, who has been waiting for a chunk of cookie to hit the floor, hangs his head when Dad pops the last bite into his mouth. His ears perk up and he heads for the stairs. Where Miller is cleaning up the evidence of our bedroom antics. I had no idea I could have that many orgasms in a row. My thighs clench at the memory. If my parents hadn't come home, maybe my cookie would be happy this morning and not all achy. I give my head a little shake to throw off the hormone haze and realize this is my chance. "Oh! I left my bedroom door open. I should go up there and grab Andy!"

"That's okay, I can do it, you stay here with your friends," Dad says.

I suspect he's not actually being helpful, but that he wants to check on Miller. And I can't even warn him my dad is coming. Every mental plan I've made has backfired so far. Why can I plan and organize charity events with little to no issues, but I can't seem to keep everything from going sideways where Miller is concerned?

"Let's take everything outside, it's a beautiful morning," Mom suggests helpfully.

Dad kisses her on the cheek and heads for the stairs. I say a prayer that Miller has cleaned up the mess. I'm twenty, and I can choose who I want to be with and in what capacity, but my dad will want to have a safe sex talk. He did it with Kale and I when he found out we were having sex in my grade twelve year. It was mortifying.

It will be even more mortifying if my dad does it with my new boyfriend in front of my old boyfriend.

She passes items to Benji and Kale and sends them on ahead, then glances between me and Lily. "Do you two need a minute?"

"Yes, please," we say at the same time.

"I'll keep your shadows busy." She takes the cinnamon buns, which I made for Miller, out to the back deck.

Thank goodness one person is on my side when it comes to Miller.

"What the heck?" I whisper to Lily once we're alone.

"I'm so sorry. Seriously. I had no idea Kale was coming until Benji showed up at my door this morning." She rapidly blinks and wrings her hands. "I promise I'm not trying to sabotage you and Miller. I might have my feelings about him, but I wouldn't intentionally set you up like this. And I didn't know about him and Kait breaking up either. I'd understand if you wanted to bail." She bites her lips together and her chin wobbles.

Lily isn't a crier.

She was raised by her mom because her dad is a deadbeat and not involved in her life. She's been my best friend for years, and I know that her feelings about Miller have a lot more to do with her history than mine. Her dad isn't in her life because he couldn't be bothered to take responsibility for his actions. It's complicated.

"I'm not sending you on a camping trip alone with Benji and Kale." I might not love the predicament I'm suddenly in, but I can't abandon her when she needs me.

Besides, I'm really hoping that this is the last camping trip she ever goes on with Benji, and that she finally works up the nerve to dump him for good.

But one step at a time.

Lily's mouth tightens. "How do you think Miller will handle this?"

"Hopefully he's understanding." And hopefully I have a chance to explain before we leave.

16

Kale Sucks

-MILLER-

I quickly stuff my clothes in my duffle. Andy does a circle around me as I clean up the condom wrappers, nudging me with his nose as I tuck them into my duffle for lack of a better place to put them.

"Psst. Hey, buddy, you have to go downstairs."

Robbie calls for him. Andy ignores him, like he does pretty much everyone except Sunny—and sometimes me if a treat is involved.

"Go, Andy. Go see Robbie." I push his butt toward the door, but he runs into the bathroom and shoves his head in the garbage can. I need to get the hell out of Sunny's room before someone comes up here, especially Sunny's dad.

I scan the room one more time and notice a pair of Sunny's underwear peeking out from under the bed. I scoop them up and rub the soft cotton between my fingers. They're my First Time With Sunny underwear, which makes them special. I don't consider how weird it is to steal them as I shove them in my bag.

A throat clears, drawing my attention to the door. Robbie stands there, looking suspicious. He pops a cookie into his mouth and chews.

I make sure the panties are tucked away safely. "Hey, Robbie. Sunny must have left her door open. Andy came in here, and I wanted to make sure he didn't get into anything. You know how much he loves to eat out her trash." When he blinks at me, I review what I've said and rewind. "I mean, eat out of her garbage can. I don't want him to get sick."

He eyes my duffle. I hope I got rid of the incriminating evidence. "You should come downstairs and get one of those cinnamon buns before they're all gone."

"I'll be right there. I just need to change."

"Everyone's on the back deck." He stuffs another cookie in his mouth and waits for me to leave the room before he closes Sunny's door. I stop in the guest bathroom to change out of my wet shorts.

Less than two minutes later I'm on my way outside. Kale is next to Sunny, and Lily is on the other side. The only open seat is beside Daisy.

"Miller! I saved you a cinnamon roll." Sunny holds up the plate and smiles, but there's tension underneath.

I circle the group instead of reaching across the table. Leaning down between them, I tuck invisible strands of hair behind Sunny's ear and brush a kiss over her shoulder, keeping it polite for current company. "Thanks, sweets."

The conversation consists of a lot of inside jokes from Lily and Kale, which is annoying. Kale also tries to reminisce with Daisy, who doesn't seem all that comfortable or happy with the situation. It sounds like he used to spend a lot of time at the

Waters' place, which makes me believe that I'm right and there is a history there. I don't like it, and I don't like that Sunny's spending time with him. At best, they'll have separate tents. At worst they'll all be sleeping in the trailer together. I need to talk to her alone before she leaves today.

"Miller?"

"Huh?" I glance around the table. Everyone is looking at me—except Lily. She's busy texting under the table. I realize I've been staring off into space. Actually, I've been staring at Sunny's chest. Her nipples are saluting me from under her tank. If I'd mentioned them before, I could have had a minute with her upstairs. Then maybe I'd have some answers to all the freaking questions I have about this.

"What's the name of the camp you're volunteering at again?" Sunny asks.

"Oh. It's Camp Beaver Woods." Me and Randy had a good laugh about that.

"Why'd you pick one in Canada? It seems out of the way." Kale picks a dandelion fluff out of Sunny's hair. I want to shove it up his left nostril with my fist.

"Usually I do a couple of weeks in the Chicago area so I can visit my family, but now that I'm living in the city, I thought I'd change it up. And I wanted an excuse to see Sunny. I was hoping to convince her to visit me out there for a couple of days, but it looks like you got to her first."

"Looks like." He grins.

I lean back in my chair and return the smile. "I don't mind sticking around for a few days after the camp is over, though."

The tension at the table is thicker than my playoff beard. I'm having a pissing contest with this douchebag in front of her parents, but my position feels pretty fucking threatened right now.

Lily sets down her phone. "So this camp you volunteer for, it's for hockey brats?"

I frown. "It's a sports camp, but some of the kids have special needs." It's an amazing, inclusive program.

"Miller subsidizes it so struggling families can afford it," Sunny says.

Lily seems shocked. "Oh. I didn't realize that." Everything she knows about me is based on social media, so it's a narrow view.

"It's not something I advertise."

"What's it called again?" Lily asks.

"Camp Beaver Woods," Sunny replies for me.

The conversation makes me feel uncomfortable—like I'm on the hot seat facing a bestie interrogation.

Daisy pats my hand. "You're always doing such wonderful things. You're so generous. Isn't he, Sunny?"

She gives me a small smile. "He is." She looks almost guilty. I can't imagine why.

"It's no big deal. I don't think money should get in the way of a kid's opportunity."

"Must be nice to have lots to throw around," Kale grumbles.

He's being antagonistic. If I was on the ice, I'd stick him in the shins, but I'm not. So words are my only option. "You think helping pay for kids who otherwise wouldn't have a chance to attend a camp like this is throwing money around?"

"I don't think Kale means it like that," Sunny says, clearly uncomfortable.

"I just think there are other causes you can donate to that would have more of an impact."

I know Kale's type. He's the same kid in high school who had a comment for everything. He'd find a weakness and exploit it to make someone feel like an idiot. I'm done with his superiority complex.

"Really? So you don't think subsidizing a camp for low-income families or financing a partnership with an inclusion program for kids with physical and intellectual exceptionalities will have an impact? That's an *interesting* perspective."

He blinks. Lily looks stunned. Sometimes the stereotypes associated with being a professional athlete piss me off. I might have struggled with academics, but not all smarts are related to books.

"Miller's involved in a lot of charity work." Sunny's eyes bounce between us.

I don't want to defend myself to this jerkoff, or have Sunny do it for me. I work hard for the money I make. And yeah, it's a lot, which is why I give back.

"I'm also aware that my current career is limited. I only have so long before I'm not fast enough to keep up with the younger players. I started doing the charity stuff so I have a focus when my professional hockey career ends," I add.

"That's just so wonderful," Daisy pats my arm again.

Lily puts an end to the smoldering argument before it can ignite. "We should get going. It's a long drive, and we want to set up camp before it gets dark."

Andy sticks his head between Sunny and Kale, nudging her with his head. "What's up, Andy?" Sunny takes his drooly face between her hands and goes nose-to-nose with the dog. Usually she'd get a kiss, but he keeps his mouth shut. "What're you eating? Give." Sunny holds out her hand. "Drop it."

A gummy, green blob covered in drool lands in her palm.

"What is that?" Kale gets in closer.

It's one of my green condoms—we ran out of the normal ones. Andy must have dug it out of the trash. I'm out of my chair and around the table with a napkin before anyone else can identify it.

I scoop it out of her cupped palm. "I got this, sweets. You should wash your hands."

"It looked like chewed gum," Daisy exclaims. God bless her.

"He was digging around in your bathroom when I went upstairs to change. You know what he's like, always loving on your used tissues and stuff."

"Oh no! Bad Andy! That stuff makes you sick!" She gives him a tap on the nose. He whines.

Robbie makes a noise from the other side of the table while frowning.

We help Daisy clean up the plates and cups and bring them inside. Lily excuses herself to the bathroom while Sunny gets her bags. Anything I want to say I can't, like *don't go*, or *I hate this Kale dude and I want him to get eaten by a bear.*

I'm searching for a reason to run upstairs when Lily returns from the bathroom. I need to get her on my side; so this camping trip doesn't turn into a freaking couples' road trip.

"I think we've gotten off on the wrong foot."

She crosses her arms, looking like she wants to be anywhere else. "What makes you say that?"

"Oh, I don't know. Maybe it's the way you hate me."

"I don't hate you, Miller. I just don't trust you. You're too smooth and too..." She waves her hand around.

"Too what?"

"Too... Ken."

"Ken?"

"You know, like Barbie and Ken."

"What does that even mean? Ken's not a bad guy." Randy's little sister used to watch Barbie movies all the time. We'd babysit when his mom had to work.

"You're a player."

"You think Ken's a player?" He was head over ass in love with Barbie. I see the parallels. Wait. *Am I in love with Sunny*?

Lily rolls her eyes. "All this charity stuff doesn't change the reputation you have. Sunny's my best friend. I don't want to see her get hurt, and you seem like a guy who does that often."

"How do you get to decide what kind of guy I am based on the little you know about me? I'm not looking to hurt Sunny. I care about her. I'm trying here, Lily, but it seems like you've already made up your mind about me."

She plants her hands on her hips, but before she can go at me, Sunny appears at the top of the stairs.

"I'm ready!"

She has two wheelie suitcases. It seems like she prepared for an all-inclusive vacation rather than a camping trip. I sprint up to help her. It's unnecessary. She's more than capable.

"What's the deal with Kale?" I whisper.

"I swear I didn't know he was coming, Miller. Not until he showed up at the door." She bites her lips together, eyes wide. Like she's waiting for me to freak out on her.

"I believe you." Her shock was written all over her face, just like her anxiety is now. I ask the question, even though I'm not sure I'm ready for the answer. "Were you two a thing?"

She grimaces. "We dated in high school. It was a long time ago."

Fuck, fuck, *fuck*. Sunny is twenty. She graduated three years ago, so a long time is pretty damn relative. "Are you over that relationship?" My stomach feels like it's trying to turn itself inside out.

She nods. "Yes. Completely. We had to stay friends because he's Benji's best friend and well…I didn't know he was coming. I don't want to bail on Lily. Please don't be mad at me."

This is an opportunity to be the understanding boyfriend. To not freak out and be a completely possessive douchebag, even though that's exactly what I'd like to do. "I'm not mad at you, Sunny. I trust you." That ex of hers though? Not even a little.

"I promise I'll message every day, and video call if I can."

"That sounds great, sweets. I want you to have fun." And if this is the jackass who never got her off even once, I should be okay. That's the only reassurance I have at the moment. That my ability to fulfill her needs usurps her fresh-on-the-rebound ex-boyfriend.

"We should hit the road," Kale says from the bottom of the stairs.

I help Sunny bring her bags down. Everyone shoves their feet into sandals and heads outside. I have my bag with me, too.

The door opens to reveal not a Magic Bus, but a for-real camping trailer. Where people can sleep. It's old, but seems well-maintained. Still, I don't want Sunny stranded anywhere with Kale. I also want to check out the inside so I can assess the sleeping situation.

Daisy hugs everyone while Robbie shakes hands with Ben and Kale, then hugs Lily and Sunny. I stand back, observing the interactions, wishing I was going instead of that Kale fucker. When it's my turn, I go for Lily first. It's like hugging a steel pipe. I shake her boyfriend's hand, then I turn to Kale. He's too smug. I need to fix that.

I take his hand and squeeze. "Take care of my girl for me." Sunny will probably be annoyed by my territorial nonsense, but I need to make it clear I'm in this for the fight.

"You have nothing to worry about. I always do." He pats me on the shoulder, his satisfied smile pushing my last damn button.

I lean in close and clap him on the shoulder, lowering my voice so only he can hear. "Not as well as I do." I wink and turn to Sunny.

She still looks anxious. I pull her into my arms and hug her tight. Putting my lips to her ear, I whisper, "He gets you for a week. I only got you for two days."

I take her face in my hands, wishing her parents weren't witnessing this. I brush my nose against hers, then kiss the tiny dimple on her left cheek. "Have fun, Sunny Sunshine."

"I'll try."

"But not too much." I press my lips softly to hers.

She holds onto my forearms, fingernails digging in. "I won't."

Benji and Kale get into the front seats, and Lily and Sunny get in the back. I can see inside. There's a table with cushioned seats that turn into a bed. I grab the door before Sunny can close it and step inside.

"Wow. This is spacious. How many does it sleep?" I wait for one of them to meet my eyes.

"There are two double beds." Kale is back to being a smug jerkoff.

"And we have tents," Sunny reminds me.

It's a shit situation, having to pretend I'm cool with the woman I'm deep in my feels over going on a camping trip with her ex. I drop my bag on the driveway and cram myself into the confined space. I'm blocking her parents' view since I fill the entire door.

This time I lay one on her. She gasps, and I slide my tongue between her parted lips. I suck on her tongue, and she fists my shirt, making a plaintive, needy sound. Lily coughs, reminding me we have an audience. Like I'm not aware.

I break the kiss. "I'm sorry I keep messing things up. You're the only one I want, Sunny. Just remember how good we can be together while you're away with your friends." I pull my phone out and snap one of the selfies I usually hate while I kiss her on the cheek.

I point at Lily. "Make sure no bears eat her."

Sunny's confusion matches my frustration as I close the door.

Everything good about this weekend evaporates as they drive away.

"I hope she has an okay time." Daisy pats her hair.

"Yeah. Me, too." I pick up my bag. "I should head out. I'm picking up a buddy at the airport on the way to the camp."

Daisy goes in for a hug. I turn my face in time to avoid the hairspray assault. "It was nice of you to stop by, Miller. I hope we get to see you real soon." She pats my cheek and sighs.

Robbie stays behind while I throw my bag in the back of the SUV. I shake his hand, wanting to get the hell out of here. I need to call Randy and check flight times, and I need to call Violet. I'm not feeling great about how things ended here. I also want to text Sunny, and I need to use the voice-to-text function, so it doesn't take a year. Thumb typing is the worst.

"Thanks for the hospitality, Robbie. I'm sure I'll see you before the season starts."

"You take care of yourself, Miller."

He stands by my door as I turn the engine over. As I'm about to pull out of the driveway, he knocks on my window. I roll it down. My palms are clammy, and I have the lip sweats. "Yes, sir?"

"I know Sunny lied to us." Leaning on the edge of the window he makes a clicking sound with his tongue. "The neighbors said this vehicle has been here since late Friday night."

"I didn't want to get her into trouble—"

He holds up a hand. "Sunny's a big girl, but she's still my

little girl, so I'm asking you to be careful with her. I like you, Miller. I think you're a nice kid, and I know the media skews things, but I'd hate for my baby to get hurt by someone who's stringing her along."

"It's not like that. I really like Sunny."

"Then I suggest you step up your game." He taps the hood of the car as he strolls up the driveway, Andy following.

His parting words don't make me feel better at all.

17

The Kicker of Pants

-MILLER-

I drive around the corner and park the car. I have an entire day to kill, and all I can think about is how this weekend went from awesome to total shit. All because of Kale.

I pull my phone out and check my messages.

Sunny Sunshine: *I wish we'ed had alone time b4 I left. Thx 4 coming 2 visit me.*

I had fun. <3

I send her one back, along with the selfie, using voice-to-text so I don't mess it up:

Miller: *Me too. I can't wait to see you again. Message me when you get to camp if you have reception.*

When I'm finished, I set the picture as my wallpaper, and then I post it to social media, and tag her. I add the caption "Spending time with my favorite Canadian girl." It's not as in-your-face as I'd like to be, but I think it gets the point across.

I check my emails while I wait for a reply. Randy's sent

two. I use text-to-speech to listen to those. His flight times have changed, and he'll be in a few hours earlier, which means less waiting around for me. Sunny hasn't responded to my message yet, so I call Vi. She answers on the third ring.

"Buck." My name sounds like a swear word. "Care to explain the hat trick message you left for me yesterday before I beam myself to Canada and beat your ass with a nine iron?"

I forgot about that message. "You don't golf."

"I might start. It seems like it might be fun if I'm aiming for your balls. Please tell me you didn't call me to brag to me about bagging three bunnies when you're supposed to be with Sunny."

"I hat tricked *with* Sunny."

"You did what?" Her voice is muffled for a moment, "Everything's fine. I'm talking to Charlene. She bought another purse off the shopping channel." Then she's clear again, "You better explain yourself. Quickly."

"So, Sunny had a boyfriend in high school, right?"

"What the hell does this have to do with a hat trick?"

"I'm getting to that. So get this, he was terrible at sexing."

"Everyone's terrible at sexing in high school."

"Fair, but this guy never gave Sunny an orgasm. Not once."

Violet gasps. "That's awful."

"Right? That's poor boyfriend form." My first responsibility is learning what makes my partner tick.

"If that's true, it really is terrible."

"What do you mean, 'if it's true'?"

"You're sure Sunny didn't tell you that to boost your ego?"

"Do women really do that?" I can't imagine lying about orgasms, and Sunny isn't much for dishonesty.

"I don't know. Sometimes? I've lied to Alex about...never mind."

"You can't not tell me."

"You don't want me to finish that sentence. I promise it won't make a difference to this conversation, other than causing irreparable emotional damage."

"I highly doubt that. What have you lied to him about? Sex stuff? Orgasms? About never having one before?"

"You're sure you want to know?"

Vi tends to say exactly what's on her mind at any given time. If she's censored herself, it must be bad, which makes me want to know even more. "I'm sure."

"Once I lied about my level of...leakiness."

"Leakiness?"

"Yes."

"What does that even mean?" I immediately regret the question.

"How wet I get."

I gag. "You're right. I didn't need that information."

"I warned you, but you wouldn't listen. It's not my fault I'm a naturally lubey person."

"Okay. Enough. Sunny wouldn't lie about her lack of orgasms. She looked way surprised every time I gave her one."

"Maybe that's her O face."

"I don't think so. I also gave her her first orgasm by mouth and her first sex-gasm, so there's my hat trick. It totally kicks Waters' fake hat trick's ass."

A long time ago, a rumor circulated that Waters had slept with three bunnies in one night. It wasn't true, but it caused a shitload of issues for him and Vi. Eventually he set things straight, and it ended up being a prime example of how the media can twist information.

"You do realize you called to brag about sleeping with my fiancé's sister, right? Super classy, Buck. Who else have you told?"

"No one. Believe me, if I could talk to anyone other than you, I would, but I can't. So I'm oversharing, Vi. You do it all the time."

She sighs. "I suppose you have a point. I'd rather you tell me than one of your hockey buddies. Those guys have big mouths. Obviously Sunny forgave you."

"Yeah. She got over it." That's not one hundred percent truth, though, considering where she is right now versus where I'd like her to be.

"That's good. I'm glad. So your weekend has been good?"

"It was up until an hour ago."

"What happened?" She doesn't immediately throw the blame at me.

I explain, including the part where Sunny is now camping with Lily, her boyfriend and her high school ex-boyfriend. "I should've had the entire day with her. Now she's camping with her bearded hipster ex Kale."

"Oh." She chews loudly for several seconds, maybe processing. "Did you meet him?"

"Yup. They all showed up at the house this morning, right after Robbie and Daisy came home early." I roll down the window and recline the seat.

"Was everything okay with the 'rents?" Vi's aware of how protective Sunny's parents are.

"It was mostly fine. Sunny didn't tell them I was visiting. They almost walked in on us getting it on. Robbie knows I spent the weekend. He had the neighbors watching the place."

"Oh, shit."

"Surprisingly, he didn't seem too upset. But he gave me the 'don't fuck with my daughter' talk." Now that I think about it, it seems like Sunny might have purposely forgotten to mention my visit. It makes sense if she wanted us to have the house to ourselves. "But Lily thinks I'm playing Sunny."

"Of course she does. It's not as though your reputation will evaporate because you're dating someone."

"I haven't been with anyone since I met Sunny."

"I know that, but Lily doesn't. You're still at the bars with your buddies all the time, and the pictures with the bunnies haven't stopped. And then there are the parties at Lance's. Where the media is concerned, you're not acting like a guy in a relationship. People believe what they see, even if it's not true. You know that better than anyone. It's the situations you get yourself into that are the real problem. Anyways, we're off-topic. This is about the vegetable dude and Sunny going camping. You said they dated in high school?"

"Yeah."

"You're sure about that?" Her tone makes me nervous.

"That's what Sunny said."

"I think Sunny only had one boyfriend in high school."

"So she didn't do a lot of dating. That's not a bad thing." The asshole in me likes the idea that Sunny didn't engage in all the teenage hormonal experimentation.

"Not necessarily..." She hedges. "Hold on a second. I need to ask Alex something." She covers the receiver. Her voice is muffled and then she's clear again. "Charlene returned the purse. I'm talking to Buck now. No. No. Don't even." There's some fumbling. "I won't touch the MC for a week if you do that! I mean it! Stop." When Violet turns her attention back to me, she's slightly breathless. "I was right. Kale's the only guy Sunny dated in high school."

"But that was a few years ago, so it shouldn't be a big deal, right?" I need confirmation this will be okay.

"Sure. Yeah." Her lack of confidence is disconcerting.

"You're not making me feel better about this."

"Did she tell you when they broke up?" Violet asks.

"During senior year, I think? That was three years ago, though. That's plenty of time to move on." Three years seems like a small eternity. I waited all of two days to move on when I found out the girl I'd been dating was screwing around with half the hockey team at her college, two states away. Then I fucked all the depression out. It wasn't the most effective strategy, but it kept me busy. That was five years ago.

"In theory."

"Why in theory?"

"They started dating when Sunny was a freshman and Kale was a sophomore. He stayed an extra semester after graduation so he could be with her. He planned to take the last semester off to work and then they would go to college together. She broke up with him because he was being a clinger and not very motivated or something. That's Alex's version of the story. I don't know Sunny's side." I must not say anything for a long time as I process this shitload of important information. "They dated for four years," Vi finally adds.

"I can do the math." That's almost as long as I've been playing professional hockey. I should have asked more questions. But I didn't have time and now look where I am. "I can't believe he never gave her an orgasm. Seriously. What the fuck is wrong with that guy? We've been together for three months and I've already given her, like, fifty."

"Unfortunately, relationships are not just about orgasms."

"Well, they should be. That's the first thing I give myself in the morning, and the last thing I take care of at night. They're essential. Orgasms are like breathing." I'm panicking. I know this. I'm also sharing a lot of information I probably shouldn't— not that this whole conversation hasn't been an epic overshare. We should be drunk so we can forget all the crap we've just told each other.

"Look, I know this is hard for you to understand. You've been engaging in meaningless sex for a long time, but in real relationships, it's about a lot more than the number of orgasms you can provide. Sex is awesome. Orgasms are awesome. Someone else providing those orgasms is the best thing ever, but that's not the only thing that matters."

My panic turns into full-blown hysteria. Okay. No, it doesn't, but I'm freaked out. I already know this—it's why Sunny and I were taking it slow until this weekend. We spent months talking almost every day. I know what she loves, what makes her happy. *But I didn't know about this four-year relationship.* And I stupidly put all my eggs in the orgasm basket, thinking it was the key to taking this relationship to another level.

"I put all this energy into making Sunny feel good this weekend. No one has ever given her what I have. That has to mean something."

"I'm sure it does. But you also have to remember that for the past three months she's been seeing pictures of you with puck bunnies all over social media. One weekend without media coverage doesn't negate that. I'm sure there was more to it than a fuck-a-thon. At least I'm hoping there was. Did you act like an asshole when she left with veggie man?"

"No." I reconsider my answer. I might have been a bit dickish with him; only because he was being that way with me. "Maybe a little. But mostly no."

"Care to elaborate?"

I explain what happened with Kale and try not to leave out details or paint myself in a more favorable light. It's hard. I feel like shit. Sunny still hasn't responded to my text. I want to be cool about this, but I'm not sure I am.

When I'm done, Vi exhales into the receiver. "You haven't

done anything wrong. He provoked you, and you responded. I'll ask Charlene and maybe one of the girls at work for their opinions, because I'll be honest, I think it's hot when Alex gets all possessive. Remember that guy in my building, Melvin? The one who smells like dick cheese and two-year-old socks?"

Vi is notorious for going on tangents. "I remember him, yeah." I have no idea what this has to do with me and Sunny and her being with her ex-boyfriend who she dated for four years. It seems like a significant detail to leave out. I'm kind of hurt.

"He used to ask me to hang out all the time. Even though he wasn't a threat, Alex always wanted to get it on in the living room when he came to my place. I think it was so Melvin could hear my MC love professions."

"MC?"

"Monster cock."

"For shit's sake, Vi. I have to play hockey with this guy. How am I supposed to look at him, let alone talk to him, when you tell me shit like this?"

"I'm making a point. And you guys walk around naked in front of each other all the time, so you know what Alex's junk looks like. Anyway, as much as I'm an independent woman, I appreciate that Alex gets a little territorial over me. But I don't know if Sunny feels the same."

"So I might have fucked things up again?" I can't win at all.

"I don't think you fucked up. All women are different. I think you're used to women only expecting one thing from you, and while orgasms are nice, that isn't what it's about between you and Sunny."

"Dating is hard."

Violet sighs. "It sure is. Relationships aren't a game. No one wants to get screwed around, except maybe people who like a lot of drama and want to end up on those terrible reality dating shows."

"I'm not playing Sunny. I told her I wasn't upset, that I trusted her. Even though the first part isn't true, and I also don't trust her ex for shit."

"That's a great step in the right direction. Now your goal this week is to message her every day, call her, say nice things, make sure she knows you're thinking about her," Violet says.

"I can do all of that. "

"Yeah, you can. I have faith in you, Buck. You've got this."

"Thanks for the vote of confidence."

"No problem. You off the ledge now?"

"Yeah."

"Cool. Alex has the Scrabble board set up, and I plan to kick his ass."

"Have fun with that." Scrabble is my least favorite game in the entire world. "Thanks for the advice and your usual overshare."

"I don't know if I'm the best person to ask for advice on relationships, but I'll help where I can. Sunny will only tell me so much. She's smart enough to know I'll share the important shit. Make sure you message her every day, at least twice. Even if she's in the middle of nowhere and can't get the message. You need to be as persistent as a yeast infection."

"What if it's not enough?"

"You can't control other people's feelings. All you can do is put yourself out there and hope she reciprocates."

"And if she doesn't?"

"You'll move on. But you can do this. Relationships are scary. Especially new ones with guys who have seriously questionable reputations. Sometimes it's easier to go back to what we know because it's familiar and comfortable rather than put ourselves on the line. If you want this—if you want her—it's you putting yourself on the line, not the other way around. Call me tomorrow if you need to; Alex has a workout scheduled at nine in the morning. I'm planning to watch him sweat while I pretend to exert myself on a recumbent bike."

She hangs up with a screech and a giggle.

I don't want Sunny's orgasm-challenged, jerk of an ex to be the safer option. I need to prove that I can be the boyfriend she needs. It'll be tough with her all the way in Chapleau, but I'm up for a challenge.

18

Big Bets and Vague Memories

-MILLER-

After the call with Violet, I find a buffet and eat my feelings. Then I head to the airport. I check social media while I wait for him to land. Kale has tagged Sunny in pictures. She and Lily are sitting at the table in the backseat, arms around each other with big grins. There's another one of Sunny with her face right next to Kale's scruffy beard, holding a bag of those damn kale chips. I hate him and his stupid name.

I comment on every post, so Kale knows I'm watching his ass. I desperately want to talk to Sunny about the whole four-year thing, but I don't want to rock an already rocky boat. And having that talk with hours separating us seems like a recipe for disaster.

Randy's all smiles and "fuck yeah, camping!" when I pull up to arrivals and he tosses his stuff in the back of the SUV. I try not to let my crap mood ruin his. He reclines his seat and adjusts his baseball cap. He's a walking billboard for Chicago.

"So? How was the weekend with Sunny? I figured it couldn't have gone too bad since I only heard from you once."

I struggle to maintain a neutral expression. "It was good."

"Just good? Come on, you've been radio silent all weekend. Did you finally get some action or what?"

In the past talking about this stuff didn't bother me, but now...it feels wrong to talk about what Sunny and I do behind closed doors.

The GPS pipes up and tells me to get on the 401 East. I follow the signs, avoiding an answer.

"Miller?"

"Yeah?"

"You planning to answer or what?"

"We had a good time. Let's leave it at that."

"Oh, shit. How fucking blue are your balls right now?" He pulls out his phone.

"What are you doing?" The traffic here is unreal. People cut across lanes without even looking. There are signs everywhere and assholes going ten kilometers under the limit in the slow lane, forcing everyone behind them to slam on their brakes.

He's thumb typing, and the sound is on, so I hear every annoying click. "Texting Lance."

"What the hell for?"

He stops typing to talk. "Because I owe him a case of beer."

"For what?"

"I lost the bet." He's got that cocky grin going again.

"Bet?"

"Yeah. We put a case of beer on your weekend adventures."

I slap his phone out of his hand. I also swerve and accidentally cut into the lane next to me. A woman in a sporty car honks and gives me the bird.

"Dude! What's your deal?" He bends to retrieve his phone,

but I crossbar him with a forearm to the neck.

"Text Lance and I'll leave you on the side of the highway."

"I won't. Jeez, man, what's going on with you? What happened? Did you and Sunny get into a fight? I figured you'd smooth things over with your sweet talking like you do with the bunnies."

"Sunny's not a bunny." The rhyme irritates me.

"I know that."

I run a hand through my hair and give him the side eye. "You want to make bets on the bunnies, you go right ahead. But don't bring Sunny into your bullshit. She's not some woman whose pants I'm trying to get in."

Randy settles back in his seat when I withdraw my arm. "I know that, man, but you know how Lance is; everything's a game for him."

"You'd think it was obvious at this point that I'm serious about Sunny."

"Right? Who keeps seeing the same woman for three months if it isn't about more than sex." Randy looks out the window and rubs at his beard. "I know I sure as hell wouldn't."

I don't say anything while Randy fiddles around with the radio and finds a station he likes. He's big into country music.

Here's the thing: I know I shouldn't say anything, but like Randy said, I've been waiting for months to get to this point. I can't give details to Violet, because that shit's awkward and weird. I mean, mostly she's like a girl version of Randy, but stepsister or not, we're quasi-related, and we're close. I can't go there. However, Randy's one of my closest buddies. I should be able to trust him not to run his mouth.

"You can't say anything to Lance."

He stops messing around with the radio. "I won't. Scout's honor." He holds up two fingers and gives me a cheeky-ass grin.

"I'm serious."

"Sorry. I can't help it. But yeah, I won't say anything—not to Lance or anyone else."

"So Sunny was pissed when I got there, but we talked it out, and I smoothed it over."

"So you did get some action?"

I fight a smile.

"I knew it! You owe me a case of beer, asshole. How was it? She teaches yoga right? I bet she's super bendy." He makes thrusting motions.

I want to punch him in the side of the head. I suck my teeth.

"Sorry. Sorry, man. That was out of line." He pats me on the shoulder. "I know you've been blue-balling it over this girl, so I'm glad you finally got some."

I can tell he wants details. Before Sunny, I would've given them. Often the bunnies like to share details—some of them seriously exaggerated—in online groups. Up until now it didn't feel wrong to share, but Sunny won't post anything about our weekend sex-a-thon, so I feel like I should keep most of it to myself.

"What about you? How was your weekend?" I ask, shifting the focus.

"You know how it goes when Lance is on a bender. He keeps inviting more people. When I left this morning he was looking rough."

That's not an answer. Not the kind I expect from Randy. He's usually all over providing excessive details. Right now he seems irritated more than anything.

"Natasha was pretty annoyed?" I probe.

"Right? She was a drill sergeant. Lance puked his guts out later."

I hit the brakes when the guy in front of us slams on his.

Ahead of me is a sea of red lights and a lot of pickup trucks with huge tires. It's like we're on the way to a monster truck rally. It's Sunday afternoon. We're in Canada, with an endless supply of land, and we're sitting in bumper-to-bumper traffic. I don't get it.

"You think there's anything going on there?" I ask.

"Between Tash and Lance? He flirts with her, but then he flirts with everyone. That would be stupid on Tash's part. Lance is fun to be around, but he's dirty. Why? Tash say something to you?" Randy messes with the radio.

"No. Just a feeling I get."

Randy's a fidgety guy. If I didn't know him as well as I do, I'd think he was strung out on something most of the time. He's not. I don't think he even smoked weed in high school. He taps his fingers on his knees and hums along to the song.

He stops drumming. "You know, maybe you're right."

"About Tash and Lance?"

"He was in a shitty mood after she left, bitching about how she didn't even say she was going and how she short-changed us on the workout. I figured he was in one of his moods, because he was hungover as shit, and it wasn't like he was actually doing anything other than being a pain in the ass. But that was when the party started to get out of hand. He was slamming back the shots. Then he took a porcelain throne break. He came out an hour or two later, called half his bunny list, and went back to getting wasted. I stopped drinking because I was worried he'd get into a fight, and flying hungover sucks."

Lance has a short fuse on the ice and an even shorter fuse when he's wasted and someone says something he doesn't like. I have my moments, but Lance is way worse. He blames it on the ginger in him. I blame it on his messed-up childhood.

"Anyway, he passed out around eight, and I figured that'd

be the end of him, but he got back up at midnight and kept going. He was still asleep when I left today. I should call later and see how he's doing."

Sometimes I worry about Lance. He's two years into his career and still a hotheaded rookie. He's stupid with his money— blowing it on parties and his collection of cars. I'd probably be doing the same if it wasn't for Violet. She essentially gives me an allowance so I don't waste what's supposed to be my savings on frivolous crap—not that I don't useless things. I just buy them less often. Plus, living in a condo makes it impossible to have fifty people at my place. Having Lance as a friend allows me to experience the parties without managing the cleanup or the actual expense.

"Whatever happened to those women you guys brought home?"

"Which ones?"

"The ones from the bar the night before I left."

His expression is still blank.

"The woman in the dickface pictures. The ones that got me into trouble with Sunny."

"Oh. Yeah. Lance felt bad about that."

Not so bad that he apologized, but that isn't Lance's style. He doesn't do apologies. He lives like the world revolves around him. It's another reason I'm not so sure he'll make it too many more seasons. He isn't much of a team player. That doesn't work well when you play professional hockey.

"So what happened to them?"

Randy shrugs. "Who knows?"

"One of them knew Lance, eh."

"Eh?" Randy smirks. "Sunny's starting to rub off on you."

My response is automatic. "She's done a lot more than rub off on me."

Randy laughs. "You better not say that in front of Waters or he'll use your balls for shoot-out practice. What do you mean one of them knew Lance? Pretty much everyone's had a piece of that guy."

"The girl who cleaned my forehead said she went to school with him back in the day."

"Seriously? Did he sleep with her?"

"Nope. I don't think he recognized her. She said she was younger. Like middle school or something. There was some party her older sister dragged her to, and they ended up in a closet together."

"No shit! Are you going to tell him about it?"

"I don't see the point. It's not like he gives a shit. Besides, she seemed like a nice girl. I felt bad that he took her friend to bed."

Randy makes a disapproving sound. "What was her name?"

"Poppy."

"Poppy what?"

"I don't know. Poppy from the garden. I'd say ask Lance, but he won't remember. Anyway, she was a nice girl, definitely not a bunny. Apparently Lance was her first kiss."

"Wow. That sucks for her." Randy reclines in his seat again and stares out the window, tapping his fingers on his lips to the beat. "You know, I don't even remember my first kiss. There've been so many women. I can't keep track anymore."

He's not bragging. In fact, he seems sad about it.

19

Ground Rules

-MILLER-

The traffic thins once we're outside of Toronto. Randy and I stop at a burger joint on the way up and scarfed down half a dozen burgers each, so we're not starving when we pull into camp at dinner time. Having volunteered at these things before, I'm highly aware that keeping up with the quantity of food Randy and I can consume takes effort.

This isn't the same as the training camps for future professional players. These kids are here for fun and the experience. While a few may have serious potential, most of them are here for the love of the sport. The camp is heavily subsidized, partially by me, partially by other foundations that work with underprivileged families or kids with medical needs. One of the kids this year might not even make it to his teens. That's why I chose this camp. No one appreciates—and deserves—life's joys like someone who knows life is short.

I follow the directions of one of the junior counselors, who gets all bug-eyed and excited when we tell him who we are and what we're here for. We park in the staff lot and cut the engine. Two girls in shorts and camp shirts that read STAFF come out of the mess hall.

The boys' camp is on the south side of the lake and the girls are on the north side. The mess hall is central, so they eat together and there are coed events during the day, and campfires in the evening. It doesn't stop them from trying to pair off and disappear into the forest.

I press the lock button before Randy can get out of the car and keep my thumb on it. "We need to set some ground rules for the week."

"Huh?"

"Ground rules." I snap my fingers to get his attention. "The junior counselors are sixteen and seventeen. The senior counselors are eighteen and up." I know this because Amber read me the program information when I said I wanted to volunteer here instead of at one of the serious hockey camps this summer. "There's a no-fraternizing policy in effect."

Randy snorts. "Does anyone actually take that seriously?"

"You need to take it seriously."

"Do you remember hockey camp, Miller? I sure do. It was a no-holds-barred fuck fest."

"This isn't that kind of hockey camp, and we're not attending, we're volunteering. Don't make me regret inviting you."

A group of four girls comes out of the mess hall; one has a staff shirt on, and the other three are dressed in regular summer clothes. "How do I know if they're senior or junior counselors?"

"You ask."

"Awesome. Let's go." He reefs on the door again.

"We're not done laying ground rules yet. If you're going to

hook up with a senior counselor, you need to limit it to one."

"One?" He looks like his head is going to explode.

"Yeah. One. All these girls know each other. They've probably been coming here since they were little kids. They're going to talk, and if you bang your way through them, I'm never going to be invited back. And I don't need the drama."

"So just one." He cracks his knuckles and rolls his shoulders like he's getting ready to take on an opponent. "Okay. I can do that, I guess."

"Choose wisely, Balls."

I release the lock, and he gets out of the car, stretching before he leans against his door and watches another gaggle of teenagers burst out of the mess hall. This time one of the counselors pushes a kid in a wheelchair. Randy's up the stairs and offering assistance before I can unbuckle my seatbelt.

My phone dings several times in a row with new messages.

Sunny Sunshine: *<3 the pic!*

Made it 2 the camp. How are you?

Forgot my charger :(going to town in a couple of days to get one

Fuck. This isn't good. I don't bother with messaging. I hit her contact and call right away. She picks up on the second ring. The connection isn't great.

"Hey, sweets."

"Miller! I don't have much battery left."

"That's okay. I wanted to make sure you made it up there all right."

"You're sweet. The drive was great! Kale and Benji are making a fire, and then we're going to make dinner."

It's like a double date out in the middle of nowhere. The only good thing is the lack of shower options. I'm hoping Sunny also forgot deodorant and soap. With my luck, that would probably be an aphrodisiac for Kale.

"We won't get to town for a couple of days. I'll message from Lily's phone, but her reception is almost as bad as mine."

"That sucks. I was hoping for daily updates."

"I know. I'm sorry, Miller. I'll message as soon as I get a new charger. I still need to call my parents, so I should go before my phone dies." The static makes it hard to hear her.

"Okay. Be careful up there. When I see you next, I think we should talk—" I want to put the exclusivity card on the table.

Her shriek forces me to pull the phone away from my ear. "Kale! Stop it! I'm on the phone with Miller! Put me down—"

The call drops; beep-beep-beeping is the last thing I get.

I stare at the blank screen, heat creeping up the back of my neck.

This is going to be a long, shitty week of worrying.

20

Not the Trip I Wanted to Go On

-SUNNY-

The call drops before I can tell Miller I miss him already.

It's only been eight hours and I'm already fed up with Kale. My relationship with Miller might not be perfect and we may be working out the kinks that come with long distance and the nightmare of social media fodder, but the differences between Kale and Miller couldn't be more glaring.

Miller is altruistic, kind, and sweet. He's a caretaker in the best ways, patient and giving. So giving. My body warms at the memory of his strong arms looped gently around my thighs, his mouth soft and sure, lips and tongue gentle as he learned my body and brought me to orgasm again and again.

But it's not just about the sex, which I had no idea could feel that good every single time. I might not have a ton of experience, but I have enough to know that he's a rare and precious gem.

What made it even more special, was the way he gathered me in his arms and snuggled with me while we talked into the wee hours of the morning (between more rounds of sex). He asked if he could fly me out to Chicago in September during exhibition games so we could have more time together. He asked about my classes, and what kind of internship I wanted, and if there was a possibility for me to do it outside of Guelph. It gives me hope that he wants what I want. When we were sufficiently exhausted, and heavy-lidded, he tucked me into his side and held me all night.

The other parts of our relationship might be challenging, especially with the way my brother is always interfering with his love and concern. But it's the memories of our time together and the way we connect both inside and outside of bed that reassure me when my insecurities get the better of me.

I plant my fists on my hips frustrated that our call ended prematurely, all because Kale is being a problem. "Why would you do that?"

"I didn't realize you were on the phone."

I arch a brow. "Who did you think I was talking to?"

His nose twitches and he tugs at one unruly sideburn. It's one of his tells.

"Not myself, surely," I press.

He blinks. "Come on, Sunny. You can't be serious about that guy. He's a total player."

"You don't know the first thing about Miller."

He opens his mouth to argue.

Usually when my brother pulls one of these "I just want what's best for you" spiels or "I worry about you" lectures, I let him yammer on and tell him what he wants to hear. But I'm tired of everyone telling me what to do. I'm sick of the interference. They see one side of him that's warped by a singular, inaccurate perception. So I roll my shoulders back and hold up a hand. "No."

"But—"

"I'm a big girl. I can and I will make my own decisions."

"I'm just trying to be a—"

"Good friend? If that's your goal, you'll respect my choices and stop being passive-aggressive."

"I'm not—"

I arch a brow.

Kale's lips thin in a line.

Internally I give myself a back pat because standing up for myself sure feels good. And I'm hoping that this week I can help Lily do the same with Benji.

"You're doing it wrong!" Benji snaps from the campfire. "Give it to me!"

"Fine. Here! Do it yourself!" Lily stalks across the uneven terrain toward the trailer, wearing her frustration on her face.

They've been bickering the entire time. Well, Benji has been bickering with Lily and she's been trying to keep the peace. Looks like both of us are tired of the bullshit already.

"Maybe go help Benji," I say flatly to Kale.

He sighs and turns sideways as Lily brushes by him, then leaves when she promptly bursts into tears. I wrap my arms around her.

"I think this was a really bad idea. I don't know why I thought a camping trip would fix things. I'm sorry I dragged you into this mess." She hiccups.

"It's okay." I pat her back. "If there's anything you and I know how to do, it's make the best of a bad situation."

And honestly, if a week of camping with Benji and Kale is what Lily needs to finally end things for good, then it's worth the headache.

21
Big Balls

-MILLER-

Randy is on his best behavior for the first two days, which is a miracle. There are way more counselors than I'm used to, probably because the kids require more supervision and assistance. At least I have Randy as my shield against the interested senior counselors, who are in abundant supply.

I thought the Sunny wallpaper on my phone would function as a deterrent, but I discovered that girls like guys who have pictures of their girlfriends on their phones. At first I think they're hitting on me, but then I realize they want to be my friend. Girls are funny about the whole *being friends with a guy* business. They're flirty, and overly touchy, but there's no expectation that we're going to sneak into an empty cabin for reasons. It's like having a whole bunch of Vis who engage in the overshare.

Randy has the opposite issue. Once it becomes clear he doesn't have a girlfriend, he's fair game. It's like watching turkey vultures fight over a carcass on the highway. They'll peck each other's eyes out to get to him.

By the morning of day three, I still haven't heard from Sunny. Between coaching sessions and games with the kids, I check her social media accounts, but there's nothing new apart from a picture posted on the first day—not by her or Lily, but Kale. The four of them have their arms wrapped around each other, standing in front of the camping trailer-van, being all happy together. I get it better now more than ever why she reacted the way she did to those bunny pics. Kale has his arm around Sunny. I want to rip it off and beat him with it, but I also know that things aren't always the way they look.

The longer I don't hear from her, the more antsy I get. I know they're all friends, and that they obviously didn't work out for a reason, but I hate the way this feels. And I realize that this is probably how Sunny has felt every single time a bunny posts a picture. And that's a seriously shitty realization. Especially because I can't tell her.

I combat the happy, smiley picture with multiple pics of me and Sunny from our weekend at her place. Even though I'm anxious and frustrated, I message her every day with little updates. I tell her I miss her. That I can't wait to see her again.

The reception up here isn't the greatest unless I'm in the mess hall or by the water where there aren't as many trees obstructing the signal. This means I'm forced to type most of my messages. I won't use voice-to-text in front of other people when some of what I want to text is private.

I'd vet them through my PA like I sometimes do, but she's still out in the middle of the wilderness, so it's not an option. And there's no way I want Randy to see these messages.

By the end of the fifth day, I'm bagged. Kids are a lot of work. I must've been hard for my dad to manage as a kid, especially having hockey practice five days a week. But it was a good way to get me out of my dad's hair so he could get shit done. And eventually my practices were a good place for him to scout.

While I never had a problem with practice, schoolwork was always a fight. I feel like it's the same way for some of these kids. I've already sent my dad an email with the names of a couple kids who have serious potential, but likely can't afford the training they'll need to make hockey a career. I don't expect to hear from him until he's back from his cruise, but I like to keep him informed.

After six rounds of ball hockey I hit the staff showers, and use the privacy to handle my issue. Randy and I are sharing a cabin with two other counselors, and those two do not need to see my morning wood.

I cut the water and towel off, putting on a fresh pair of shorts and a T-shirt. I almost bowl over one of the female counselors on my way out.

Randy's standing beside her with his towel and a change of clothes. "You go first." He nods to the open stall.

"You're sure?" She's all blush-y and lip bite-y.

"Yeah. Definitely. I'll catch up with you later."

"Okay. I'll see you in the mess hall before the campfire?" She twirls her ponytail around her finger.

"Sure thing." He winks, and she practically trips over her own feet getting into the shower.

As soon as she's locked inside, I ask the most important question: "How old is she?"

"Nineteen."

"You sure about that?"

"She showed me her driver's license." He pats me on the shoulder. "Don't worry, Miller. I've got a handle on the situation."

Another stall comes open, and he grabs it before I can question him further.

I have time before the campfire, so I walk down to the lake where the reception and privacy are better. Sunny said she'd try to call tonight. The last I heard from her was two nights ago. I missed the call because I was leading a session. She left a choppy message saying her reception was terrible, she missed me and she would try to call me later if she could get enough of a signal. She didn't sound particularly happy. It shouldn't have made me feel good, but it did.

Tonight, they're supposed to be at some live music event in town. Lily isn't much of a drinker, so she's the DD. Which I'm grateful for. I don't want anyone taking advantage of her when she's under the influence, especially not Kale.

The first night I met Sunny, she was blitzed after three drinks, two of which I bought for her. I ordered her a non-alcoholic mojito while she was in the bathroom to help sober her up. We ended up at an all-night breakfast place. She ate an unholy amount of food and we talked for hours.

I made sure she got back to her friend's place and we made out on the front porch for a good ten minutes. Then I asked for her number and gave her mine. On the way back to the hotel, I voice-texted her so autocorrect wouldn't mess shit up for me and told her I had a great time and wanted to see her again. And now I'm here and she's in Chapleau and I regret not asking her to be my girlfriend so she would know, without a doubt, that I'm serious about her.

The sun dips toward the treetops in the distance, but dusk is an hour away, so I should be safe from the mosquitoes. They're terrible up here. I have clusters of bites all over the place. I've been bathing in bug spray every night before the campfire, but it's not helping much.

I drop into one of the chairs on an empty dock, brushing away a few cobwebs and a spider or two. It's quiet out here with everyone getting ready for the fire. I'm hoping to get directions from Sunny for when camp is done.

Pulling up my messages, I find nothing new from her. Since I'm out here alone, I can use the voice-to-text function. I dictate a quick message telling her I miss her and can't wait to see her soon before I check social media. Sunny isn't big on updating, but Kale has tagged her in half a dozen pictures. There are a bunch of Sunny with Lily. One caught them in a candid moment with their arms around each other, laughing. They look happy and like they're having fun together.

But the farther I scroll through the feed, the less happy I am. There are pictures of Sunny in my favorite bikini and Kale is right freaking there, all smiles. I hate that she's so far away and it's so hard to contact her.

I'm about to comment on a couple of the pictures when a sharp sting has me out of the chair and on my feet. My phone clatters to the dock and bounces once. It spins on its side before falling away from the crack in the boards. My relief is short-lived. A huge spider falls out of my shorts and lands on top of my running shoe. I shout and kick it off, then stomp on the fucker until he's nothing but a splatter mark.

Making sure I'm still alone first, I unbutton my shorts to check my parts. It's hard to see without dropping my shorts completely and mooning anyone who might accidentally find me. I stick my hand down there, feeling my balls where the sting is the worst. There's a bump on my left nut. It hurts to touch.

"Um...is everything okay?" The voice is female and vaguely familiar.

I immediately retract my hand and button my shorts. Once everything is tucked away, I turn around. It's one of the senior counselors. The same one who's been following me around for the past few days. She turned eighteen last week. She's told me seven thousand times already. It's a harmless crush—I think—but I've been trying not to end up alone with her. Like I am right now.

She looks around, confused. "I heard a girl scream."

"A spider bit me."

"Oh. Are you okay?"

I'd be embarrassed by the pitch of my scream, but the bite stings, and it was a big fucking spider. "I'll be fine. Nothing some anti-bite cream won't fix."

I'm not sure that's true. It already feels like I dipped my balls in acid.

"Do you want me to take a look?" She takes a few steps toward me, and I take a couple back.

"That's okay. I can handle it."

"I should check it out for you. I might be able to figure out what type of spider it was. Last week one of the kid's hands swelled up to twice its size because she got bit by a dock spider. Sometimes when they're pregnant they lay their eggs under the skin."

I shudder at the thought of a thousand baby spiders exploding from my balls. It's like a damn horror movie.

She moves closer. "Are you sure you're okay? I have first aid. Where'd it bite you?"

"Not in a spot I want you to look at." It feels like something is happening in my pants, and it's not good.

I move her out of the way by her shoulders. In my hurry to escape, I almost step on my phone. I scoop it up and rush toward the cabins. She calls after me, but I wave over my shoulder and start jogging. It's uncomfortable. I have to throw my leg out to the side so I don't cause unnecessary friction.

My cabin is empty, thankfully, so I drop my shorts and inspect the damage. My left nut is now significantly larger than the right one and the bite is red and angry.

I remember one time at hockey camp, way back when I was a teenager, a spider bit me and it swelled. That was my foot, though. It was uncomfortable, but it could have been worse. This isn't the same. I need an antihistamine at the very least. This bastard will be itchy as hell, and if my ball keeps swelling, I'll be sporting one hell of a moose knuckle. I can't have that when I'm dealing with a bunch of pre-teens.

I pull my shorts up and check the first aid kit. The medicated wipes and bandages won't cut it. My only other option is to visit the clinic. Because of the nature of the camp, there's always a nurse on call. I almost trip over the girl from the dock on my way out the door.

"Everything okay? They're starting the campfire soon. You're coming, right?"

"I'll be there. I need to make a quick stop first."

My shorts chafe against my swollen ball, forcing me to hobble. The girl bounces along beside me. She's got great energy when it comes to working with the kids, but right now I find it irritating, mostly because I'm in pain.

"Oh wow. You're limping. Did it get you on the leg?" She bends until her head is almost at crotch level.

I want to get to the clinic, but the faster I move, the more it hurts. "I didn't get bit on the leg."

"Where'd it bite you?"

"On the balls."

"Oh. Oh, God." That stops the questions.

We run into Randy. He's with that girl from the showers. He frowns when he sees me walking like someone gave me a Charlie horse. He glances between me and the girl. It's the first time I've noticed she's blond and looks a little like Sunny. That might explain my subconscious attempt to get away from her.

"What happened to you?" Randy asks.

Sunny's doppelgänger bounces excitedly. "A spider bit him on his balls!"

"How did that happen?" Randy's suspicion is offensive. I've been faithful to Sunny for three damn months. I'm not going to fold after five days because the woman beside me looks like my sort-of girlfriend, who's currently seven hours away. Without cell phone reception. And whose ex-boyfriend probably wants her back.

"I'm assuming it crawled into my shorts, took one look at my balls, thought, *hey man, those look tasty*, and chomped down. But I'm not a spider-whisperer, so I have no idea how spiders make those kinds of decisions. That's just a guess."

Randy has the audacity to check with Doppelgänger to verify whether I'm indeed telling the truth.

She lifts one shoulder and lets it fall. "I heard a scream and went to check it out. I was worried some of the kids might have snuck down to the water without permission. I found Miller on the dock. He squished the spider. It was hard to tell what kind it was, but it was probably a dock spider because he was on the dock."

This whole conversation might be okay if it didn't feel as if my balls were about to explode like the sun. "I need to hit the bathroom."

"I still think you should let me check it out. You look uncomfortable." She makes a face. "And you're sweaty."

Randy pats me on the back and steers me in the direction of the staff bathroom. "Come on, let's go."

I'm relieved to find the bathroom empty. I close the door, and Randy stands in front of it. There's no lock on the inside, so he's my barricade while I'm checking the damage. "You need to tell me how bad it is. I can't see the bite."

Randy crosses his arms over his chest. "I'll man the door, and you can check it out in that mirror."

"Fine. But don't let anyone in here." I hobble across the room. The mirror is so old it has a cloudy haze to it. It's also high up on the wall. At 6'2" I'm tall, but the mirror only reaches my waist. I drop my shorts and jump up, but it's painful and ineffective. "I can't see anything."

"Try taking the mirror off the wall."

"It's fastened with screws." I turn around, prepared to show my irritation with a hand gesture.

The color drains from Randy's face as he gets a load of my junk. "Holy fucking shit, dude. You need to see a medic."

I glance down. I don't need a mirror to see the problem. In the time it's taken me to walk from the cabin to the bathrooms, my left nut has swollen to twice its normal size and it feels like I've given them a bath in lava. "I need an antihistamine, some Tylenol, and maybe a bag of frozen peas."

"I think you might need more than that." He moves closer and leans in.

I'm assaulted by a flash of light. Momentarily blinded, I raise my hands, and my shorts drop all the way to the floor.

"You can't post that anywhere!" I grab for his phone, but he holds it out of reach, clicking buttons with his thumb.

"It's just your junk, dude." He shows me a close-up pic of my branch and berries. "There's this site where they can identify medical stuff through pictures. Maybe they can figure out what kind of spider bit you."

"I don't want pictures of my dick on the Internet!"

This is the exact moment the door flies open, slamming into Randy from behind. He stumbles forward and almost face-plants into my giant balls. I stop him with a palm on his forehead. A senior counselor—I recognize him from mess hall duty—stands inside the door. He starts to apologize, but it turns into a croak as he takes in the scene: me cupping my balls and Randy on his knees in front of me with his phone in his hand.

Because this day wasn't bad enough already, shit had to get even stupider.

22
Nothing is Easy. Ever.

-MILLER-

"Uh—" Bathroom Interloper's eyes dart back and forth between us.

"A spider bit me on the balls." I put both hands in the air before he gets the wrong idea. Which he clearly already has, so it's useless.

"I'm going—" He thumbs over his shoulder and starts to back out of the bathroom.

Randy grabs him by the shirt and yanks him inside, slapping his free palm against the door to prevent anyone from entering or exiting. "You're not going anywhere."

"I-I don't—I'm not. I won't tell anyone."

"Randy, chill out and let him go." Bathroom Interloper looks like he's about to pee his pants. Which is understandable considering the situation he walked in on and Randy's misplaced aggression. "This isn't how it looks. A spider seriously bit me on the balls."

I've got enough crap to contend with where Sunny is concerned. I don't need more rumors circulating.

His eyes drop down and then flip right back up. His horror confirms what I already know. I need to get this taken care of. Sooner rather than later.

To drive the point home, Bathroom Interloper says, "That doesn't look normal."

"No shit."

"You should probably see someone about that."

"That's the plan."

He nods like it makes good sense, because it does.

I carefully zip my shorts to avoid any additional unnecessary pain. Randy and our new friend walk two steps in front of me, acting as a shield so I don't traumatize any of the kids or junior counselors or campers. The girls run up as we head for the clinic. Sunny's doppelgänger gets in front of us and throws open the door. "Miller has a spider bite!" She pauses for greater effect. "On his balls!"

If it was just me and Randy and Bathroom Interloper, plus the two girls it would be embarrassing but manageable. But there are several tables full of kids, some playing cards, others on their devices, since this is the best place to get reception. Several junior counselors are preparing snacks for the campfire. We're having banana boats. They're my favorite. I hope my balls don't prevent me from being able to go. I really want one. Or six.

Everyone stops what they're doing to stare at my crotch. I can understand why; my shorts are tight across the front, the outline of my now oversized balls clearly visible. I shield myself with my hands, but it's too late. They've all seen the monstrosity taking up way too much real estate in my shorts.

"You should probably see the nurse," one of the girls at the table says. Her eyes are still below my waist.

"I need an antihistamine. You got a bag of frozen vegetables in the kitchen I can borrow?"

Everyone continues to stare. Randy coughs from beside me.

"Fine. How about a bag of ice instead? That way I won't have to return it after I put it on my balls." I glance at the kids in the corner. They're all gaping, too. "I mean my testicles."

That gets a few giggles. It's nice that this is entertaining for someone.

Bathroom Interloper puts in his two cents. "I still think someone should check that out."

"I offered!" Doppelgänger's hand shoots up in the air. The girl beside her forces her hand back down to her side.

"*I've* checked it out." I point to my chest. "It's just a little swollen."

Randy coughs again.

"Okay. It's a lot swollen. But I've had way worse, so this is no big deal." The burning in my balls is now accompanied by a horrendous itch. It's unreal. I have the strangest urge to dip them in ice-cold water. It's about the last thing any guy usually wants to do, and a sure sign things are way worse than I thought.

"Let's go find Nurse Debbie," Doppelgänger suggests. "She'll take care of you."

I stop arguing. Not accepting medical attention is setting a bad example. Plus, no one's balls should ever be this big. My growing entourage accompanies me through the mess hall to the medical center. When we get there and no one moves to leave, I clap my hands. "Okay, everyone. Thanks for getting me here. I appreciate all your help, but I don't think I need a cheering squad for the rest of this."

"Um..." Doppelgänger raises her hand like we're in class and I'm the teacher. "Can I get a quick picture with you?"

"Group photo!" Randy says, a stupid, jerky grin on his face. "Everyone in!"

He mashes everyone together, Bathroom Interloper and Doppelgänger on either side of me. My smile is more grimace than anything else. I'd flip the bird, but this will undoubtedly make it to someone's socials. I hope he doesn't get my actual package in the picture.

Finally, once the photo shoot is over, they all leave.

In the far corner of the clinic, a kid is hooked up to a bunch of machines, an IV bag running to his arm. As soon as he sees me, he ducks his head like he's embarrassed to be here, or he witnessed that display of idiocy.

I recognize him from earlier in the week. He hasn't signed up for any of the competitive hockey business, but he's been to every lesson. He's an amazing player, but he's quiet, always leaving as soon as the lesson is over before I can talk to him. He's missed the campfire a couple of times.

"Hey, man. I'm Miller. I've seen you playing this week. How's it going?"

He lifts his head, his eyes widening in surprise. "Uh, I'm Michael." He looks at the IV drip. "I guess it's okay."

"You getting gassed up so you can play with me tomorrow?" I nod to all the shit he's hooked up to.

He smiles, but it's sad and old, way older than it should be for a kid. "Something like that."

Nurse Debbie appears in her white running shoes and scrubs. I'd like to say she's in her mid-fifties and looks like my aunt. She doesn't. She's probably in her early to mid-thirties. I'm not sure how I feel about her having to look at my junk. But the itch has become as pervasive as the burning sensation.

She clears her throat and props her clipboard on her hip, flipping into professional mode. "How can I help you?"

"I got bit by a spider, and it's swelling." I want to shove my hands in my pockets, but there's no room.

"Why don't you have a seat so I can take a look?"

"Uh..." I incline my head in the direction of my young friend. "We'll need privacy for this."

Nurse Debbie's eyebrows shoot up into her hairline. She does that strobe-light blink thing. "Privacy?"

"It's not in a PG spot."

She strobe blinks a couple more times and gestures to one of the cots. She hands me a gown and closes the curtain while I drop my shorts. This is beyond mortifying.

When I'm gowned up, I invite her in. Nurse Debbie doesn't mask her shock when I show her my junk. "Oh my God."

I'm not sure if it's an optical illusion, but my balls seem even bigger than they were the last time I looked. They're about the size of a softball now, with one side significantly more swollen than the other. They usually resemble a couple of plums hanging out together. The left one is massive, and the swelling has traveled to the other side

"It's a little swollen."

Nurse Debbie's eyes flip up to mine, her disbelief obvious. "A little?"

"Okay. A lot. But it's not a big deal, right? The swelling should go down if I take an antihistamine and ice those babies."

"Do you know what bit you?"

"A spider. I squished it when it fell out of my shorts."

"It fell out of your shorts?"

"Yeah. I was chilling on the dock after dinner, checking my emails, because it's peaceful out there, and the reception is decent." I don't know why I'm explaining. What I was doing isn't important. It's the state of my balls that matters.

"If you were on the dock, it was probably a fishing spider.

It's hard to know for sure until I get a better look." She snaps on a pair of gloves. "This is a pretty extreme reaction, though, possibly because of the location. Do you have any allergies?"

"I'm only allergic to penicillin."

"Ah. That could explain this." She motions to my huge balls.

"An allergy to penicillin can explain my nuts turning into grapefruit?"

"The spider venom has similar properties to penicillin. It means you'll have a more significant reaction."

My balls do seem damn significant. I glance at the clock; it's already after eight. "How long do you think this will take? I need to go to the campfire tonight; the kids are expecting me. Tomorrow morning we're playing kids-versus-counselors before their parents pick them up. I need the swelling to go down so I can play." Plus there will be some local journalists, as per Amber's suggestion.

"We can get your teammate to cover for you."

"I don't need Randy to cover for me. I want to hang out with these kids and play hockey and roast banana boats on an open fire. Just give me some antihistamine and a couple of painkillers. I'll be good to go."

My man unit is still hanging out. Nurse Debbie is still staring. I can understand why. I'll snap a couple of pics before the swelling goes down because they're unreal. I'll threaten Vi with them if she gets on my nerves.

Debbie crosses her arms. I should know better than to tell a medical professional what she needs to do. "I need to take a better look at the bite before I do that."

She makes me put my legs up on the cot and spread them. It's an awkward, exposed position, way worse than *look to the left and cough*. She gets right in there and fondles my fuzzy, burning balls. Then she makes me roll over on my side and lift a leg. It's not a pleasant position.

The longer she's down there, the more worried I become. My biggest concern is that some spider has mutated into a highly venomous ball biter and moved to Canada.

I calm my anxieties by reviewing the list of Canada's most dangerous creatures while Nurse Debbie pokes at my balls. Moose are lethal if they're threatened. Beavers get territorial over their wood. Bears are bears. I'm not sure about the rest of the animal population here. I guess it's tame, like the people.

Eventually I'm allowed to sit up. Nurse Debbie hands me a sheet to cover my business.

"As suspected, it's a fishing spider bite. It won't cause lasting damage if it's treated properly, but with your allergy to penicillin, it's worse than it should be. Plus the location is sensitive, as is the tissue there. I'd like to do a blood test to rule out toxicity, and I'll give you something for the swelling and pain. I'll need you to come back in a couple hours so I can check again, and then again tomorrow morning before I can clear you for games."

"It'll be fine by morning. I've taken a puck to the balls before, and my junk works fine. No spider will stop me from playing tomorrow."

"If I don't clear you, you can't play."

I'm about to plead my case, but she raises a hand. "I deal with athletes with medical issues for a living. You can argue with me until you're blue in the face, but if I tell you it's not safe to play, it's not safe to play. You'll find another way to do what you came here to do."

"Come on, Debbie. It's the last day."

She puts one hand on her hip and points at my sheet-covered crotch with the other. "You only get one set of those. They're not car parts. You can't replace them. It'd be a shame if nothing worked because you decided to be stubborn, wouldn't it?"

I've had so many hockey injuries; ninety percent of the time I'm fine in a couple of days. Sometimes there are creaks and cracks that shouldn't be there, considering I'm only twenty-three.

The occasions when it takes longer to heal, I dial back the workouts, do some physio, swim instead of run, and take the required herbs and supplements to get my body back in order. The possibility that my man unit might not work thanks to a spider bite is some scary shit. I've just started using it again. I need to make sure I'm functional when I see Sunny, which I'm hoping is soon.

I expel a heavy breath. "Okay. But let's do what we can to make this better as quick as possible. I want to make tomorrow count. Plus I'm supposed to see my girlfriend, so the faster things are back to normal, the better."

"You'll need the better part of a week to recover from that bite."

"Yeah. That's way too long."

"We'll discuss options after the blood tests." She slips out through the gap in the curtain, leaving me alone.

I take out my camera and snap a few pics of my swollen nut sac. From below it looks massive, and my dick looks average. It's not flattering.

I check my messages while I wait. I still haven't heard from Sunny, but Kale posted a while ago, so I send her another text. I've been dealing with this for less than a week, and I'm already frustrated. If this is how Sunny felt every single time another picture appeared on social media, I have an incredible amount of apologizing to do. For the first time since fifth grade—when I got my nickname—I'm insecure. Today can suck my gigantic balls.

Next I search the Internet for images of fishing spiders. I shudder as countless pictures pop up on the tiny screen. Those things are huge. I'm almost positive that's what bit me. Because I'm curious, and sometimes stupid, I add the word *bite* after *fishing spider*.

"Holy fucking shit." I clamp a hand over my mouth. Then I start to hyperventilate. The bites featured are right out of a horror movie. I'll be lucky if I still have my balls when this is over.

Nurse Debbie comes back, and I hold the phone up. "You said the damage wouldn't be lasting!"

She takes the device from me. "That's a brown recluse bite, not a fishing spider bite." She clicks on another picture and hands me the phone. It's bad, but not nearly as terrifying. Still, it's my balls.

Nurse Debbie takes some blood and offers me painkillers and a strong antihistamine.

"How long do you think it will take for the swelling to go down?" I put my shorts back on. Tucking everything in is a feat.

"It depends. It could take several hours or a few days."

"A few days? Is there any way to make that happen faster?"

She taps her pen on the clipboard. "Antihistamine injections work faster than taking them orally."

"Do you have to inject it into my balls?" I can't hold back the shudder.

She laughs. "Oh, God no! The arm or the butt works best."

"Let's do that, then."

She gets a syringe and stabs me in the arm. It doesn't deflate my balls instantly, or relieve the burning itch. If this is anything like an STI, I never want one. "So I'm good to go?"

"For now. I'd still like you to check in after the campfire, and then again in the morning. I should have the blood test results by then as well, although I expect they'll come back clean."

"Sure. Sounds like a plan."

"I'll see you in a couple hours." She opens the privacy curtain and heads over to see my buddy across the room. She checks the monitor and pats him on the shoulder. "Okay, Michael. It looks like you're all set."

He looks tired and embarrassed as she sets about removing all the stuff that keeps him tethered to the bed.

"You coming to the campfire tonight?" I ask him.

He throws his legs over the side of the cot, his eyes on the floor. "I don't know if I'm allowed."

Nurse Debbie shoots me a look that tells me I've made her life difficult.

"It's the last night. We're having banana boats. You should come." I throw on my best panty-melting smile.

Michael looks at Nurse Debbie. "Can I go?"

She hesitates. "I don't know if that's a good idea. You should probably rest up tonight if you want to participate tomorrow."

His head drops in a curt nod, like he expected as much. Long hair falls forward to cover his face. He can't be more than twelve, thirteen at best. He's got the lanky build of a kid who will be tall and broad in a few years. His sullen attitude is another sign the teen years are about to hit, although I feel like his might be justified.

"We'll be sitting the whole time. It'll be low-key."

I can tell she's debating. I can also tell Michael is resigned to being told he can't.

I give it one last shot. "I'll make sure he doesn't try to run a marathon or anything."

"Give us a minute, okay, Michael?" She crooks her finger, and I limp behind her until we're out of hearing range.

I speak first. "It's the last night. He shouldn't miss this."

She rubs her forehead and closes her eyes. "This is the second time he's been in the clinic this week. He's tired, and he's been pushing the limits. Last time he went to bed straight away. He won't tell you if he's feeling unwell. He'll want to stay to the end, and he doesn't want to be left out."

"He looks like a healthy kid. What's he been in here for?"

"He was diagnosed with cancer two months ago."

He's one of the kids I sponsored. "He has a brain tumor."

Her eyes go wide. "Did he tell you that?"

"Will he be all right?"

She purses her lips. "They rescheduled a radiation treatment so he could be here this week."

"But it's working, right?" I focus on the present, not the few memories I have of my mom in a hospital bed, in too much pain to even hug me.

"They're hoping they can reduce the size enough to make it operable. I shouldn't be telling you this."

Vague answers suck. "I won't say anything." I stuff my hands in my pockets and instantly regret it.

Brain tumors are tricky. Even if they can take it out, it doesn't mean he'll be the same kid when they're done, or that the cancer won't come back.

"Let him come to the campfire." I glance at the kid. He's sitting on the edge of the bed, head still hanging, looking like he hates his life. "I'll keep him with me the entire time. I'd hate to be the kid who has to lie in bed, wishing he wasn't so damn sick that he couldn't even handle a campfire. It's the best part of the day."

I can tell how hard this is for Nurse Debbie. The medical professional in her wants Michael to rest. The human being in her wants him to have this experience. If treatment doesn't work, he might not be able to have it again.

"I'll take good care of him, and I'll make sure he doesn't push himself." I make a mental note to get more information on his family and their financial situation when I'm in Chicago.

Nurse Debbie releases him with some trepidation. She fusses over him, much like he's her own kid, and finally sends us on our way. The stipulation is that I take him in a wheelchair since he's sloppy about walking. He doesn't seem all that excited, but when Randy and the girls meet up with us, and they fight over who gets to push him, he eases up.

The campfire is awesome. The counselors tell stories. We eat treats and talk about what's planned for tomorrow. The kids share their favorite part about being here. A few of them say it makes them feel normal. Michael holds up through the entire thing, but at the end I can tell it's taken everything he had to stay awake this long. One of the other counselors comes by to collect him—sleepy and happy and full of treats.

By the time the campfire is over, the pain in my balls has reduced to a slight ache. I'm still straining the front of my shorts, but Michael's situation puts mine into perspective.

As directed, I check in with Nurse Debbie on my way back to the cabin. She still seems concerned by the swelling, but happy about the lack of pain. In the cabin, a few of the senior counselors are playing cards and drinking contraband beers. Randy is nowhere to be seen.

I check my phone, hoping Sunny's called. She hasn't. It's already eleven.

The connection is in and out, but I pull my socials anyway. While I wait for the page to load, I stare at the wooden slats of the bunk above me. We decided it'd be best if I didn't sleep on the top, in case I ended up being too heavy. Nothing says shitty camping experience like being crushed by a bunkmate in the middle of the night. It happened back in high school during one of my summer hockey camps. Carved into the wood are names. Some are tagged with "was here" and others say "+ so-and-so."

The first girl I ever made out with I met at hockey camp. I was a junior counselor. My teeth—which were a mess thanks to my thumb-sucking as a kid—were finally being fixed. I started the bad habit after my mom died, according to my dad. I didn't do sleepovers with friends because there was a damn good chance I would wake up with my thumb in my mouth. It was embarrassing.

Anyway, this girl was amazing at hockey, so I liked her. We were walking from the lake to the mess hall, and she pulled me off the trail, behind some big evergreens. Then she laid one on me, just crushed her mouth against mine and rammed her tongue right in there.

I didn't know what to do. Well, that's not true. I'd watched enough movies and checked out the magazines my dad had hidden in his workshop to understand the mechanics, but she took me by surprise. When I recovered from the shock I kissed her back.

It was dusk, and the mosquitoes were terrible. I was covered in bites when we came back out five minutes later. Sadly, I found out later that night that she had kissed almost every junior counselor in the camp. I imagine the number might have been a bit of an exaggeration. Either way, it took some of the shine off the moment.

I think about that Michael kid, and how his future is up in the air. If treatment doesn't work, he might never have a first kiss. All those experiences, the good and the bad, will only ever be ideas in his head. Sometimes the world sucks.

My phone vibrates with an alert. There are new pictures from Sunny, Lily and Kale. They're all smiles and arms around each other's shoulders. At first glance she looks happy, but upon closer inspection her eyes are puffy and her cheeks are blotchy.

My phone rings, but it's not Sunny; it's Violet.

"Why are your disfigured balls all over the Internet?"

I'm going to drown Randy in the lake when I find him.

23

Always With the Overshare

-MILLER-

I roll off my bunk and limp-run to the porch for privacy.

"Seriously, Miller, what is even going on? You're supposed to be at a camp, not flashing your balls all over the place. And there's another picture of you in the same damn shorts with a Sunny look-a-like! She's been posting the picture everywhere, which wouldn't be so bad if one of your damn balls wasn't right beside it. You better not be messing around on Sunny. Alex won't have to kick your ass. *I* will!"

"Hold on."

"Don't tell me to hold on—"

I take the phone away from my ear. I can still hear her giving me shit as I type in a search of my name + dick. The first link is a medical site with the picture Randy took, along with the question. "What kind of spider bite causes this sort of swelling?"

After that is the group photo with me and my unfortunately

swollen nuts. My balls are circled in red, and Sunny's doppelgänger has reposted it, along with the ball pic. And she's also posted one where she cropped everyone else out but the two of us and made it her damn profile picture. So much for her concern about me. It's amazing how quickly pictures I don't want circulating can go viral.

There's nothing I can do to stop this train wreck. I've been tagged by an unholy number of people. There's loads of bunny love offering to take care of my balls, and wishing me a speedy recovery.

"This looks so bad." Why can't I ever win?

"Bad? It looks like you're messing around on Sunny with someone who looks like Sunny! How am I supposed to help you when things like this keep showing up?"

I scrub a palm over my face and explain what happened with the whole spider bite fiasco.

"I don't even know what to say anymore," she mutters.

"Thanks a lot, Vi. You're an awesome source of support."

She sighs. "I love you, but sometimes you make it harder than it needs to be. Why aren't you posting pictures of you with all the kids at the camp? You must have taken a million of them by this point. You always do. You need to jam your feed with something positive, not all this garbage about your balls being swollen."

"It takes the altruism out of it if I post the pics of the camp."

"No, it doesn't. Not even a little. All those kids' families sign a waiver for that purpose."

"How do you know that?"

"Because I read the emails Amber sends me. We've been over this before. I get that this is personal for you, but it doesn't help anyone if you aren't more vocal about all the good things you do. How do you expect to inspire other people if you keep it to yourself? All the positive things get shoved under the blanket of puck bunny pics. Your life isn't a frat party, but that's the only version of you that people see. You've got all these great plans, but you're not doing anything to promote your goals—unless your plan is to set up a puck bunny support group."

I stare at the sky, a million stars winking at me. Violet has a point. Amber has been on me about this for a long time. She's been asking me to be more of a spokesperson for the charities I support. I need to put some energy into following through. The offseason is a good time to get this ball rolling, and do something on my own. My end goal is to create a foundation to help more kids like Michael.

"Okay, Vi. I'm listening and I hear you. I'll put a few posts up about the camp. I also have an idea of where I want to start with a project I manage. I'm thinking a charity game might go over well, especially preseason. I'll talk to Amber, and we can start planning when I get back to Chicago. And I'll email Dad and get him in on it since he's got so many contacts."

"You need to do something that showcases your generosity beyond sharing your yeti love."

I roll my eyes. "You can't help yourself, can you?"

"I really can't. I should go."

"Wait. I have another problem."

"Not the kind that might make Alex try to break your dick off, I hope."

"Pfft. Waters couldn't break my dick off if he tried. It's made of straight magic, like a unicorn horn. Except not sharp. And made of flesh instead of whatever mythical substance unicorn horns are made of. But it's unbreakable."

"Have you been smoking the greenery while you've been up there in Canada?"

"No. Why? Never mind. So you know how Sunny's on that

camping trip with Kale?"

"I couldn't forget if I tried."

"I'm worried she may have forgotten about my superior snuggle skills, or how fun naked movie-watching was, because there are pictures of him all over her like a horny dog."

"There's so much about that sentence I don't even want to think about. I don't need an overshare right before bed."

"Can we not debate what constitutes an overshare right now? I don't know how worried I should be."

"Sorry. Okay, tell me about these pictures. She's not naked is she? Alex will flip his lid."

"He's got his arm around her."

"While she's naked?"

Sometimes Violet is frustrating. "No."

"Is he fondling her?"

"No."

"So he's trying to kiss her or something?" She sounds disgusted, which would make me feel justified in my anger, if that were the case.

"No. His arm is around her."

"Oh. Well, what's she doing?"

"Smiling. They're both holding beers. She posted it recently. They're at a bar."

"There's no inappropriate hand placement?"

"I'd be on my way there right now if there was."

"Hold up there, Ragey McRagerson. Think about what you're saying. Some guy has his arm around her shoulder, and you're considering driving eight million hours north into the middle of nowhere to do what? Yell at him? Yell at Sunny? Throw her over your shoulder and move to a cabin in the woods so no one can be with her but you?"

"You're making me sound like a caveman."

"If the loincloth fits…"

"He's her ex. They dated for four years, Vi. What if their history wins over our potential future?"

"Didn't you tell me you trust Sunny?"

"Of course. It's Kale I don't trust. These pictures are fucking with my head."

"You don't say."

"Fu—dge. Fudgerson fudgey fudge."

"Are the dots connecting for you now?"

"Yeah, they're connecting." I've put Sunny in this position countless times. "She's been so patient, hasn't she?"

"Yeah, Buck, she has. Because she sees the real you. So deal with your jealousy and trust in her the way she's been trying to with you. You of all people know what it's like when photos are taken out of context. Stop borrowing worst-case scenarios. When you talk to her, put on your big boy pants and tell her how you feel about her. Tell her you understand how hard it's been for her and that you're all in with her."

"What if she isn't all in with me?"

"What if she is?"

I exhale loudly into the phone. "Are relationships always this hard?"

"Not always. But the ones that are worth it are the ones you have to fight for."

24

Video Killed the Bathroom Stall

-MILLER-

I'm half a second away from calling Sunny when my phone rings. At first I think it's Violet with some final insult of the night, or parting words of wisdom—both are equally likely. But it's Sunny on a video call.

I answer it, but the screen remains black for several seconds before Sunny's tear-stained face appears.

My worry compounds. "Sunny? What's wrong?" I try to assess her surroundings, but she's holding the phone close to her face.

"You promised!" She's been drinking. And crying. I've seen Sunny tipsy a couple of times. She was cute and fun and touchy. That's nothing like she is right now.

I can only assume she's seen the pictures of my dick. "Sunny, sweets. I can explain."

"You always have an explanation ready! Why did you have to be so sweet last weekend and now this? You've been all I can think about and—and—and—" She breaks down in a fit of tears.

I can't see her face anymore. I think I'm looking at her hair, but it's hard to tell. Music gets loud and then quiet again. Voices in the background sound male. I wish I had my earbuds.

"Sunny Sunshine, take a breath. It's okay. I wish you would've called me or messaged this week, then you'd know you don't have anything to worry about."

"We didn't have very good reception. Every time I sent a message it would come back as undelivered. I shouldn't have gone with the cheaper phone package. I mostly only had one bar. Sometimes I could see your texts, but I couldn't reply. Lily's reception wasn't any better. I tried to use her phone tonight, and there were all these pictures—" She hiccups.

"Let's talk it out."

She lifts her head and looks blearily at me. "Your penis is all over the Internet. It was supposed to be *my* penis."

"It is yours, sweets. I'm sorry about the picture. I got bit by a spider today. I didn't know Randy was putting that picture up."

"I don't care if everyone sees your penis. It's a nice penis. Except your balls looked really big. Like, not-right big, which I guess is from the spider bite? It was the comments on your wall. I didn't like them. I can't—" She hiccups. "Did you know there's a bunny group dedicated to you?"

I sure do. I stumbled on it one day when I searched my own name. What's in that group won't help make things better between me and Sunny. "You shouldn't look at that stuff. You know how things get skewed." As for the comments on the picture of my balls, I can't control condolences.

Sunny sits up straighter and flips her hair over her shoulder. She twirls a thin braid between her fingers and rubs it over her lips. "I didn't try to join the group. I already know what the rumors are. I've known the entire time, and I still—" She sighs. "Lily and Benji have been fighting the whole trip. It's been so bad. I was going to sleep in the tent last night, but there's bear poop around the site so I didn't. I don't think Kale is over me. Are you over me?"

I'm definitely worried about how drunk she is, based on her inability to stick with one train of thought. I'm also concerned about her location. I have a million questions, such as where is she sleeping if she's not in the tent, and what has Kale done to make her say he's not over her.

I address the last question, because it's the most important and likely the only one she remembers. "No, of course I'm not over you. Why would you think that?"

Her eyes drop along with her voice. "We had sex. I thought you wouldn't want me anymore." Tears slide down her blotchy cheeks. "That's why I held out for so long."

"Why would you think I wouldn't want you anymore after we had sex?" This is not a conversation I want to have on the phone. Especially when I can't go to her. Console her. Reassure her.

"You're so good at the sex, and I don't have a ton of experience. I thought I would never measure up." She picks up the end of her braid and swipes it back and forth over her lips. "I miss you. I don't know what I'm supposed to believe. There was a picture with a girl who looks like me and I was so worried, Miller. Everyone is always chirping in my ear. I like you so much, but I'm so scared you're going to break my heart."

Her honesty makes me feel ill. There's so much about what she's said that's unsettling. This isn't how I want things to be between us. I didn't push for sex because I didn't want her to think that was my only reason for being with her. I thought I'd made that clear. But this is something I want to talk about face to face, not while she's crying on the phone. "That girl is a camp counselor. The only person I want is you. You're the only one for me, Sunny. No one else compares. Last weekend was the best weekend of my life." I don't know if she'll remember any of this. "Where are you? Where's Lily?"

"She's fighting with Benji." She shifts around, leaning against a wall. Words are written on it in marker, or scratched into the surface, exposing silver where there was paint before.

"Are you in a bathroom?"

She nods and sniffs. The sound of toilet paper being pulled from a roll follows. She brings the wad to her nose and blows. "It smells horrible in here."

"I bet. Why don't you go outside? It'll smell way better and be quieter."

She drops her voice to a whisper. "I'm hiding."

"From who?"

"Kale. He close talks too much. He hasn't brushed his teeth since we got here. Or maybe he has cavities. Anyway, his breath is bad. I didn't want to leave Lily alone with Benji and now I regret coming at all." She dabs under her eyes. "I'd rather be where you are."

Her candidness gives me a lot to process. There's a quick burst of noise. Country music and male voices filter through the phone, along with a flush and the sound of water running.

"Sunny, can I ask you a question?"

"Sure."

"Are you in the men's bathroom?"

"Uh-huh. No one will look for me here because I have a cookie, not a penis."

She'd be funny if I was there to take care of her. I'm angry at Lily for not being a better friend and Kale for making her feel like she needs to hide. "You need to get out of there, sweets."

"I can't. There are urinals. They're right outside the stall. I'll see penises. Or is it peni?" She wrinkles her nose and whispers, "I only want to look at your penis."

"I'm glad you feel that way. But the men's bathroom isn't a good place for you to be. Just cover your eyes and head for the door."

She takes a couple of deep breaths.

"You can do it, Sunny. I'd come get you if I could. Camp's done tomorrow. I'll come as soon as the kids leave."

"I'm self-sufficient."

"I know that. I'm just worried, and I don't like that you're upset. I want to be there so I can keep you safe."

She licks her lips and her eyes grow sad. "I don't want to fight when we see each other, but I know we both have things we're upset about. I'm sorry I went on this camping trip. I wanted to be a good friend to Lily, but all being here did was make me feel bad."

"We don't have to fight, Sunny, we can just talk it out and go from there." We both have things to be unhappy about. "Should you leave the bathroom?"

"Okay." She nods, resolved, and presses the phone against her chest. The screen is dark and deep voices issue shouts of surprise and a couple of whistles.

"Sunny? What are you doing in here?" It's Kale.

There's fumbling and arguing. The music gets obnoxiously loud, then there's crunching. Gravel, maybe. More muffled talking. All of a sudden it's not dark anymore. Sunny's phone clatters to the floor of the trailer.

A hand covers the screen like a spider. But it's not Sunny's face I'm met with; it's Kale.

I point at him. "I'm coming for you, asshole."

He ends the call before I can say another word. I try to call back, but I get voicemail.

It's on. I'm taking that fucker down.

25

It's Time for This Nightmare to End

-SUNNY-

This entire week has been one big giant cluster.

Benji has spent the entire week being the biggest dick of all time.

Kale has been a pain in everyone's ass.

Lily has spent most of it crying.

And I've spent the past twenty-four hours trying not to let every worst-case scenario live rent-free in my head. It hasn't been easy. Especially not when my boyfriend's (swollen?) body parts have become a viral sensation along with some girl who looked like my twin.

Not living in the land of panic has been the challenge of all challenges.

But lessons have been learned.

Big, ugly lessons.

I've spent my entire life going with the flow, allowing other people's opinions inform my decisions. I'm done with that.

Well, I'm trying to be done with that. But I'm stuck with Kale and Lily is stuck with Benji until we leave this freaking town.

Lily slams through the door of the trailer. "We're leaving."

"Where's Benji?" Kale asks.

"Right here." Benji appears in the doorway. He's drunk.

I'm tipsy. Tipsier than I'd like. I had three coolers and two is my absolute limit. But Kale kept trying to take a trip down relationship memory lane. He also tried to argue his case as to why he's a great boyfriend. It's been a long, long week of nonsense. Especially since my phone plan is garbage and I can't keep a signal long enough to send a freaking text or voice message, which means none of my standing up for what I want or asking Miller to explain what's going on has managed to reach him. It's just a sea of red circles with exclamation marks pronouncing each message as undelivered.

"What are you doing?" Benji asks Lily as she turns the engine over.

"Driving the RV."

I slide into the passenger seat and fasten my seatbelt as she puts it into gear.

Kale and Benji aren't smart enough to take a seat before she hits the gas. They collide and fall to the floor like bowling pins.

"Are you okay? What's the plan?" I ask.

Lily white knuckles the steering wheel. "We take down the tents and then we're heading home."

"Or we could go to Alex's cottage. It's three hours closer." And it's already late. We'll have to drive through the night. Alex's cottage also has reception, so I'll finally be able to message Miller and sort out the crap that's been happening without me breaking down in a men's bathroom. At the time it seemed like a good place to hide.

Alex's cottage is also very close to Miller's camp.

He can meet us there and we can have the conversation we need to without my parents or my brother there to interfere. All these misunderstandings would be a lot more manageable if everyone minded their own damn business.

"Alex's cottage it is."

26

Deflated

-MILLER-

The next morning I get up early, partly because I can't stop thinking about Sunny, and partly because my balls hurt, and I have to pee. I hobble to the bathroom. I'm unhappy to see that my balls are still bigger than they should be. The swelling hasn't gone down the way I'd hoped it would.

I stop by the medical clinic before breakfast. I'll get another shot of antihistamine, participate in closing activities, and get my ass to Sunny.

I drop my drawers; Nurse Debbie's expression remains neutral as she inspects the situation.

"Shouldn't the swelling have gone down more than this?" I ask.

"It's not the swelling that's the issue. It's the fluid."

"Fluid?"

"Sometimes this happens, especially when there's an allergic reaction to the bite. The site fills with fluid."

"Like a blister?"

"That's a reasonable comparison, yes."

"Okay. So will it go down on its own?" I can't be walking around with balls the size of grapefruits. And I have a long drive ahead of me. Most importantly, I need my parts to work again. Soon.

"Eventually, yes."

"How long is eventually?"

"It could take a few days, maybe longer."

"That's no good. Isn't there something we can do? Something you can give me?"

Nurse Debbie clears her throat and looks at her clipboard. "The antibiotics I gave you last night should help. There's another option—"

I slap my thighs. "Well, what is it? Anything is better than having a giant nut sac."

"I can drain the bite."

"Drain it?"

She nods. "That will definitely alleviate swelling."

"So you'd do that by…" I let the question hang. There's only one way to drain fluid.

"Using a needle."

"Right. Okay."

I run my hands up and down my thighs. My stomach is now hanging out in my toes. I've had stitches plenty of times without any freezing. I've watched the team doctor put a huge needle in a gaping wound on my arm, and it didn't even faze me. But a needle in the balls is different. They're attached to the center of my universe.

"My balls will go back to being their regular size?"

"It should help significantly."

"I'll be in working order sooner?"

"You should be if you take it easy and don't overexert yourself. You'll have to sit out today, and no strenuous activity for the next few days."

"What's considered strenuous?"

"Anything high impact. I'm also recommending that you wear briefs to reduce friction."

"I'll get briefs today." I can make sex with Sunny low impact for a few days. "Okay. Let's do this."

"If you're sure." She's giving me an out.

I can't take it back now even if I want to. "I'm sure."

"I'll numb the site first."

"Sounds good."

Nurse Debbie gives me a hospital gown to change into. It's ironic that she gives me privacy for that, since she'll be spending time with my nuts again shortly, but I put it on and sit back down. After the numbing, Nurse Debbie leaves me alone again while we wait for it to take effect.

Since there's no one else around, I use the voice-to-text function to send Sunny a message.

Miller: *How are you feeling this morning?*

I flip through my emails while I wait for a response. It looks like Amber had access to the Internet yesterday. I have twelve new emails from her. Most of them are audio messages.

Nurse Debbie comes back with a covered tray. I let her do her thing, keeping my eyes on the ceiling. I have no interest in seeing the needle she plans to use.

"There will be a pinch, but I need you to stay as still as you can."

"Got it. Be a mannequin." The "pinch" feels more like someone jabbed me in the balls with a hot poker.

When she's done, she swabs the site and covers it with gauze and medical tape. That won't be fun to remove. I sit up and check my package. It's not as swollen. I'm given another shot of antihistamines, a straight shot of antibiotics, and more painkillers. I'm still not allowed to play in the tournament this morning, which blows, but not as much as giant balls.

I slide off the bed and give walking a shot. My limp isn't as pronounced anymore. Still, I'll take Nurse Debbie's advice and get myself some briefs.

After the clinic, I hit the mess hall. I can sit with the counselors, but sometimes it's nice to hang out with the kids and shoot the shit. It's still early, and they're trickling in a few at a time. My buddy Michael sits at a table by himself, poking at his pancakes.

I gingerly sit beside him and ruffle his hair. "How you doing this morning?"

He gives me a halfhearted smile and lifts one shoulder. "All right."

"You party it up last night?"

"We stayed up 'til midnight." He gives me a cheeky grin.

"Hardcore. You tired today, then?"

"I'm okay." He looks around, making sure no one else is near. "The medication they give me makes me feel sick. I didn't want to have the treatment yesterday, but they said I had to, and now I can't play today. I hate this."

"I bet. That has to suck."

He pushes his food around his plate. "It does. I never used to get sick, and now I always feel crappy."

"You have to take care of the body first, though, right? So it can get better?" I cut into my short stack, which is actually seven pancakes layered with margarine and fake maple syrup. "I can't play today, either." I shove food in my mouth and chew. Now that my balls aren't the size of my head, I'm hungry again.

"Why not?"

"I got a spider bite."

His cheeks flush. "I wasn't sure if it was a rumor."

"I wish. I'm on coaching duty; you want to be my junior coach today?"

His eyes light up like I've told him I'm buying him a Ferrari. "Seriously? Like f'reals?"

"Yeah, man. I need some help. You in?"

"For sure."

"Cool." I take off my ball cap and put it on his head. It's way too big, and I probably have the worst case of hathead ever, but I don't care. I've got that warm feeling I get when I do something that makes someone else feel good. It's a rush. I pull out my phone and snap a couple of pictures. "Is it okay if I post these?"

"Yeah. Totally."

I put up one of the pictures and caption it: *Strategizing with my junior coach over bfast. Team Butterson has it in the bag.*

• • •

Four hours later, Randy and I are in the parking lot, autographing hats, hugging kids, and taking pictures. I haven't had a chance to give him shit over the balls picture, but we'll be in the car soon enough.

The people from the local paper are here, just like Amber said. They interview me and Randy, as well as a few of the kids. Amber was right; they're not like the usual reporters I deal with. Everything is way more relaxed up here.

Michael's parents pick him up in an older van. His mom's out of the car before it's even in park. She embarrasses the shit out of Michael by hugging him while crying. She checks him over the way moms are supposed to, with a critical eye full of love.

When she's done making him wish he could sink into the

ground, she drags him over to me and Randy. Michael stuffs his hands in his pockets and mumbles an introduction. His mom cries even harder and hugs me, thanking me for giving him this opportunity.

They're a great family, and they look like they're managing, for now. I don't know if that will change with Michael's treatment. He's a kid. He could need full-time care for months, which would mean someone staying home instead of working. I get their information so I can keep in touch. I know exactly how I want to move forward now with the fundraiser. If Vi and Amber want positive media coverage, they'll get it.

Once all the kids are gone, I throw my bags in the back of the rental and check my messages. I have five new messages from Sunny, all of them sent within the last hour.

The first one makes no sense:

Sunny Sunshine: *Rsodfld fluck bod*

The next one is super clear.

Sunny Sunshine: *Don't come to Chapleau*

It's a kick in the already achy balls until I read on.

Sunny Sunshine: *We're at Alex's cottage. Let me know when you're coming*

She links directions. The final message makes me wonder how much of last night's conversation she remembers.

Sunny Sunshine: *Can't wait to see you*

I might not love how things have gone down recently, but I still want to see her.

Miller: *We're on our way*

Waters' cottage is only about a forty-five-minute drive from camp. I wait for Randy to finish consoling the girl he's been spending time with. She's a puffy-eyed mess as he hugs her goodbye.

Once we're on the road, he lowers the window and heaves a

sigh of relief. "I don't know why I do that to myself every time."

"Because you don't like being alone?"

"Maybe. How're your balls?"

"Thanks for posting the picture of them, even though I told you not to. It caused me an assload of problems with Sunny last night."

"What? But your face wasn't even in the picture. How could she know it was you?"

"Because you posted it using your own damn name and Sunny's doppelgänger reposted it every damn place, and my shorts are the same in both pics, obviously. That's how Violet knew it was me, and everyone else too."

"I'm sorry, man." Randy looks horrified. "Is Waters shitting a brick? Do you need me to talk to him? Explain what happened? I'll talk to Sunny for you."

He means it. Which is why I can't stay mad at him for long. He wouldn't have posted the picture if he'd known it would mess things up.

"What's done is done," I tell him, checking the GPS to make sure we're still on track. "So there's a change of plans. I'm not heading to Chapleau anymore."

"I messed things up that bad for you?"

"Sunny's at her brother's cottage, not all the way in BF Nowhere, so that saves me seven hours of driving."

"So what's the deal? You still dropping me at the hotel?" He checks the time. "I should be able to check in. I'm kicking around until tomorrow for that charity car wash."

"Cancel the reservation; you don't need it. Waters' cottage isn't far from here. You can come with me, but that means dealing with Lily and the khaki twins."

"I'm in. I'm looking forward to the entertainment. Will you come with me tomorrow afternoon now? We could wash this kickass rental."

"I should be able to. I want to talk to the guy who runs it. After this week I want to get started on that project I've been talking about." Other than Vi, my dad, and my PA, Randy's the only person I've talked to about setting up a fundraiser.

Randy pats me on the shoulder. "I think that's a great plan. Whatever help you want, I'm in."

. . .

We make a quick stop on the way to Waters' cottage in a tiny town called Bracebridge. I pick up a six-pack of briefs. They're red. I'm not a big fan of wearing them, but they do a good job of containing my boys and reducing the friction like Nurse Debbie said they would. The swelling has gone down since this morning. I've got small apples instead of grapefruits.

From there, we drive the rest of the way to Waters' cottage, which isn't really a cottage. It's two stories of stained cedar and floor-to-ceiling windows with a wraparound deck. The landscaping is incredible. Huge pines and birch trees provide natural privacy. The camping trailer is parked in front of a three-car garage. There's music coming from inside. I peek in one of the windows. Lily's boyfriend is passed out. He's shirtless. And Violet thinks I'm hairy. I've got nothing on this guy. He has tufts on his shoulders.

"I'll pretend I'm a bear and scare the piss out of him," Randy whispers.

"They're probably his distant relatives."

He grabs the door handle, but I put a hand on his shoulder to stop him. "Later. I want to find Sunny first."

Randy shrugs and follows me down the driveway to the deck. From where I'm standing I can see all the way to the lake. Kale is sitting on the edge of the dock with his feet in the water.

I hope one of those fishing spiders climbs into his shorts and bites him on his balls.

I find Sunny around the other side of the deck, lying in a hammock. She's in the bikini I love. The top is untied, the straps tucked into the cups. She's fast asleep, her soft lips parted. The bridge of her nose is pink from too much sun. She has scratches on her arms, scabs on her knees, and a load of bug bites, along with several bruises on her shins. I don't like all the damage. She looks like everything I've been missing.

My frustration over the past week merges with the unsettling need to touch her. Hug her. I want to fix this mess so I can tell her how important she is to me.

Randy elbows me. "I need to find a bathroom."

I nod and crouch beside Sunny. Seeing her, finally being close to her again, settles me. Especially after spending a week with a kid whose life is up in the air. I run the tip of my finger across her blond lashes. She shakes her head and bats at her face.

"Sunny Sunshine, wake up."

She hums, but doesn't move otherwise.

I trace the contour of her jaw with my fingertip, moving down the side of her neck to her throat and over her collarbone. The sound that comes out of her is more moan than hum. Her eyes flutter, and she blinks against the sun. Surprise crosses her delicate features. It's followed by recognition, relief, and then uncertainty.

Despite the final emotion, Sunny reaches up and strokes my beard. I haven't shaved since I left for the camp. "You're here."

"I am."

She licks her lips, eyes roaming over my face. "I'm glad."

"Me, too."

"I was a mess last night," she says sleepily.

"I could tell." I take her hand in mine. Her nails, usually filed into gentle curves, are ragged and chipped. "I hated seeing you so upset and being too far away to do anything about it. I also didn't like that you were stuck in a men's bathroom, hiding from Kale." I brush wayward strands of hair away from her face. "When did you get here?"

Her gaze moves over my face. "Around eight this morning. Everything came to a head last night. Lily is fed up with Benji, I was fed up with Kale, so here we are. Lily drove the whole way." She glances around. "I don't know where she is."

"Probably inside." Or it's a full moon and she's changed into a werebear.

"Probably." Sunny cups the back of my neck and tries to pull me down.

When I'm an inch from her lips, I resist. "We should talk."

"We should." Her voice is soft, almost breathless.

I don't want to say what I'm about to, but I liked what we had before sex and orgasms became part of the equation. It felt like a real relationship. "Before we make out."

"Just one kiss, Miller, then we can talk." She strokes my bearded cheek. "I missed you this week."

"I'm weak for you, Sunny," I admit.

She searches my face. "I'm the same for you."

When her tongue peeks out to wet her bottom lip I give in. I brush my lips over hers. Her grip tightens on the back of my neck. Sunny sucks on my bottom lip, then slips her tongue inside my mouth. Something hot and needy simmering below the surface. My rational side takes a back seat to the hormonal, caveman side that desperately wants to stake my claim. It would be so easy to get lost in feeling good, but then we'll be right back where we started, both uncertain as to where we stand outside of this incredible chemistry we share.

A shriek comes from somewhere in the cottage. Sunny sits up with a start, ending what we just got started. Her bikini top falls, her boobs popping out as the sliding door opens and Randy comes tripping out onto the deck. His hands are over his head like he's protecting himself.

Lily skids to a stop behind him. She's wielding a toilet paper holder. Three rolls flutter in the breeze, the paper unraveling like surrender flags behind her. She's wearing a towel with shoulder straps. Her legs are covered in shaving lotion.

"Someone just tried to—"

She stops when she sees me. I'm cupping Sunny's bare breasts to protect them from everyone else's eyes.

"This asshole must be one of your friends!" She jabs the toilet paper holder in my direction and then swings it toward Randy.

"I was looking for a bathroom, honey."

"Don't honey me, you, you—he tried to…he was going to…"

His eyebrows lift, along with the corners of his mouth. "What exactly do you think I was trying to do, sweetheart?"

Lily is shaking and brandishing the toilet paper holder like a sword. She seems to be having trouble with words. And her face is bright red. It's the most flustered I've ever seen her. Sunny pulls the cups of her bathing suit up over my hands. I reluctantly let them go.

"I was in the middle of shaving my legs! You burst into the bathroom. I'm naked under this towel!"

"Oh, I'm well aware of what's going on under that towel." Randy smirks. "If you'd locked the door maybe I wouldn't have gotten a front-row seat to the show."

"You—I—you're disgusting!" As she spins around, the two sides of the towel fly open, giving everyone another shot of beaver.

"I like the natural look," Randy says.

She flips the bird over her shoulder as she storms away. "My waxer's been sick."

"I'm happy to help out, if you want," Randy calls after her.

"You're an asshole." The screen door slams shut.

"So... I guess you met Lily." Sunny swings her legs over the edge of the hammock and uses my shoulders as a brace to stand. "She's not usually like that. She and Benji broke up last night. Again. For the fourth time on this trip, so she's in a bit of a mood."

"Is that the guy sleeping in the trailer out front?" Randy asks, staring at the screen door. He takes off his hat and spins it on his finger. That's his contemplation move. It means he's sizing up the competition and coming up with a plan of attack. I wish him luck. Lily's vagina probably has teeth—like Jaws.

"Mm-hmm." Sunny runs her fingers absently through my hair. "He's been in there since we got here."

I catch movement in my peripheral vision. Glancing toward the lake, I spot Kale on the dock, shading his eyes from the sun as he frowns up at us. I stand, enjoying Sunny's shiver as I skim her sides with my fingertips. "We should find a place to talk."

"Okay." Her hands are still on my shoulders. She pushes up on the balls of her feet and kisses my cheek and Kale heads for the stairs. Looks like today is going to be all about confrontation.

27
Motherpucking Fail

-MILLER-

Kale comes storming up the stairs.

Sunny sighs. "Here we go. He's about to throw another tantrum."

"I thought those were reserved for hangry toddlers."

"And Kale. It's one of the many reasons I broke up with him."

"And yet he's still here," I mutter.

She laces our fingers. "It's...complicated."

I hate that word. I've spent my entire life managing complicated bullshit. School was complicated. My mother's death was complicated. My career makes this attempted relationship complicated.

"You could avoid him if you go inside and find a room to hide in," Randy suggests.

I'd forgotten he was on the deck with us.

"Seriously. Go. I can deal with him." He cracks his knuckles

and grins. "It should be fun."

Sunny tugs me toward the door. I follow her inside, through a huge living room with vaulted ceilings and a massive stone fireplace. We pass through the dining room. On the table is what looks like a giant, sculpted, orange penis. Sunny shoves her feet into sandals and we leave through the front door. Passing the trailer and turn right, through a narrow gap in the trees, onto a path.

"Where are we going?" And why are we avoiding Kale and *not* telling those douches to take their trailer and GTFO?

"There's a trail up here; it leads to the water. It's private. Make sure you stay on the trail; there's tons of poison ivy out here."

"I'm immune, but thanks for the warning."

"Immune? How do you know that?"

"I fell in a patch when I was a kid. Nothing happened."

"Wow, that's lucky, isn't it?"

"Yeah. Real lucky." The kid I was with had to go to the hospital. He was covered in the rash.

Sunny glances at me. "Are you limping?"

"I'm fine."

"No, you're not. Is this because of the spider bite?" Sunny slows to a stroll.

"It's a lot better, way less swollen than it was." I don't need to tell her it was drained. I'd rather leave that memory in the discard pile. "Don't worry about me. I'm full of antibiotics and antihistamines. I'm good to go."

"I'll make you an antiseptic compress when we get back to the cottage."

"Sure, if you think that'll help." Who am I to say no if Sunny wants to make my balls feel better?

A minute later we reach the edge of the lake. Boathouses

and cottages dot the opposite shore. Sunny sits on a fallen tree close to the water and pats the spot beside her. I straddle it so I'm facing her. Birds tweet overhead. All we need is some cheesy music and a unicorn trotting by to make it perfectly romantic, apart from the fact that we need to have a difficult conversation.

The part of me that doesn't know how to navigate a relationship like this would like to skip the talking and go right to what I know best. Which is making her feel good. But then we'll be stuck in this loop.

Sunny shifts to face me. She's only wearing a bikini, so I take off my shirt, fold it in half and offer it to her so she has something less uncomfortable to sit on.

I rest my elbows on my thighs and go with honesty. "I understand why you've had such a difficult time trusting me."

Her eyes flare. "You do?"

"I haven't made it easy on myself or you. I can't control who posts what, and I can't erase my past, but seeing all the photos of you popping up this week while you were with your ex has been…the opposite of awesome. I don't love the way it's made me feel. Especially with the lack of reception and how difficult it's made communication. And I imagine that it's been just as shitty for you. And I'm sorry about that. I bet the last few months have been tough for you, huh?"

She bites the corner of her lip and swallows thickly. "I let too many people influence my decisions."

I can't read her expression and it makes me nervous. "How do you mean?"

"I love my brother, but the way his exploits were splashed across social media before he met Violet…it was hard to see. I tried to avoid it as much as possible, but he didn't always make it easy. And when I met you, I felt this instant connection.

Being with you settles me. I wanted to believe in that, but then there was always a new picture on social, or another party...and Alex...he's always been protective—" she sighs. "But at first he was convinced that you were only interested in me because he was with Violet. And I let that get in my head."

It hurts in ways I can't explain to hear her say that, even though I can understand the protective brother situation. I might not be related to Vi by blood, but she's my family and I don't ever want anyone to fuck with her. "And it didn't make it easier when the pictures kept surfacing."

She nods. "That's why Lily is so on the fence about you."

"And you? Are you on the fence about me?"

She shakes her head. "At first I felt awful about this trip. And there are definitely a lot of things I don't ever want to repeat, but I also learned a lot of valuable lessons. Even the ones that hurt. I wish I'd been able to really talk to you before I left and set your mind at ease the way you always try to with me." She smiles softly. "Kale and I will only ever be friends, and even that's questionable. The only reason I've been friends with him at all is because he's Benji's best friend and I care too much about Lily to let him affect my friendship with her."

My relief is immediate and astounding. "Well that's good news."

She takes my hand. "If anything, having to spend a week with Kale has made me hyper-aware of just how incompatible he and I are. And how much I care about you. I think we just need to be considerate of each other when it comes to the parts of our lives that we allow the world to see. I know this incredible version of you, Miller. You're kind, you're sweet, you're giving, you do so many wonderful things for so many people and yet you give the world a one-dimensional side of you. I have all these feelings tied up in how my brother used to present himself to the world, and it's made me scared of how I might appear. But I don't want to hide from the world, not who I am, and not who we are to each other," she says softly.

This is exactly what I'd hoped for, and while I hated where she was this week and who she was with, if it brought us here, I guess the pain was worth it. I shift closer until my knees are on either side of hers and I'm inside her personal space bubble. "I wanted to ask you a question before I left for camp."

She bites her lip. "Okay."

"Will you be my girlfriend?"

She ducks her head, and a soft smile curves her perfect lips. "I would love to be your girlfriend."

I grin. "Yeah?"

She nods and her eyes well.

"Whoa, what's this?"

She waves a hand in front of her face. "I have so many feelings. I was so worried I'd messed it all up by going on this camping trip, and it all sort of compounded and turned into a perfect storm of insecurity. I was afraid you were going to show up and break things off."

"That's not going to happen. But I worried about the same thing." I gently sweep her tears away. "Let's make a deal, okay?"

She nods once and sniffles.

"From now on we're honest with each other about how we're feeling, even when it scares us."

"That's a good deal. I like it."

"I like it too. Come here. I missed the fuck out of you, and I need a hug." I beckon her closer.

She laughs and shifts forward on the log until I can wrap my arms around her. I press my nose into her hair. She smells more like the outdoors than her shampoo, and there are a few pine needles stuck in there, so I rest my chin on top of her head and hold her.

I get why she's scared. I feel the same way. It's not horror-movie scared, or spider-bite-on-my-balls terrifying, but an inside kind of fear. Because we have the potential to hurt each other with our actions. Or in my case, my inaction.

"You're the only one for me, Sunny Sunshine." I drop my head as she lifts hers. Her fingers dance across my lips. "I feel like we did a good job talking things out?"

"We did." She nods.

"Are we okay now?"

"Yeah. My heart feels better."

"Mine, too." I stroke her jaw, palm resting against the side of her neck. Her heart is beating almost as hard as mine.

I brush my lips over hers, and we both sigh. It's a relief to be with her again, to have her in my arms and the taste of her on my tongue.

Sunny scrambles into my lap and wraps herself around me. "I missed you so much, and I really, really hate camping."

"Same about missing you." I don't mind camping, but cabins make it more appealing.

She runs her fingers through my hair, gripping it hard. Her tongue slides against mine aggressively. I don't try to take over or tone it down. Whatever she needs from me, she can have. She fumbles with her bikini top, pulling at the string around her neck, and then the one at her back. She tosses it on the ground.

I cup her breasts and drop my head on a low groan. It feels like forever since I've been able to touch her, make her feel good. Covering the tight bud, I lift my eyes as I graze her nipple with my teeth.

"You should do that again, please." She runs her hands down my biceps and over my forearms until her hands cover mine.

I make the same deep noise and repeat the action.

I'm rewarded with an amazing moan. It scares the birds above us, sending them fluttering away. I pepper kisses over her chest, so damn thankful that we've managed to work things out and that we're here again. And that I get to show her how much she means to me.

Sunny pops the button on my shorts and breaks the kiss, glancing between us. "You're wearing underwear."

"I'm trying something new."

"Hmm. I like the color..." She fingers the red band.

I catch her before she can slip a hand inside. "Uh...go easy. Things are tender after my run-in with the spider."

"My poor baby." She cups my chin and the heel of her hand rests above my Adam's apple as presses a soft kiss to my lips. "You tell me if it's too much."

"Just be gentle, sweets."

She pulls the band back and peeks inside. My excitement is pretty damn obvious.

"He looks okay," she muses.

"You can touch him if you want to make sure."

She gives me a saucy look and strokes the head with a single fingertip. "It would be easier if you were naked."

"Good thinking," I agree.

Sunny moves off my lap and I step out of my shorts, laying them over the log

I hook my thumbs into the waist of my briefs.

"Wait! I want to take them off." She bites the tip of one of her fingers. "If that's okay with you."

This woman might as well put a collar on my cock and walk it around with a leash, because she owns me. "You do whatever makes you feel good."

I stand in front of her, straddling the log, hands at my sides.

My cock kicks behind the confining fabric in anticipation.

Sunny squeals.

I wink. "I think we're all excited here."

She giggles and squeezes my butt. I like this side of her. She's bolder, more confident. Sunny carefully pulls the briefs down, the tip of her tongue caught between her teeth. My cock springs free. She drags them lower, eyes widening as she takes in my not-quite-back-to-normal-situation.

"Are you sure—"

"I'm totally fine." I probably, most definitely shouldn't be entertaining any of this. As good as it feels to have her hands on me, it's also slightly uncomfortable. I'm willing to power through, though.

"Is this okay?" She gently cups my balls, stroking me.

I groan in response.

Sunny's grip loosens. I clamp my hand over hers. "It's good. You're good. Please don't stop."

"You're sure?"

"Positive."

"Okay." She's still for a few beats. "You can let go of my hand now."

"Oh, right." I stroke her cheek. She smiles up at me, before her gaze drops to my cock. It's at face level.

"Sweets, you don't have to..."

She frowns. "Don't you want me to?"

"I mean...the number of times I've fantasized about this is obscene." I trace the curve of her pouty bottom lip. She lifts her chin and bites the end of my thumb, sucking the tip softly.

"Are you too uncomfortable still?" She circles the head with her fingertip. It feels amazing. Even though the dull ache in my balls occasionally becomes a sharp stabbing pain, I won't ask her to stop.

"I don't want you to feel obligated or anything."

"I don't feel obligated." She licks her lips. "But fair warning, I haven't had a lot of practice."

"That's okay. You can practice on me all you want."

"Okay." She nods once. "But, you'll tell me if I'm doing it wrong?"

"Just don't use teeth and you're golden, sweets," I assure her. I'll be her BJ cheerleader if she needs me to.

She kisses the tip and brushes it back and forth over her lips, like she does with the end of her braid. Then she kisses down the shaft and back up before running her tongue around the ridge.

"You are so fucking beautiful." I keep my hands fisted at my sides, taking in the sight of her, the feel of her soft mouth on my skin. When she engulfs the head, she sucks hard, like my cock's a lollipop someone's trying to steal.

I groan and sift my hand through her hair, ready to guide her mouth.

"Okay?" she asks, the word distorted by my cock.

"You're perfect."

No sooner are the words out of my mouth than I feel the distinct press of teeth below the head. My loose grip on her hair tightens reflexively. "Wha—"

Sunny's eyes lift, and she strokes the underside of my cock with her tongue. Strangely, as panicked as I am over the possibility that she might bite me, it feels good.

"Easy," I murmur.

She grins, and sucks softly. She takes more of me in her mouth, every soft moan and wet kiss sending me closer to the edge. When I'm close, I ease her off, not wanting to finish like this.

"You didn't come."

I sit down on my shorts, which are draped over the log, and lift her so she's straddling me again. My wet cock rests against the inside of her leg, the head pressed up against the bathing suit material. I kiss her puffy, wet lips. "I want to be inside you for that. I want your mouth on mine when I come." I suck her bottom lip. "But you were perfect, and tonight, when we're alone in your bedroom I'm going to eat that sweet little cookie of yours."

She runs her hands through my hair. "I love your mouth on me."

"Me too, more than you know."

I pull the ties on either hip and the front folds down, exposing her pink slit. I slide a knuckle low, rubbing her clit as we kiss. When she starts making those soft noises, I slip one finger inside her and then another to make sure she's ready.

And then I remember one important detail: my duffle and all the important things are still in the rental.

28

Mine

-SUNNY-

Miller's fingers still for a moment, then curl again in the way that always makes my entire body feel like a shower of shooting stars is inside me. I moan his name softly; a plea, a prayer.

I've missed him. Missed every part of how good it feels when we're together. How all the noise is gone and nothing matters but him and me. As awful as last week was for both of us, all the pain and uncertainty has brought us here. To this place where we can be honest with each other. Where I've discovered this inner strength I didn't know existed. We're closer than ever, he's mine and I'm his. Heart and soul.

I cover his hand and push his thick fingers deeper, grinding down, craving more.

More of his hands on me. More connection. More of everything.

He curls his fingers again and I whimper at the jolt of lust that shoots through me.

"That feel good, sweets?"

"Mm-hmm." I wind my arm around his neck and bite along the edge of his jaw. "I want you in me."

He makes a needy sound. "I want the same, but first I want to feel you come on my fingers."

I shudder as he brushes over my clit with his thumb.

I'm so close. The shimmer of an orgasm making my toes and scalp tingle.

His lips skim my cheek. "All I could think about this week was how good it would feel to touch you like this again. I missed how soft you are." He nibbles a path up my neck. "And I missed the way your skin tastes."

I moan and roll my hips, grinding on his fingers, desperate for the feel of him filling me. To have our bodies connected in the most primal, intimate way.

And Miller keeps whispering in my ear while he strokes that perfect spot inside me. "I love those sounds you make when you're getting close, and how soft your mouth is, and that thing you do with your tongue when we're kissing. I wish you could see how amazing you look, naked like this, ready to come on my fingers. When we get back to the cottage, I'll eat your—"

I groan and crush my mouth to his as the orgasm rushes through me. The most incredible meteor shower of sensation takes hold. I pull back so I can see his face, his expression one of complete satisfaction, like it's not just my orgasm, but his too that pulses through me.

I sag against him, sated and yet still needy. I run my fingers through his thick hair and smile contentedly. "You're my orgasm soulmate."

"I'll be any kind of soulmate you want, Sunny Sunshine." He strokes my cheek, eyes soft now. "I told you I'd make you feel better, didn't I?"

"You always do." It's true. He knows how to fix things, how to show me with actions and softness that he cares, that I'm important to him, that I matter.

Miller slowly withdraws his fingers and I brace a hand on one of his thickly muscled shoulders, gripping his straining erection with the other. I sigh as I run the head over my still-sensitive clit.

He grunts and curves his fingers around my hip. "Sweets, we have to wait until we're back at the cottage before we take this any further."

I frown. I don't want to wait. I want him here, now, where we have privacy. "Why? You haven't come yet, and you look like you need to." The tip is already weeping.

"I don't have a condom with me." His tone is all apology.

"Oh." My disappointment leaches into that one word.

"They're in my bag, back at the car." He kneads my hip.

"I'm on the pill." I'm the only person he's been with since we met. "And I'm good about taking it."

His eyes heat and his tongue drags across his bottom lip. "You're sure?"

"You could pull out, just to be safe," I offer as I rub the head over my clit.

"I don't want to push you." His eyes fall closed and his fingers flex on my hip.

"You made me feel good. I want to make you feel good, too," I whisper against his lips.

"I want that, too," he groans.

I brush my lips over his, emboldened. "Look, Miller." I glance between us as I sink down, the head disappearing inside.

"Fuck me, sweets." His grip on my hips tightens.

I give him a saucy wink. "That was my plan."

He grins. "You're forever my favorite."

His smile turns into a slack-jawed groan as I sink down, slowly, gently. It's an incredible, powerful feeling to know that I make him feel good like this. That I can give him what he needs just like he does with me.

He holds my hip with one hand and cups my cheek with his other. "Stay like this for a minute, please. I just want to feel you." He threads his hand through my hair and pushes his tongue past my lips, kissing me with the same gentleness as the way he rocks me over him. "I've been waiting my whole life for you, Sunny."

I wrap myself around him and we move together, skin slick with sweat, emotions and sensations mixing in the most incredible way.

This time the orgasm is like an atomic detonation. It's a week of pent-up insecurity and frustration, rolled together with an argument and our make-up talk. As soon as I've crested the orgasm, Miller lifts me off him and angles his erection away from us. A moment later he settles me in his lap and wraps himself around me.

"That was amazing." I kiss a path across his cheek.

"You're amazing." He brushes his lips over mine, then smacks the side of his neck, squashing a mosquito. "We should probably get back to the cottage before the bugs make lunch out of us." He slaps another one. "Or Lily murders Randy, or Randy murders Kale."

"Agreed." I lean back and cup his face in my palms. "Thank you for being you, and for being willing to talk this through." I search his soft gaze, shoring up courage. "I like you a lot, Miller. Like, really a lot. We fit, and that scares me sometimes."

"I get it. I know I haven't made it easy." He picks up the end of the thin braid at my crown and brushes the end over his lips in contemplation. "I want this to be fun, not scary." He presses his palm to my chest. "I'll do my best to keep this safe."

29

That Girl is Poison

-MILLER-

I help Sunny tie her bikini bottoms before I put my shorts back on. She picks up her top and shakes off the dirt.

"That isn't poison ivy, is it?" I point to the plants her bikini top was lying on.

She barely glances at them. "It's Virginia Creeper. They look a lot alike."

The Boy Scout in me wants to question that, but she's been up here enough to know the difference. She ties the string behind her back and adjusts the cups so they cover her nipples.

My clothes didn't get too dirty, thanks to the moss, but I'll have to change when we get back to the cottage. Especially since I managed to hit my T-shirt of all things when I came instead of literally any other forest location. I rinse it in the lake, and follow Sunny back to the cottage.

"When do you think Kale and Benji will leave?" I ask as the camping trailer comes into view, still parked in the driveway.

"They don't need to be here anymore. We can take you and Lily back to Guelph whenever you're ready to go."

"Benji won't leave until he and Lily are back together."

"Will that happen anytime soon?"

Sunny shrugs. "Who knows with those two?"

I grab my bag from the rental. "Does this break-up thing happen a lot?"

"I guess it depends on what *a lot* is. They break up three or four times a year."

That sure seems like a lot. "What's the point of getting back together at all?"

"Lily says the sex is really good."

Really good wouldn't be good enough for me to put up with that shit, but I don't say anything. Lily is Sunny's bestie.

I peek inside the trailer as we pass. Benji seems to have gotten his ass up. The question is, where is he now, and how soon will he leave? His location becomes obvious when we walk into the cottage. Lily and Benji are in the kitchen arguing. Lily's all flailing hands while Benji leans against the counter looking like a smug asshole.

Randy sits at the table across the room, eating a bowl of cereal and browsing a magazine like nothing is happening. The weird dick sculpture wearing the superhero cape is still on the table. I need to check that out later. Kale is nowhere to be seen.

"We're done, Benji! I'm not doing this anymore with you! How many times do I have to say it's over before you get it?"

"You say this every time, and then we get back together." He's cocky about it, smirking like a jackass.

"Not this time!" Under all that anger are tears. She's fighting them. Her chin trembles and her eyes are watering.

Benji laughs. Maybe it's because he's got an audience. Then again, maybe he really is a giant dick. "If I leave, you know you'll be calling me in a couple hours, crying like you always do. So why don't you take the bitch down a notch?"

Now Lily has been a serious pain in my ass where Sunny's concerned. But no matter how I feel about her interference, I'm not cool with this kind of blatant disrespect. It's demeaning. And he's doing it in front of other people, which makes me wonder what he says to her when no one else is around.

Randy pauses with his spoon halfway to his mouth. "The fuck you say to her?"

"Mind your own business," Benji snaps.

Randy's eyebrows lift, and he drops his spoon in his bowl. Milk splatters the table, his beard, and his shirt. He doesn't seem to notice or care as he pushes his chair back. "Mind my own business?" Randy crosses the kitchen until he's towering over Benji. Randy's tall, but not as built as me. I tell him he's skinny all the time. In hockey he's lean; in the real world he's intimidating, and he has about fifty pounds on Benji.

Randy thumbs over his shoulder at Lily. "You've been following her around the house like an untrained puppy for the past twenty minutes, needling the shit out of her right in front of me. Maybe it's time you take a fucking hint and leave like she's been asking you to."

"I'm not going anywhere."

"You sure about that?" Randy cracks his knuckles.

"I have a brown belt in karate."

"And I have a black belt in kicking your fucking ass."

Then the weirdest thing in the world happens. Lily grabs Randy by the shoulder, spins him around, and suctions her mouth to his.

"Is there a full moon?" I ask Sunny, who looks as shocked as me.

She doesn't even have to think about her answer. "It's not

until next week."

Randy's hands are up in the air. His eyes are as wide as Sunny's—and Benji's. It'd be comical if it wasn't so fucked up.

"Fuck you, Lily!" Benji yells and stomps off.

Lily breaks free from Randy's mouth, covers his ears with her palms, and shouts, "No. Fuck you, Benji!"

He turns around to say something else, but Lily glues her lips to Randy's again. Benji slams through the front door in a snit.

At this point it's safe for Lily to disengage, but that doesn't seem to be happening. Eventually, Randy takes her face in his hands and unlocks their mouths. Both Sunny and I are still staring.

"I think you proved your point, honey."

Lily blinks. "What?"

"I think he got the message. You're good."

She shakes her head. "Oh. Oh! I'm sorry. I didn't mean. Shit." She lets go of him like he's a grenade without a pin.

"Unless you want to keep going. I've already seen you naked, so we're halfway there, right?" He grins and winks.

"Ugh. You're a pig!"

Randy laughs as she pushes past him and heads for the stairs, her face an interesting shade of red. "I like your friend, Sunny. She's fun."

Randy laces his fingers together and stretches his arms over his head as he watches Lily run up the stairs. "I think I'll go for a swim."

It's hot, and I smell like sex, so joining him seems like a smart plan. "Me, too. You coming?"

Sunny scratches the underside of her boob. "I'll change my bathing suit first. I think there might be pine needles stuck in this one or something. I'm itchy."

"You want help with that?" I slide a finger under the fabric and graze her nipple.

"Later I want help with a lot of things. I'll check on Lily first."

"Sure thing, sweets."

She kisses me on the cheek and heads for the stairs.

I grab my bag and find a pair of swim shorts. Randy puts his cereal away and we head down to the dock together.

The camping trailer is gone. Good riddance to Kale. Things are finally looking up.

$$\cdots$$

We spend what's left of the afternoon down at the dock. When the sun hangs over the tree line and my stomach starts to rumble, we head back up to the cottage to make dinner. While Sunny prepares stuffed peppers, I check the fridge for an animal product accompaniment. I should know better—it's full of tofu and fresh produce. I check the freezer, and find lobster tails and crab legs. If I'm eating Waters' food, it might as well be the expensive stuff.

We don't eat dinner until almost nine, which Sunny tells me is typical at the cottage. As long as there's lots of food and it tastes good, I don't care about timing. Lily comes down and surveys the table. It seats eight comfortably, but the only unused place setting is beside Randy. None of us—apart from Sunny—has seen her since the blowout with Benji and the face sucking with Randy. She doesn't so much as look at him, but her face is red again, and she's uncommonly quiet.

She guzzles her glass of wine and tops it off, staring at the contents while the conversation goes on around her. Sunny and Randy get along well, which is a bonus. If I could find some common ground with Lily, we'd be golden. She's clearly uncomfortable, but she stays, maybe because she doesn't want to be rude.

"What is this thing, anyway?" She picks up the orange sculpture from the center of the table. The cape around its neck looks like it's meant for Superman, except it has the letters MC on it, and it has googly eyes and a mustache.

"Let me see that." Randy holds out his hand, and she passes it over. He flips the cape up and starts laughing so hard he almost falls off his chair. "It's a superhero dick."

"I bet a million dollars that's Violet's work," I say.

"What's the MC stand for?" Randy asks.

"I think that's what Vi calls Waters' dick. Monster Cock or something," I offer. Everyone stops eating. "She does a lot of oversharing."

Randy snorts. "Waters isn't that hung."

"That's what I thought, but he's got a stash of Magnum XL in his bedroom," I reply. "Sunny can vouch."

"No shit. He must be a serious grower." Randy stabs a green bean and bites it in half.

"I can't deal with this conversation." Lily drops her fork on the table and grabs the dick sculpture. She and Sunny decide to take pictures of it all over the cottage.

The two of them are ridiculous, giggling their asses off as they hide the Superhero dick behind pillows, on the fireplace mantel, and in the fridge. It's the first time Lily's smiled since Randy and I arrived.

When they're done, Lily and Randy take care of the dishes while Sunny and I go outside to build a campfire. She swats at the back of her neck and scratches under the collar of her shirt.

"You okay? Still itchy?"

"It's fine. I think it was a mosquito. I'll put on some bug spray once we get the fire started."

I wait until we're away from the cottage before I say anything about our friends still inside. "You should probably warn Lily about Randy."

"I already did."

"Yeah, but—"

Sunny puts a hand on my shoulder and pushes to her tiptoes to plant a kiss on my lips. "They're adults."

"Yeah, but she's probably not going to be making the best decisions, and Randy can be smooth."

"Like you?"

There's a difference between me and Randy. He's a different kind of smooth. He'll get involved with a bunny until it gets too serious, and then he cuts ties. Completely. I've watched him shut girls out like a door in the face. I know why he does it; he doesn't want to end up doing to someone else what his dad did to his mom. Unfortunately, it means he leaves a trail of discarded, emotionally bereft bunnies in his wake.

We were eleven when Randy's parents split for good. His dad was mostly farm team with only a couple NHL seasons under his belt. He wasn't very good about keeping his dick in his pants on the road. Randy's mom put up with it until she couldn't anymore. I think Randy's afraid he'll follow the same path, so whenever it starts to get too real, he bails.

Until Sunny came along I didn't want to get serious with anyone. She makes me see the value in being vulnerable with someone.

Still, her comment hits me right in the chest.

She must read it on my face. Her fingers curl around my chin. "I don't mean it the way you're taking it, Miller. Well, in some ways I do. You know what to say and when to say it, and you definitely know what to do and how to do it well, but I never feel like you're feeding me lines."

"That's because I'm not."

"I know. Lily's been with Benji for a long time. She hasn't been happy for a while. I think this week made her realize things won't get better." She picks up a stick and twirls it between her fingers. "You can understand now why I didn't want to bail on Lily. Benji has some...issues. Sometimes he can be mean. Anyways, it might be good for her to have a fling."

"As long as she gets that that's all it is."

"She knows all about you hockey boys." She grabs my hand and moves toward the forest. "Come on, let's get some kindling."

We end up making out in the forest against a tree. Making out turns into sex against a tree before we return with just enough kindling to get the fire going.

Once it's blazing, I go back to the cottage to look for marshmallows and roasting sticks. Campfires aren't campfires without them. I also want to head off any potential fuckery between Randy and Lily.

I'm too late, though. I find them in the kitchen. Randy has Lily pinned against the counter. Maybe *pinned* isn't the right word. Lily is fisting his shirt, and he's got a hand braced on either side of her, with one knee between her legs, while they suck face.

I close the screen door harder than I need to. Lily shoves him away and spins around, dunking her hands in the sink. Her back expands and contracts with every heavy breath. Randy wipes his mouth with his sleeve as he glances over his shoulder. "'Sup, Miller? You get a campfire going yet or what?"

"It's marshmallow time." I wrangle up a bag from the pantry along with graham crackers. I can't find a chocolate bar, so I make do with Nutella. "You coming, or are you planning to get it on in the kitchen some more first?"

He slips an arm around Lily's waist and nuzzles her neck. "I'm partial to option two, but I'll leave the decision to Lily here."

"We'll be right out," she croaks.

Randy chuckles. I shake my head and shut the screen door behind me. For someone with a big hate-on for players—perceived or real—Lily seems intent on hooking up with one. I wonder how long it'll take for her to regret it.

• • •

I learn that Sunny doesn't eat marshmallows. Gelatin is made from bone marrow, and bone marrow comes from animals, so they're a no-go.

We stay outside for a few hours, but Sunny's itchy, even with all the bug spray. Everyone's drunk by the time we decide to call it a night. Sunny sets Randy up in the room right next to Lily's. I'd say it's a bad idea, but based on the way those two were glued to each other at the fire, they'll find a way into each other's beds regardless. I hope Sunny's right and Lily takes it for what it is: a fun rebound.

Sunny's bedroom is decorated for her. The walls are painted a soft, pale yellow. The comforter is covered in sunflowers. It's everything she loves, and it shows me exactly how important she is to her brother that he decorated a room just for her.

"I need a shower; my hair smells like campfire," Sunny says once we're behind closed doors.

I wrap my arms around her and shove my nose in her blond waves. "You smell like toasted marshmallows. I like it."

"I smell like smoke and bug spray. And I'm itchy."

"I'll give you a hand, then, eh?"

She turns around, her grin sloppy and her eyes glassy from all the mojitos. "I love that my Canadianness is rubbing off on you."

"I like it when you rub your Canadianness all over me."

I brush my lips over hers. Even they taste smoky. Easing my hands down her sides, I give her butt a little squeeze before I reverse the circuit and pull her shirt over her head. Which is the moment I notice the rash. Streaks of red cover her chest. I move her hair out of the way and note the same rash around the back of her neck, as if it's followed the line of her bikini.

"Do you have any allergies?"

She looks down and screams, then brings her hands up to touch her boobs. I grab her wrists before she can make contact.

"Sweets, are you sure that was Virginia Creeper in the forest today?"

Her eyes shoot up to mine, tears already brimming. "Oh no! No, no, no! I have poison ivy on my boobs?" It's a question, even though the evidence is streaked across her chest in a red, blistering rash.

"Are you itchy anywhere else?" I just hope it hasn't spread.

"No. I showered as soon as we got back from our walk in the forest." She goes for the button on my shorts.

"What are you doing?"

"Checking your lightning rod."

"I would've noticed if I had poison ivy on my dick, Sunny. Remember I told you I'm immune?"

"What if you're wrong? Why aren't I immune?"

I move her hands away, unbutton my pants, and drop my shorts, along with my underwear—to humor her. Everything is almost normal again. "See? No rash."

The door bursts open. "Is everything okay? I heard Sunny sc—" Lily stops short. "Holy geez! You weren't lying." Her eyes are fixed on my half-mast lightning rod.

Randy's right behind her. He's in a pair of boxers, and Lily is wearing his shirt. That didn't take long. I pull the underwear back up, but leave the shorts where they are, wrapped around my ankles, and put my hands up to shield Sunny's boobs.

Randy has already averted his gaze. "Nice tightie-whities, Butterson."

"Nice patch of chest hairs, Ballistic. What are you up to now, three or four? And my underwear is red. Not white."

"Would you two stop! What am I going to do, Miller? I have poison ivy on my boobs, and it's itchy!"

Lily closes the door on Randy and elbows me out of the way. She pulls Sunny into the bathroom and flips on the light. "Get me baking soda, please."

"You got it." Baking soda is one of the few things that can take the itch out of poison ivy. I learned that in Boy Scouts.

I hunt down the baking soda while Lily calms Sunny. By the time I get back, the shower is running and Lily is standing in the hall with Randy. They're close-talking and so absorbed they don't even notice me ease past them into the bedroom. I rifle through my bag until I find the box of condoms. I toss it to Randy. "I've got Sunny from here. You two play safe." Then I shut the door and lock it.

I make a paste out of the baking soda, and when Sunny gets out of the shower I slather it all over her chest while she lies on the bed and sniffles.

Then I eat her cookie to make her forget about the itch.

It works. Twice.

30

Car Wash Problems

-Miller-

The distractions worked well enough last night, but they're not so effective this morning. Overnight the rash has gotten worse.

"This looks awful!" Sunny gestures to her bare chest.

It doesn't look great. "It's not that bad, sweets."

She can tell I'm not being honest. "I have to teach yoga in three days. I can't do that like this!"

"You'll be wearing a shirt, though. Won't that cover it?"

"I wear tank tops. They won't cover this!" She motions to her neck and collarbones.

It isn't until Randy knocks on the door and reminds me we have to get a move on that I remember the charity car wash this afternoon. It's already eleven forty-five. I need to shower and get dressed, but first I need to calm Sunny down again.

She wouldn't have sex this morning without a shirt on no matter how much I assured her that I don't care, and the rash isn't contagious. She's self-conscious. Overnight it's crept up her throat, blossoming into blisters that nearly reach her face.

I feel terrible. If we hadn't had sex in the forest, she wouldn't have this problem. The only upside is that I don't have to make excuses as to why she can't come to this fundraiser with me. Any other time I'd want her there—but since I want to pick the dude's brain who's running it, and it pertains to a venture I'm hoping might eventually include Sunny, the poison ivy is an unfortunate blessing.

"Maybe it'll clear up by then."

"In three days? I'm blistering. Do you know what happens to blisters? They turn into scabs. I'm going to be scabby. I'll be disgusting!"

I run a hand through my hair, searching for a solution. "Should we take a trip to a medical clinic?"

Her frustration softens. "They can't do anything about it." She sighs. "I wanted to come with you to the fundraiser, but I can't go looking like this."

"I still think you're beautiful." At least where she isn't covered in poison ivy she's beautiful. And on the inside.

"Can you imagine if people took pictures and posted them on the Internet? The rumors would be awful. Neither of us needs that."

While Sunny and I haven't been out much in public, the few pictures of us from my weekend at her place are now hashtagged with #thebarbieandkenofhockey. The recognition that we're a couple is something, but the nicknames are not my favorite. Sunny with blisters all over her would probably be tagged with something even worse.

I pull her into a hug. "I shouldn't have used a log as a bed."

"You weren't alone. I'm just as much to blame. It was fun at the time. Nature makes me horny."

"Me too. Next time we'll bring blankets."

"Next time?"

"If you want there to be a next time. Otherwise we can stick to indoor sex." I kiss her forehead. "I'll bring back Calamine lotion. I'm glad it wasn't your cookie." I kiss the edge of her jaw.

"Oh God. Don't even say that! We would've had matching damaged parts!" She pats me through my shorts. "I'm so relieved everything's almost back to normal."

There's a little residual swelling, but it's healing up nicely. Sunny keeps patting; we stop talking and start kissing. Clothes come off—except for Sunny's shirt. We have slow, easy sex on her sunflower comforter. If it weren't for wanting to keep her in my life in a more permanent way, I'd blow off the fundraiser and my research mission to stay in bed with her all day.

. . .

Randy knocks on the bedroom door ten minutes after I give Sunny her second orgasm. "We'll only be gone a couple hours, Miller. Give your girl a break."

Sunny lifts her head from my chest and smiles. "You should go so you can come back."

"Good call."

I throw on a golf shirt and a pair of shorts and fix my messed-up hair. By the time I'm ready to go, Sunny's curled up in bed, reading a book for one of the classes she's taking this fall. She wants to get a head start. The book part is tedious like it is for me. It's when we get to put it into action that we shine. We're the same in a lot of ways. I kiss her on the forehead and then the lips. She looks sad when I pull away.

"Are you okay?" I tuck a few strands of hair behind her ear.

"Just tired from all the exercise." She stretches and puts the book down on her stomach, her grin cheeky.

As I stare down at her, a weird, unsettled feeling makes my

chest clench. "I don't have to go if you don't want me to."

"It's for a good cause, so you should go." She covers her yawn with her hand. "I'll catch a nap, maybe paint my nails with Lily or something else girly so I can find out what happened last night."

I'll be fishing for the same information on the ride to the fundraiser. "You're a hundred percent sure?"

"Yup. You go do good things."

"Okay." I drop another kiss on her lips before I head for the door.

"Miller."

I turn to find her twirling her hair around her finger. "'Sup, sweets?"

She hesitates and then asks, "There won't be any bunnies, will there?"

I come back to the bed and lie down beside her, stealing the lock of hair from between her fingers. "It's not like one of those parties at Lance's. It's a fundraiser for breast cancer. I don't know who will be there, but people will take pictures. It's inevitable. This is where that whole trust thing comes in, Sunny. It's a social event. I'm there to make a donation, and then I'm coming back to you, because you matter and I care about you. Okay?"

She nods.

"I should put on some bunny repellent to be safe, shouldn't I?"

Grabbing her by the ankles, I drag her to the edge of the bed until her legs hang off the end.

"What are you doing?"

I hook my thumbs into the waist of her shorts and pull them down, along with her panties. "Putting on bunny repellent." I drop to my knees on the floor. Her book is still lying open on her stomach. "I'll be thinking about you the entire time I'm there. As soon as I get back I'll rub some of that pink lotion on your poison ivy."

"'Cause that's so sexy and all."

"You don't think so?" I kiss the spot below her navel. I don't have time to warm her up.

Randy knocks on the door. "Butterson, we really need to go."

"Two minutes!" I shout back.

Then I put my mouth on her and erase the sad look from her face, replacing it with another orgasm.

. . .

Waters has two cars in the garage so we borrow one instead of showing up in the rental. One's a truck with sweet rims. The other is an old-school Iroc Z with an eagle painted on the hood.

"Waters is a weirdo, isn't he?" Randy eyes our ride.

"He's marrying my sister, so yup."

"Not that I'm complaining." He slides into the red leather interior. The whole thing has been redesigned so the inside looks like a racecar.

I don't expect we'll be gone long. All we need to do is write a check, get the car washed, schmooze with the host, and I can get back to Sunny. We only have another night or two at the cottage before Sunny has to return to Guelph for work.

As soon as we pull out of the driveway, I start with the questions. "So? What's the deal?"

"Huh?" Randy's on his phone, texting. He pauses and sniffs. He lifts the bottom of his shirt to his nose and follows with his fingers. "What's that smell?"

"Bunny repellent."

"Say what now?" He arches a brow.

I repeat myself, but don't elaborate.

"It smells a lot like pussy." He cracks a window and continues texting.

"Speaking of, what happened with Lily?"

She came through the kitchen to get coffee while I was cutting peaches for Sunny and me. She was wearing Randy's T-shirt. She was also friendly. It was very un-Lily.

"We had fun. Several times." He doesn't pause his texting. "I'm hoping to have even more fun tonight."

"Oh, yeah?" I try to see what's on his screen, but it's impossible to read and drive at the same time. "Who're you texting?"

"No one."

"Please tell me you don't have plans to meet up with a bunny this afternoon." I don't need more drama. I've already had enough over the past week.

"No, man. I'm not a total asshole." He sends one more message and pockets his phone. About two miles down the road from Waters' cottage, I spot a camping trailer parked halfway in the bushes. I slow down.

"Is that Kale and Benji?"

Randy frowns as we pass. "Maybe? It's hard to tell."

There's a car behind us, so I speed up again. "If it's still there on the way back, I'm stopping. Those guys are as persistent as cockroaches."

"No kidding. That dickhead kept texting Lily all night. Eventually I made her shut off her phone, otherwise I would've thrown it out the damn window. Or gone to find the fucker and broken all his cocksucking fingers."

He flips through radio stations and taps his fingers on his knee.

"So?"

He stops fidgeting to look at me. "So what?"

"That's all I get? You had fun."

"Don't forget the several times part."

"I'm guessing I was wrong about the vagina teeth if you managed to get in there more than once."

"Vagina teeth?"

"Yeah. I figured she's snarly, so maybe her vagina is, too."

Randy shakes his head. "Butterson, sometimes your brain is a fucked up place to be."

He flips down the visor and checks his reflection in the mirror.

"She wasn't snarly with me at all."

"That's because you were sexing her."

"Lily's actually a lotta fun." His mouth quirks up in a private grin. He flips the visor back up. "She has a cousin who was at Camp Beaver Woods this past week."

"With us?"

"Yup."

"No shit."

"She said he's been playing hockey since he could hold a stick, but her aunt and uncle have, like, six kids, and they can't afford all the lessons, or whatever. Don't tell her I told you, though. I think he might've been one of the kids you helped subsidize."

"Huh."

"I don't think she hates you as much as you think." His phone buzzes in his pocket, and he checks the message, ending the conversation.

Has Lily been different with me since we arrived yesterday? It's hard to tell with all the Benji BS and Sunny's poison ivy.

The fundraiser takes place at a cottage on top of a hill. The driveway curves around a rocky bend, making the actual structure impossible to see. Cars snake upward in a slow line—luxury rides interspersed with moderately expensive vehicles. Based on the sheer number of cars, we'll be sitting here for a while. It's like a small version of a car show. The rental would've sucked compared to Waters' car.

Randy pulls his phone out and sends a few more messages while we wait, so I do the same, including a warning to Sunny that we saw a camping trailer parked a couple miles down the road from the cottage.

Sunny messages back. They're hard to decipher without listening to them, but the last one has a heart and a kissy lips emoticon, which I take as a sign things are good.

Randy passes over his phone with our invitation to the suits manning the gates. The dude passes me a clipboard with a bunch of forms to sign. I pass it to Randy to scan, otherwise we'll hold up the line.

"It's a bunch of waivers for photos. The usual." He passes it back to me, I sign, and we move forward.

As soon as we round the bend, the cottage comes into view. It makes Alex's pad look like a dump, and that's saying something. Three stories of glass, wood, and stone are built into the side of a steep, rocky incline. The view is spectacular. The top floor is the only one accessible from the driveway. I'd love to appreciate the architecture more, but I suddenly realize I'm in trouble. Cars worth a quarter of a million dollars and up line the edges of the driveway. Two Ferraris—one red, one yellow, a black Mercedes, and an orange Lambo are among the nicest.

I'm a guy. I have a hard-on for cars. I don't own anything quite so wildly expensive, only because Violet won't let me. The money's there, but she wants me to wait a few years before I do something stupid with it—like throw it away on a car I'll never fit in comfortably.

But the cars aren't where the trouble is. It's what's happening with the cars: bikini models drape themselves over the hoods, or the owners who stand with them, holding fake checks that represent donations. I can't read the amounts from where I am, but based on the cars, they're significant.

One of the models saunters up to the hood of our car, a wet, soapy sponge in one hand, a half-full bucket of water in the other. For a second I think she's naked, but realize her bathing suit is the same color as her skin.

Randy and I look at each other. "Dude."

I look anywhere but the hood of the car. "This is not what I thought it would be."

Randy holds a fake smile as he gives the woman a thumbs up. "Maybe we should write a check and leave."

I know things are bad if Randy's making that suggestion. A photographer chases after the model, snapping pictures. She rounds the passenger side, then stretches out over the hood. Holding the sponge above her chest, she squeezes, releasing a white, foamy spray that bounces off her chest and lands on the hood and windshield. Then she rubs her chest all over the eagle. It's a scene right out of a B-rated movie.

"I'm not so sure your bunny repellent is working," Randy says as she comes around to my side of the car. She drops the sponge in the bucket and takes a towel from one of the men lining the driveway.

She picks up a clipboard and a pen and struts over to my window. "Fun ride, boys! You can pull into that spot right there. Fill out this form with your donation amount, and we'll get you set up so the team can start washing. You've already signed the photo release form?"

"Yup. We're all set." I make sure I hold eye contact and don't look down again.

She guides my car into a spot like she's getting ready for a drag race. Her hair's in a swishy ponytail.

"Did you know there would be models?"

"Well, yeah, but I didn't think it would be like this." Randy runs an anxious hand through his hair, messing with his ponytail stub.

"What are you all worried about?"

"I don't know. There are a lot of models."

"No one said you had to hook up with any of them."

"Screw you, Miller. That's not what I mean. It won't look good."

"No shit."

Now that we're in, there doesn't seem to be any way to get out, based on the unreal lineup of cars filtering in behind us. I assumed because it was a cause I could get behind, the event would be all civilized. I should've known better.

Apparently, a magazine is shooting its annual bikini model edition as part of the event. That would've been good to know. I scribble my way through another release and the donation form, while Randy does the same.

Randy leans over and checks out my papers while I flip to make sure I've signed in all the right places. "Miller, that's—"

Another model sticks her head in the window. "All set?"

"Good to go." I hand over my forms and pass her his as well.

"It's good; don't worry about it," I tell Randy, who looks seriously stressed.

The model checks our information and gives us a megawatt smile. "I'll be right back."

"Sure." I want to text Sunny and let her know I'm stuck and it's not what it looks like, but I don't have a chance. Models swarm the car. They hold open the doors; Randy and I have no choice but to get out. One of the women passes us fake checks with our donation amounts on them. They prod Randy into a picture with me.

"Dude," he hisses out of the corner of his mouth. "I would've bumped my donation amount if I'd known you were throwing in fifty grand."

I meant to donate twenty. "Sorry, man. I flipped the numbers," I whisper back.

Two other models—ones wearing normal bikini tops and shorts—flank us, and two more drop into odd, contortion-y poses in front of us. The women on either side put their hands on our shoulders and lean in, making kissy lips. I turn toward the model with the intention of protesting. Her lips are hot pink and half an inch away from mine—thanks to her monster heels—which is the exact moment the flash goes off. I've been here for less than five minutes, and already I'm screwed.

As soon as they're done, I try to get my phone out of my pocket so I can warn Sunny, but the model links arms with me and ushers us toward the house. I want to shake the bikini model entourage, but I don't want to be rude or attract more attention. I let them guide me around the back of the mansion and up stone steps to a massive deck. It drops in tiers to a stone surround and an Olympic-sized pool. I'm not sure what the deal with the pool is since there's a lake below us. It seems wasteful and excessive. Sunny wouldn't approve.

Music blasts from the speakers, and more bikini-clad models with trays of drinks and appetizers strut around, posing every time they stop to offer a snack. I decline the booze. The whole scenario is exactly what I promised Sunny I would avoid. Unintentionally, Randy has screwed me again.

But I'm here, so I don't mess around. I seek out the host, Gene. My intention is to chat with him about the business side of setting up a fundraiser—with less partial nudity—and make a plan to talk more at a later date, when he's not hosting a party with hundreds of people. Then I need to find Randy, so we can get back to the cottage, and I can get back to Sunny.

I manage to find Gene and secure an introduction. He's a big hockey fan, so we end up talking about the coming season and training for a bit. Then I get sucked into an hour-long conversation about endorsements, career longevity, and philanthropic pursuits. He's business savvy. Apparently he knows all about my involvement with the summer camps, including the one I left yesterday. The interview I gave has already been printed in the local paper. It's sitting on the coffee table in his living room, open to a picture of me with Michael and his family.

My phone buzzes in my pocket more than once while we're talking. I don't want to be rude, not when this could be a once-in-a-lifetime opportunity. Gene and I exchange contact information, which is exactly what I'd hoped would happen.

I'm searching for a way to end the conversation—dude is seriously chatty—when Randy finally shows up. He's wearing a strange, fake-looking smile. Gene gives him one of those back-pat hugs and invites us to stay for dinner.

"We'd love to, but we've got to get back. Butterson's girlfriend's sick." Randy's still wearing that messed-up smile.

"I'm sorry to hear that."

I take the cue and stand. "She'll be okay. I just don't want to be gone too long."

Gene nods and Randy ushers me out of the house, but it's another half hour before we get back to the car with all the handshakes and conversations we're forced into on the way.

"We need to get back to the cottage *now*," Randy says as he slides into the passenger seat.

I check my messages. I have tons of texts from Sunny and

several from Violet. Reading them all will take forever. Based on Randy's panicked expression, I shouldn't be wasting time. I toss him my phone. "What's going on? I need you to read those to me."

"Waters and your sister showed up at the cottage a while ago. According to Lily, Waters is raging. Lily is pretty pissed too. She called me a ball-licking anus pimple."

"She's creative. Is Waters upset about us taking his car?"

"Probably? It's hard to tell from Violet's messages. She mentions something about the poison ivy and veggie man. There's a lot of autocorrect going on." Randy scrolls through my messages. Some of it is probably personal, but he knows most of my business anyway. He flips back and forth between his phone and mine.

"Fuck."

"What?"

"The exes came back to the cottage."

He hits a button and brings the phone to his ear, tapping the dash with anxious fingers. Whatever's going on can't be good. "Hey. Shit. I'm glad you finally answered. I was getting wor—"

He stops abruptly, his eyebrows pulling down. "Whoa. Hold up a second. What do you mean you're leaving? He can't do that—Can you stall? We're on our way back now."

I can hear Lily through the phone, her voice high. Randy bangs his head against the back of the seat. "Come on, Lily. It's not like that." After a brief pause he holds the phone away from his ear and checks the screen. "Fuck."

"What now?"

"She hung up."

"On purpose?"

"Maybe? I don't know. I could hear Waters in the background. I think he might have been arguing with Sunny.

We need to get back. There's a lot of misinformation happening, and it's making us both look like assholes."

I rub my forehead and take a bend in the road too fast, almost fishtailing around the corner. Waters will have my balls if I ruin his car. Randy checks my messages every few minutes, but the ones from Sunny stopped about an hour ago. The last one I received from her was about Waters being at the cottage and how he wasn't happy.

I almost ram Waters' car into the back of the camping trailer when I pull into the driveway. They're backing out as I'm pulling in. The unsettled feeling from earlier slaps me in the face as I park the car, blocking them.

Kale sticks his fuzzy, patchy face out the open window. I shift the car into park. I can see Sunny in the back window, twisting her hair around her finger.

"Get your car out of the way, asshole, before I back over it!" Kale yells.

"Go ahead and try it!" I jump out of the car, leaving the door wide open, and head for the trailer. Kale backs up, almost hitting me. Before I can get to Sunny, the door of the cottage slams open.

Waters takes up almost the entire frame. "I'm going to fuck you up, Butterson!"

We're close to the same size. I'm a little broader and I might have a few pounds on him. He's a center; I'm defense, so being lighter works in his favor on the ice. I don't think the slight size difference is going to mean much if we get into it. He looks pissed.

For a split second I consider running back to the car and locking myself inside. He won't beat on his own car. But backing down means I have something to feel guilty about. And I didn't do anything wrong.

"Alex!" Violet grabs his arm and hangs off it.

He stops with the stalking business and gives her his attention. "I just want to talk to him, baby."

"You said you were going to fuck him up!"

"With my words." He pries her off his arm and goes back to stalking toward me. He's wearing flip-flops. They slap against the ground and kick up stones with each step. He doesn't acknowledge Randy when he gets out of the car. His rage is all for me.

Randy decides now is a good time to come to my defense, and his own. "I think there's been a misunderstand—"

Before he finishes the sentence, Sunny throws open the trailer door. She must not realize how close I am; the steel frame hits me in the face, the sharp edge bashing into my forehead.

"Oh God!"

"Alex, don't!" Lily yells.

I don't have a chance to recover before Waters' fist slams into my face.

There's a crunch inside my head. Pain explodes, turning my vision white.

"Alex! What's wrong with you?" That's Violet screaming.

"You didn't need to punch him in the face! He's already hurt!" Lily yells.

I don't know why the hit is unexpected. Waters has been dying to get me back for breaking his nose when he screwed Violet over. I fall backward, like a cut tree. Pines and birch rise around me, blue sky broken by fluffy white clouds. My head hits the gravel. The sun is a bright ball in the middle of it all. It expands, filling up the blue and eclipsing the clouds until it's everywhere.

I blink and the clouds are gone. There's just white and a spot of black in the center. I try to sit up, but I can't. That was a hard hit.

I hear screaming. Girl screaming.

"What happened to using words?" Violet's yelling again.

"Baby, calm down. He's fine."

"He's not fine! You knocked him out!"

A disembodied hand appears in my vision. I think it's mine. I swipe across my face. My palm comes back wet. Pain radiates through my skull in more than one location, multiplying the black spots in my vision. White turns to red as I hold my hand in front of me. Those black spots take up more room.

Gravel digs into the back of my head, and there's a huge rock under my right shoulder. I want to move, but I've had the wind knocked out of me. I might even be concussed.

Sunny's voice permeates the fog. "Oh my God! He's bleeding!"

I want to tell someone to make sure she doesn't come near me; Sunny and blood aren't a great combination.

"Sunny, you should sit down," Lily says. She must know what happens when Sunny sees blood.

"Catch her!" That's Randy. He's a good friend, watching out for my girl.

I should be the one to do that. I struggle to sit up, but Alex moves fast, getting to her before she hits the ground.

A shot of cold has me sitting up in a rush. It's Kale, with a bottle of soda. Asshole. Geez, Waters hits hard. Kale empties the rest of the soda on my face.

"Keep it up, Kale, and I'll shove that bottle up your dick hole!" Randy yells.

With Waters as his bodyguard, the little fucker has grown a set of balls. He sprinkles the last few drops on the ground next to me and backs away.

"Get her in the trailer," Waters orders.

Kale struggles to pull an unconscious Sunny up the two steps into the vehicle. Once she's mostly inside, Lily pushes him out of the way and drops down beside her. I try to stand, but I'm way off balance. Waters will definitely gloat about this. I manage to get to my feet as Kale turns over the engine.

Randy hands me a shirt to wipe my face with. It's sticky from the soda. And bloody from one of my face wounds.

I take a stumbling step towards the trailer. "You can't send Sunny home with him."

Waters puts a hand on my chest and pushes. I drop back to the ground on my ass.

"Enough, Alex!" Violet gets between us. It reminds me of what she did in the locker room after I discovered her and Waters going at it in there—except that time she was defending Alex, not me. "Do you realize what a hypocrite you're being? I don't even like you right now!"

"He's been fucking my sister around for months!" Alex snaps.

She throws her hands in the air. "No, he hasn't!"

Kale pulls the trailer forward and manages to avoid hitting all the other cars.

"Get over your goddamn ego, Waters." I try to stand, but my head is swimming and I'm dizzy. "If you use that tone with my sister again, I'll beat your ass."

"You can't even stand up right now, Butterson."

"Alex! Just stop!" Violet is equally fired up.

Kale starts backing down the driveway. I make another attempt to stand, but I only make it a couple of steps before I stumble and go back down, gravel digging into my knees and palms.

Randy tries to chase after them, but Kale's already down the driveway, gravel spitting from his tires. He spins around and pins Alex with a glare. "Congratulations fuckhead, you just sent Lily home with her verbally abusive ex-boyfriend. You're really winning right now, aren't you?"

"What are you talking about?" Alex seems confused.

"That's the question, isn't it? You didn't even ask it. Just came in, fists first. Good job." He slow claps and gives Alex the double bird.

"Alex, you should probably follow your sister home," Violet says.

He pulls her aside and they have a tense conversation.

When Waters goes to hug her, she puts her hands on his chest, expression pinched.

He pulls her close anyway, her hands trapped between them. When he tries to kiss her, she gives him her cheek. I don't want to feel responsible for their argument, but I do. He takes her hands in his and clasps them behind his neck. Then he tilts her chin up. I'm an interloper on their private moment. His expression is earnest as he close-talks, their noses almost touching. Eventually Violet lets him kiss her, but she's still stiff.

She shoves her hands in the pockets of her shorts and watches Waters leave.

If everyone would let Sunny live her own damn life, maybe I wouldn't be sitting here, bleeding, feeling like my heart has just been cleaved in two.

31

Fix It If You Broke It

-MILLER-

Eventually Violet crouches beside me. "I'm sorry."

My head throbs in multiple places. "What for?"

"This whole clusterfuck." She looks so sad. It's an echo of what's going on inside me. "Let me look at your head."

I tip my chin up, and even that makes the world spin. "I was trying to do a good thing with that fundraiser."

"We didn't know it was going to be like that," Randy says from behind her.

"Balls, you mind giving us a few minutes? Maybe get your bag together. Clean up all your used condoms and such." She doesn't even thrust once.

His head drops, and he rubs the back of his neck. "Sure thing, Vi." He disappears inside the cottage. A bird twitters somewhere above, and a squirrel makes that weird clicking sound. Fuck the happy sounds of nature.

Vi's angry. And emotional. She's on the verge of tears. I've witnessed a lot of crying lately. I don't like that I seem to be the cause of it so often. My apology is reflexive. "I'm sorry."

"Why? You don't have anything to be sorry for. Well, maybe you can be sorry for the poison ivy on Sunny's boobs, but even that wasn't your fault. It's not like you forced her to get naked in a forest at hard-on point."

"Uh, no. She took her top off all by herself."

Vi nods and keeps her hand close to my elbow as we walk over to the deck so she can inspect my forehead. "You definitely need stitches, and I think your nose is probably broken."

"I figured as much."

"I have to take you to the hospital."

"I know." I rest my elbows on my knees and press the heels of my hands against my temples, hoping to alleviate the throb. "This isn't how I thought today would go."

"That makes two of us."

"Are you and Waters okay?"

Vi shrugs. "We'll work it out. Eventually. But Boobgate is in full effect right now. Violence wasn't the answer last time and that sure hasn't changed."

"The models weren't topless, even though they looked like they were. We tried to get in and out of there as fast as we could, but it took way long, and now everything's fucked."

"It definitely didn't look good."

"We would've left if we could."

"I know that." Vi pulls up an image on her phone of what looks like me being kissed by a topless model while another one rubs her boobs on Randy's arm. "Unfortunately, this is what Alex and everyone else saw today. You could've skipped the fundraiser. Your girlfriend being covered in poison ivy is a legitimate reason to miss a bikini car wash."

"It was supposed to be a good thing, and I wanted to talk

to the guy who runs it. I didn't know it was something I should avoid until I got there, and by that time it was too late. I wanted to check in with her, but I was talking to the organizer."

Violet runs her hand over her face. "I hate the way this went down."

"Why can't Alex just let her live her own damn life?" I hate how difficult he's made things.

"He's her brother. He sees you hanging out with these guys who don't seem to care whose reputation gets dragged through the mud. Then he gets to the cottage and finds her covered in poison ivy while you're at some fundraiser that looks like a setup for a bad B movie."

"He knows things get taken out of context."

"He sure does. But you saw what I went through when Alex publicly denied being with me on national TV. You even broke his nose over it. Yet you're surprised by his reaction to this." She pulls up a video of Waters' car with the model lying on the hood.

"All I want to do is get the fundraiser stuff going like we've talked about. It backfired on me spectacularly."

"It sure did." Her phone beeps. She pulls it out. A picture of her and Waters—taken before they started dating, with her tongue in his mouth—fills the screen. She shoves it back in her pocket.

"Aren't you going to check that?"

"I will in a few minutes. He can wait."

I'm not sure me being a priority over Waters is a good thing. "Can I ask you something?"

Vi rests her cheek on her knee. "Sure."

"Why'd you get back together with Alex after the relationship denial?"

"You mean aside from the fact that he has a giant cock and

can make me come like a freight train on nitrous?"

"Don't be an asshole right now, Vi."

She sighs. "It's complicated. I love him even though he hurt me. I wanted to hate him for saying we weren't together in such a public venue, but I couldn't. People make bad decisions, especially when they're under a lot of pressure. Some are worse than others. He knows he fucked up hardcore, and I didn't sugar-coat how badly. I also don't pretend to be over it."

"You mean still?"

"I have moments of insecurity. He's good about it." She spins her engagement ring around so the diamond is facing her palm. "What I have with Alex, it's all-consuming when I'm with him, and when I'm not. And it's rare. It's not perfect, but we work, and that makes it worth fighting for."

"I thought maybe I'd have that with Sunny." I saw how hard it was on Vi when Waters screwed her over. She bawled her eyes out over that asshole for weeks. And then just like that, they were back together.

"You had a misunderstanding, Miller. That doesn't mean it's over."

"She left."

"She wasn't in charge of that situation. I'm angry at Alex for being an asshole to you. It won't last forever, but I'll let it ruminate for a while. It's why he's going back to Guelph with Sunny, and I'm here with you."

"We fucked up a vacation for you, didn't we?"

"Alex fucked it up by overreacting. I swear he could have a second career on the stage if he wanted. We can come back up once we get things sorted out. Sunny was willing to talk. I'm sure she still is. I think what it comes down to is deciding whether she's worth the effort. Relationships take a lot of energy. I get that you want her to trust you, but you have to give her some time. One conversation about it isn't a magic recipe for perfection. Loving someone is a lot of work."

"What if I'm no good at relationships?" I don't want to be doomed to a life of bunnies and no substance. They're not what I want. I want Sunny.

"You're not bad at relationships. You and Randy have been friends your entire life. You've had my back since you became my brother. You're a great guy, with a huge heart, and seeing you with Sunny has allowed me to see another side of you. A great side. You might not have a lot of boyfriend experience, but you're an amazing, caring person. You're going to make mistakes, and that's okay, as long as you learn from them."

"I thought we were making progress." I admit the thing that's been gnawing at me ever since I went to visit Sunny in Guelph. "I think I might have fallen in love with her."

"Then you need to talk to her."

"I need some time to think first." I wipe away a trail of blood from the bridge of my nose. "I wish there was a drive-thru for relationship problem-solving."

Vi laughs, but it's humorless. "Don't we all." She stands and wipes the dirt off the back of her shorts. "Come on. Let's see how Balls is doing. Then we need to get you to the hospital. You probably have a concussion, and I won't be able to forgive Alex if anything happens to you. Then my whole future's fucked, and I'll have the moops for the next year, and I'll probably start dating Balls because I'll have to break off the engagement."

I know she means it as a joke, or that's how she wants me to take it, but there's a real undercurrent of worry in her tone.

Her phone buzzes again. It's the song about peacocks. "I have to get this."

She wanders out of earshot, but I don't need to hear the conversation to read her body language. She runs a hand through her hair, stunted by her ponytail. Then she stares up at the sky.

Violet's jaw is hard; her eyes glitter. I know this face. She's holding back tears. She lifts her hand as the sun peeks through the clouds and watches the diamond catch the sun, sending prisms of light dancing over her face. Then she spins the diamond to face her palm and closes her fingers around it. She brings her closed fist to her mouth.

I hate that my relationship with Sunny is messing with their relationship. The thought of loving someone as much as Vi loves Waters is terrifying. Especially since right now, it seems to cause an awful lot of pain.

...

Apparently Lily wasn't too happy about the pictures of Randy with the models at the fundraiser. All of his clothes have *ASSHOLE* scrawled across them in various colors of permanent marker. On the front of his boxers is the warning: *SMALL DICK INSIDE.* It'd be funny if it happened to someone else.

Usually he and Lance would laugh off something like this. Not this time. Randy looks legit sick over it, and not in an I-have-a-new-stalker way. It's in a this-is-fucked-up way. He throws the last of his ruined clothes into his bag and zips it up.

"We should get you to the hospital; that needs stitches." He points to my forehead.

"Vi'll take me."

"I can follow in the rental." He picks up a note off the nightstand, flips it open and scans it, then shoves it in his pocket.

Vi appears in the doorway. "That's okay. It might take a while. You can head to Toronto, and I'll bring Buck back with me."

"Won't it be out of your way if you have to take me to the

airport?" I ask.

"It's fine. I don't mind."

My head hurts too much to argue, so I let Randy deal with the rental vehicle. I wonder if he'll stop in Guelph. If that's the case, he should probably stop at a sports store and grab a cup, just in case.

Violet runs back into the cottage once the car is loaded to grab something she forgot. She comes back holding the orange Play-Doh sculpture with the superhero cape. She hugs it, then tucks it safely into the backseat with a sweatshirt wrapped around it.

"Do you want to explain that?"

She pats the head. "It's the Super MC. It's an homage."

I shouldn't ask the next question. I'm almost positive I don't want the answer. "An homage to what?"

"The near-fatal strangling of Alex's MC when I made it into a superhero. It's a long story. I promise you don't want to hear it, but someone might tell it at our wedding—if we end up having a wedding. I hope I can convince him to elope."

I was right. I didn't need to know any of that.

• • •

The hospital in Bracebridge is small, but the people are nice, as is typical in Canada. Someone recognizes my name, and Violet knows all the right things to say, so they see me almost right away. Head injuries always take precedence. I'm concussed, but only mildly. My nose is broken, and the gash on my forehead takes six stitches to close. I'd managed to avoid breaking any parts of my face since my teeth were knocked out in high school. Figures it'd be Waters who changed that.

I get the usual spiel about having someone wake me up every couple of hours. A doctor sets my nose and bandages it. The black eyes haven't appeared yet, but they're coming. While I wait for someone to give me the requisite painkillers and sign off for me to leave, I check my messages. I have emails from Amber that, had I checked them yesterday, would have given me the information I needed about the fundraiser and why it might not be the best idea. I wish I'd read them sooner. Or checked my voicemail, since I missed a call from her as well.

Once we're finished at the hospital we drive toward Toronto. The canvas of pale blue dotted with soft white turns pink at the edges as the sun starts to sink toward the horizon. It'll be dark by the time we get to Toronto.

"I'll call the airline and see if I can get a flight out tonight."

"Why don't you come back to Guelph with me?"

"I don't think it's a good idea with Waters around. And Lily will still hate me."

"Lily doesn't hate you."

"Randy said the same thing. I have a hard time believing it, though."

"Even she was trying to get Alex to calm down. Randy's a whole different story. I don't know what happened with those two, but man, is she scorned. You're also lucky I'm the one who went through your bedroom, not Alex. Do you and Sunny even know what a garbage can is?"

"Why were you in Sunny's bedroom?"

"Alex wanted me to check her poison ivy. Poor thing." Vi grabs her own boob as if she's suffering sympathy pains. "If he'd found those condoms after seeing the pictures at the fundraiser, you'd have a lot more than a broken nose."

I want to mention the lack of fairness, considering what I walked in on with Vi and Waters, but I get that this is a different situation, and my fuck-ups outnumber his.

When we get close to Toronto, I insist she take me to the airport.

"You're sure you want to do that? Maybe you should get a hotel room for the night and sleep on it."

"I have things I need to deal with in Chicago."

"Are you still going through with that fundraiser?"

I think about that Michael kid and how much harder his life is than mine. "Yeah. I'll still do it."

"Good. It's about time you did something that shows people how great your heart is."

"I hate the interviews."

"You need to get over that."

"I have to memorize everything. You have no idea what it's like to be dyslexic."

"Nope. I sure don't. I do know what it's like to be awkward."

"That's not even remotely the same. Speeches were the worst in middle school."

"Speeches are your beef? You think it was any easier to be in the enriched math classes? Fuck that. It sucked. Like I wasn't nerdy enough without that label slapped on me. And then there was you, needing 'help'." She makes air quotes. "When really you spent all your tutoring sessions making out with whoever, because you were King Jock of Turd Hill. Being your stepsister was a pain in my damn ass in high school. But I got over it. So should you."

"Yeah, but you're super smart and shit's easy for you."

"Easy? Because I'm good at math? You do realize I have to work more than sixty hours a week to make less than two percent of your yearly salary, right?"

"Less than two percent?"

"Plus bonuses, but yeah."

"Wow."

"It's cool. I love my job. And I'm marrying a man who likes to dote on me, who happens to be a millionaire. Life could be far worse. This isn't about me, though. I get that you work hard, too, but come on! You've got an incredible skill set that allows you to get around your perceived deficiency, which, if you decided to be more vocal about it, would help so many people."

"No one wants to hear about my deficiencies."

"Are you kidding? People always want to hear about other people's challenges. It makes them feel like anything is possible. You could go into schools and talk about how hard it was for you, and how you struggled to pass your classes, but that you persevered. I mean, obviously you don't want to tell them you got it on with all your tutors, or your poor stepsister had to study in the kitchen so she wasn't emotionally scarred by the whole thing. But you can be an inspiration for a lot of kids."

I ignore the part about my tutors. "I don't know, Vi. That's... personal."

"Personal? Are you kidding? This coming from a man who lets his friends take pictures of his balls and post them on the web?"

"I didn't *let* him do that. And anyway, it was to figure out what kind of spider bit me. No one was supposed to know they were my balls."

"And that makes it so much better." She twists her ring around her finger. "I don't get why being classified as a player is so appealing—especially when being the guy who overcomes challenges, volunteers at camps and even subsidized them for struggling families is so much less offensive."

"I'm not trying to be a player. I was trying to be Sunny's boyfriend, and look how that turned out. I spent my teen years dealing with all the shit that came with being the problem kid; I'm not interested in going back to that."

"Who says you have to? Come on, Buck. Life is tough. Teenage years suck balls—cheesy ones that haven't been washed in a week. You make five million dollars a year. You weren't a problem kid. Relationship-inept maybe, but not a problem. If you want to change people's perception, you need to do something selflessly selfish."

"That doesn't even make sense."

"Let me explain. Did you know you're mentioned in an article recently that has nothing to do with who you've boned?"

"I'm not boning Sunny. That's not what you do with someone you care about."

"Sometimes all you need is a good boning, even with the person you love. Anyway, I'm talking about that camp you went to. You gave an interview, and it was awesome. People are already falling in love with you."

"That's one interview, though."

"Give more of them. The positive attention feeds on itself. Stop going to the bars, stop going to Lance's for parties, and stop getting yourself into troublesome situations. Regardless of what goes down between you and Sunny, this thing you want to do is good. The guy who volunteers at kids camps is the version of you everyone should get to see."

Funny how potentially losing someone important is the thing that makes me want to step outside my comfort zone. If only I'd learned this lesson sooner.

32

Everyone Needs to Stop Interfering

-SUNNY-

My head hurts and I'm confused. I feel like I'm in a fever dream.

"Oh, thank god." Lily's expression is full of relief.

"What's going on?" I sit up. We're bumping down the dirt road, a cloud of dust behind us. Benji is behind the wheel, Kale is in the passenger seat. Lily is beside me, looking just as upset as I feel.

"Alex punched Miller and you accidentally hit him in the head with the trailer door. There was b-l-o-o-d."

"Crap. Is Miller okay?" I sit up, but I'm woozy. All I remember is my brother and Miller fighting and wanting it to stop.

"Violet is with Miller, and Alex is following us in his car." She points to the back window. I squint and see him in the distance.

"So we're going to the hospital? Does Miller need stitches?"

"I'm not sure about stitches, but maybe? There was a lot

of…red liquid."

"Well if we're not going to the hospital, where are we going?"

"Home," Kale supplies helpfully from the front seat.

I throw my hands in the air. "I don't want to go home!"

"I know, but maybe it's for the best right now. Let everyone calm down." Lily bites her fingernail. "I think everything got blown way out of proportion."

And isn't this always the problem? Everyone reacts without thinking.

I've been guilty of it too.

"We were making such good progress," I say softly.

"I know. I'm sorry. Again."

"Me, too."

It's always one step forward and two steps back.

The question now is; have we gone too far backward to recover this time?

33

Making Ch-Ch-Changes

-MILLER-

Despite her repeated attempts to get me to stay in Toronto for the night, Vi drops me at the airport.

It's almost ten. It's been a long day. "Will you be all right to drive to Guelph from here?"

"I'm good. I'll stop at a Timmy's and get a coffee."

I grab my bags from the trunk. "Thanks for being here for me."

Vi wraps her arms around my waist and squeezes. "What are sisters for?"

We may not be blood, but she's the best sister I could ask for.

"Message when you get to Guelph so I don't worry, okay?"

"Okay. And you do the same when you get home."

I wait until she pulls back into traffic before I check in for my flight. By the time I'm in the lounge, Vi has messaged to let me know she made it to the Waters' house. I want to ask about

Sunny but I don't. I do offer to break his nose again for her if he gives her any more problems. She responds with a voice memo that she'll be the one breaking things if it comes to that. She sounds sad. I don't like it. I don't want to come between them. He might not be my favorite person, especially at the moment, but he loves the hell of my sister. I'll never forgive myself if I'm the reason she and Waters don't work out.

I set an alarm, so I don't sleep through boarding and stretch out across one of the couches. It feels like I'm only out for a few minutes when vibrating wakes me. It takes me a while to clue in that it's a call. Prying my eyes open, I hold up my phone and blink away the bleariness.

Sunny's face flashes across the screen, her bright smile makes my chest ache. I let it go to voicemail. I don't know what to do anymore. It's not just my own life I'm fucking up now. It's my sister's too. A minute later, my phone chimes with a new voicemail.

I try to resist, but I'm weak. I key in my code and listen. Sunny's voice is a warm hug and a knife in the chest.

"Hi, Miller. I guess you're not answering your phone right now." Her voice cracks. *"I'm sorry about what happened today. I don't know what the other side of the car wash looked like and maybe now I'll never know. Everything just spun out of control."* She sniffles. *"Violet got here a while ago. She said Alex broke your nose, and I gave you stitches."* She hiccups. *"Everyone I love is a mess right now. Maybe this is the universe's way of telling us...something? I don't know what the answer is anymore, Miller. Maybe you not answering is you telling me where you stand."*

I replay it several times, letting her sadness and resignation drag me farther into emotional sludge. I don't know what to do either.

. . .

The flight home sucks. My situation doesn't improve once I'm back in Chicago. I spend the first day playing video games and eating meat-lovers pizza and hot wings. I avoid Lance and Randy's phone calls. And I don't call Sunny back because I don't know what to do any more than she does. Violet is relentless with the phone calls and messages.

On day two of my undetermined wallowing period, my door buzzer goes off during an epically shitty video game session. "Yeah?"

"Buck?"

"Dad?" *What the fuck?* "I thought you and Skye were away."

"We got back last night."

"Oh. How was the trip?"

"Good. You want to let me in, son?"

"I'm here too!" Skye, my stepmom, says. "The trip was better than good, but I can't share the details without embarrassing Sidney!"

"Don't start, Mom. I'm here, too, Buck," Violet says. "Open the door."

"Sure. Okay." Violet must be the reason for the family visit. I glance around my condo. It's amazing the mess I can make in two days. I don't even have the energy to care.

Also, I'm naked, since that's how I roll when I'm alone and wallowing, or even not wallowing. Priority one is clothes.

I find a cleanish pair of shorts and a shirt on the floor and put them on. Skye's smile freezes, along with the rest of her when I open the door a minute later. My dad gives me the raised-eyebrow onceover.

Vi's holding a tray of fast-food ice cream sundaes. Her nose crinkles. "Oh. Wow. Breakup does not look good on you."

I've been avoiding that term for the past couple of days because it hurts worse than a puck to the groin. "Hey, family. Come on in. The place is a mess." The coffee table is covered in pizza boxes and Styrofoam containers of wing bones. Empty soda cans litter the floor.

"Oh, Buck!" Skye unfreezes and hugs me. She and Vi are almost exactly the same, from the way they look to the way they act. Except Skye's in her forties rather than her twenties. "I'm so sorry about you and Sunny."

I pat her on the back. "Yeah, me, too."

After she lets me go, my dad gives me a back pat. "You could've called. Even if I'm out of the country, I'm always here."

"Yeah, I know. Things were cool until a couple of days ago. I wanted some time to myself." My dad and I are close, but more in a hockey-talk way than deep feelings.

"Please tell me you didn't eat all this on your own." Vi motions to the coffee table. "Never mind. Based on the smell, the answer is yes. First things first: you need a shower. You smell like an actual yeti, if yetis were real. Then we're staging an intervention."

"An intervention?" I run my hand through my hair. It feels greasy.

"Yeah. We gave you two days to mope. That's all you get."

"Didn't you mope for weeks after you and Waters broke up?"

"He has a first name, Buck. And yes, I did. But it's a scaleable thing and this scale says you're all moped out." She searches my kitchen for a garbage bag. "You." She points at me. "Go shower. We'll clean this up."

"How are you even here right now? Don't you have to work?"

"I have an emergency business meeting with a client. Go shower."

I'd argue, but I'm ripe.

Twenty minutes later I'm clean, but still unshaven, in clothes that don't smell like stale food, and my living room doesn't look like a pizza bomb went off anymore. All my windows are open, and Vi's made coffee.

"Let's sit on the balcony."

My dad and Skye humor me by telling me about their cruise even though it's not what they're here for. After a while, Skye and Vi decide I need groceries since all I have in the fridge is soda and expired milk, so they leave me and my dad alone.

"Will you and Alex be able to manage on the ice when the season starts?" he asks.

I shrug. "I hope so. He threatened to go to the manager and have me traded if I fucked Sunny over."

"Well, you didn't, so there's no reason for him to."

"I don't know that he sees it the same way you do."

"Vi's talked to him, and so have I."

"When did you do that? And why would you do that?"

"This morning, after Vi came over, before we came here." He laces his fingers behind his head. "He's part of this family. And I did it because when my kids are unhappy, so is my wife, and none of that works for me."

"What did you say?"

"That I get that he's worried about Sunny, but punching you out over it doesn't solve any problems, or make his relationship with Violet easier. She's struggling with this, although she won't say it out loud. She already ate a damn sundae at our place and killed the bathroom."

"Wow." That's a bad sign. "Are things okay between the two of them?"

"She talks to Skye more than me, but she's stressed. She wants things to be okay with you and Alex. You know how she is." He stares out at the skyline. "I didn't do the best job preparing you for relationships."

"Hockey was my girlfriend."

My dad laughs. "You and me both. I know Skye's been good to you, but before that…"

"We're good, Dad. You did a great job. Look at this." I motion to the view of the city and the waterfront in the distance. It's a great location—close to the buzz, but not in it. "My life is good."

"It's nice to have someone to share it with, though, Miller."

"Maybe one day." I swirl the dregs of my coffee. "Did you get my email about the fundraiser?"

"I did. That kid really made an impression, huh?"

"He's an excellent player."

"I know. There was some camp footage. The interview was a smart move."

"Amber and Vi think so, and the need for positive publicity will help get this new project moving."

My dad smiles. "I talked to a few coaches for the minors about players who might want to be involved. Whatever you need, I'm here for you—and not just for business stuff, either."

"I know, Dad. It's just easier for me to focus on the fundraiser right now."

He doesn't push it, which is one of the great things about my dad. He'll offer his help, but he won't force it on me. We spend the next hour compiling a list of contacts and players we think will want to be involved in the exhibition game. I need to work fast so we can set it all up before training starts. It'll be a lot of work, but I need a distraction.

• • •

"Soooo… I talked to Daisy yesterday," Violet says, faux casually on Wednesday.

She stops by daily to help me set up the fundraiser. She maintains that things are okay with Alex, and I trust her to tell me if it's not. Also, she's a seriously sucky liar. It's a serious relief. It's one thing to fuck up my own relationship, it's another to mess with hers.

I keep my eyes on my laptop. "Oh, yeah?" I can't stop thinking about Sunny. I've been lowkey stalking her social media. The only thing she's posted is an inspirational quote about karma.

"Sunny's been moping. She won't even do a spa day with Daisy and she's been living on a steady diet of ramen and tofu fritters."

Sunny loves spa days with her mom. They go once a month. It's their thing. And tofu fritters are her comfort food. She only eats them when she's had a bad day.

"That doesn't sound good." Since the family intervention, I've hit the gym daily, and I'm back on my preseason diet. It means eating nothing I enjoy and being exhausted at the end of every day. But that makes it easier to sleep. It also means I can avoid invitations to hang with Lance because I'm not drinking.

"It's not for the people who live with her, but for you it is," Vi explains. "The stages of relationship mourning are complex for women. We have phases. Self-flagellation is next."

"Was diary part of your self-flagellating?" When Vi and Waters broke up she consumed an irrational number of dairy treats, even though she can't tolerate them.

Vi flips her ponytail over her shoulder. "Exactly. I eat ice cream because it tastes good, even though it makes me feel like crap on the inside. It gives me the moops, so it's a delicious punishment."

"That's seriously messed up, Vi."

She shrugs. "It serves its purpose."

"You were eating ice cream earlier this week," I note.

"I was sympathy eating. Sometimes I pick fights with Alex so I have an excuse to eat dairy. Don't tell him that, or I'll wax a spot on the top of your head." She makes a circle above her.

She's always threatening to wax and/or shave parts of my body. She has yet to follow through, so I'm not worried. "Why would you pick a fight with him?"

"Not like a real fight. Just, like, you know, leaving the dishes out of the dishwasher, or the cap off the toothpaste, or forgetting to buy new lube so we can't have marathon sex—that kind of thing."

I give her the stink-eye. "Always with the overshare."

"Isn't that what makes our relationship awesome? Can you imagine if you'd had a crush on me when our parents first got married? That would've been wicked messed up, eh? We'd have our own reality TV show."

I don't respond. Once I made a passing remark that I can unsay, and she's never let it go.

"So if things don't work out with Alex and me, and you and Sunny don't get back together, and your career takes a dump, and we need to make some money because you spend all yours on booze and women, we should totally pitch that idea. I bet a network would pick it up in a hot herpes minute."

"If things don't work out with Alex, I'll set you up with Randy."

I grin as her face scrunches up. She sets her coffee on the table, lifts the laptop from her knees and makes her standard thrusting motion. "It would never work. I can't control the air hump. It's embarrassing enough on the occasions when I see him now." She settles back in her chair cross-legged and repositions her laptop. "In other, more exciting and important news—sit your ass down for this—"

"I'm already sitting."

"Fuck you for ruining my intro." She pretends to wind up her middle finger like a jack-in-the-box. "Apparently, Mr. My Balls Get Fondled By the World has been trying to contact Lily since your orgy weekend at the cottage."

"There was no orgy."

"That was a test. Good to know. But anyway, your ballsy friend tried to see Lily after the car wash fiasco. It didn't work, but get this, she and Benji are through. I met him, by the way. He's a huge dickface. She could do way better."

This is news about Randy trying to see Lily. He's only mentioned her once since we've been back in Chicago. He's been doing the gym with me the past few days, and he's hung out with me instead of going to Lance's, too. I thought it was a moral support thing, but maybe he has different reasons.

"Have you called Sunny yet?"

"No." Violet asks every time I see her.

"Why not? You're obviously miserable without her, and she's miserable without you."

"I don't know. It just feels...too messy." I don't want to be honest with Vi. I'm afraid I'll keep fucking things up, and that me and Sunny won't be the only couple to implode as a result. I'm the reason my dad didn't find someone until I was nearly through with high school. I won't be the reason my sister loses the love of her life, too.

"Honestly, Miller..." She makes another one of her faces. "I can't do it. I can't call you Miller. It has to be Buck. I keep trying it on, but it's like a cheap pair of underwear. It doesn't fit right. I can't get comfortable."

"No one said you had to call me Miller."

"Yeah, but Sunny calls you Miller and so does Randy. I feel bad that I can't make it work for me."

"Don't. Buck is a multipurpose nickname. If you want to feel bad about nicknames, stop calling me yeti."

"If you had dark hair, you'd look like a Sasquatch."

"I would not. I keep everything trimmed all nice-nice. Except my balls. Those are bare, like two squishy, smooth, flesh-colored plums."

She makes a sound like she's coughing up a hairball. "Thanks, asshole. I liked plums until now. If we get that reality TV show going, we could dye your hair purple so you look like a giant wine-dipped yeti."

I shake my head and fight a chuckle. As ridiculous as Vi's tangents can be, they're entertaining, and this one has lifted my crap mood marginally. Relationship limbo sucks. Probably because I was, and still am, way more invested in Sunny than I've ever been in anyone.

"Are you going to stop with the insults and the reality TV show dream so we can talk about real, actual, important things, like this fundraiser? How are we on the finances front?" I pull up the spreadsheet with the figures and itemized lists of things we need to pull this off. If things go well, we could cover the cost of Michael's treatment and support his family.

I looked into their situation. It isn't very good. Neither parent has benefits, so they're out of pocket for all the medication. Applications for support can take months. If they can't make it work, they'll have to pull Michael out of hockey because it's expensive. Dealing with cancer as a kid is bad enough without losing his favorite thing, too.

"Sidney and I have already secured a few significant donations," Vi reports. "And you've contacted the car wash guy, right?"

"Yup. Gene's all over donating."

"Excellent." Vi types frantically on her laptop. "Overhead is almost completely covered. I have a list of volunteers for the day of, and Sidney's secured an arena, vendors, and security close to where Michael lives, so he won't have to travel. We'll start promotion once the teams are finalized."

"Awesome." I'm amazed at the number of people required to run this event and how quickly we've been able to pull it together. Gene has been great about sharing information, strategies, and his contacts. So at least one good thing came out of that car wash.

"I ordered the T-shirts," she adds.

"Nice. Wait. What? Why would you do that? I haven't made a decision about the name yet."

"I made it for you." She pretends to type so she doesn't have to look at me.

"I wish you hadn't done that. Now I'll have to look at hundreds of people wearing Project Sunshine shirts."

"They look great."

"Yeah, but—"

"Yeah, but nothing. If you don't have the balls to call Sunny, at least she can see in a real and tangible way that you care about her. Besides, it's too late to cancel the order for the shirts or the jerseys." She gives me a big, jerky grin. "Also, Alex is going to the gym this afternoon."

"So?"

"You still need a few more players, right? He's been asking about it, but it's not up to me if he can play or not. You might want to clear the air before the season starts so you don't murder each other on the ice."

"We've punched each other out; we should be even." I'd like to punch him again, but I won't. "I guess it might be a good idea since you're marrying him and all, huh? I have to deal with him no matter what."

Vi sniffs and wipes away a fake tear. "Look at you, growing up, being the man. I'm so proud."

"Suck it."

"Alex was unreasonable. We're mostly okay, but I'm still not happy with how he managed himself. I've been doing a lot of withholding. It hasn't been easy, but I think he's starting to get it."

"Withholding?"

She gestures to herself. "He gets none of this right now. So I'm responsible for taking care of my own orgasms. It's seriously fucking inconvenient, but I'm willing to take a stand for you."

I try to speak, but there aren't any words to express the level of overshare or my gratitude.

Violet waves a hand around. "Alex hasn't always done the right thing when it comes to Sunny, and he knows that, even if he won't ever admit it to you. He also knows how miserable she is, and he's worried. At the end of the day, he wants her to be happy."

He can't be all bad if Vi's willing to spend the rest of her life with him.

"I'll talk to him when I see him." I don't want to get into another discussion about calling Sunny, not until I know for sure Vi and Alex are really and truly okay, so I change the topic. "How're the wedding plans coming?"

Every time I mention it, Vi has a mini freak-out. It's fun to watch.

Her eye twitches, and she rubs her legs. "Ugh. Seriously. We haven't been engaged that long. And with all this bullshit going on...you'd think we were in a state of emergency or something. Daisy and my mom are ridiculous about it. They have a running list of, like, two hundred people, and that's just for the engagement party."

"They're excited, huh?"

"That's an understatement. I keep telling Alex we need to elope. I can't deal with a five-hundred-person wedding. It's unreasonable. I don't get the whole need to be a princess for a day. I don't want to be a princess. I want to be Violet Waters so I have a princessy, romantic name. The rest of it is total crap meant to propagate false expectations for marriage."

"Wow. Way to sell it, Vi."

"Screw you, Buck. You just wait. Your day will come. Talking about this is giving me hives."

I assume she's being dramatic, but then I note irregular red dots on her arms.

"Does Waters know you're this stressed?"

"Say one word and I'll—"

"Shave my balls. I know."

"I was about to say armpits, but you had to go for the genitalia, didn't you?"

"Shouldn't you be excited and not stressed? Don't women usually love this shit?"

Violet scratches the angry red welts expanding on her arm and ignores my questions.

The sound of the patio door opening in the condo next door puts me on alert. A new woman moved in while I was away. I haven't officially met her, but I've met her yappy dog's nose through the tennis-ball-sized drainage hole where my privacy wall meets hers. The patter of nails on the tile follows, and his little brown nose appears in the hole, it disappears and his paw shows up. He whines, aware he can't get to me.

"Doodle! Stop being a pest!" The woman next door snaps her fingers and calls out, "Hi, neighbor!"

"Morning," I call back.

Vi whispers, "Doodle? She named her dog after a penis?"

I shake my head and motion for us to go inside. This lady can be chatty for someone I've never seen, and for some reason her voice is familiar. We sneak back inside and finish planning the next phase of Project Sunshine. In two days, I fly to Toronto to see Michael for a promo video—it's been scheduled so it's before his chemo treatment. Then I'm hanging around for that to keep him company.

Vi leaves before lunch, and I head to the gym. After two hours of hardcore training, I hit the showers.

Waters is in there with his back to me. It's the first time we've been within punching distance of each other since he broke my nose. I leave a shower between us and turn on the spray, adjusting it until it's hot enough to relax my tight muscles.

"Waters."

"Butterson." He glances my way and motions to my face. "Looks like you're healing up good."

"Yup." Most of the bruising has faded to that ugly yellow-green, and I'm done with the bandage. The stitches came out a couple of days ago.

"That's good."

"Yup." I love awkward, naked conversations.

"Violet stopped by your place this morning."

"Yup. We had a breakfast meeting. Business stuff."

"She's been at your place a lot."

"We're working on a project."

"Yeah, I know." He rubs a bar of soap over his almost hair-free chest. "How's that going?"

"It's good. I think it'll be successful." Now would be a good time to get him involved. Except he beats me to it.

"If you need extra players, I'd be happy to join."

"Sure. Yeah." I cut the water. "That'd be cool. There are a couple spaces left. Vi'll fill you in on the details."

"Great. Good. I think what you're doing is commendable."

"Thanks."

There's an awkward pause and then he asks, "Vi seem all right to you?"

"She's been fine with me. Why? Is something going on?"

"Skye and my mom want to plan an engagement party. I'm not sure Vi's too thrilled about it."

"She mentioned that."

That gets his attention. He stops washing his hair to focus on me. "She say something?"

"You know how she is about being the center of attention. You can always tell how stressed Vi is by how much ice cream she eats."

"Two nights ago, she ate a whole pint and had to sleep on the bathroom floor."

I consider the conversation Vi and I had about ice cream being a punishment. I can't imagine why she would feel the need to punish herself over being stressed about their engagement party. "Sometimes I replace the ice cream with frozen yogurt. The aftermath isn't as bad. If you can get her to eat sorbet instead, you'll avoid the whole issue." This is a weird-ass conversation to have in the shower.

"Thanks for the tip. Did she say anything else?"

He's legit worried. I don't mind putting him on edge. "What Vi and I talk about is in confidence. I've already said more than I should." I grab my towel.

Waters is quick about rinsing off as I collect my shampoo and soap. "Come on, Butterson."

"Just talk to her. I'm sure she'll tell you what's what." Waters and I know that's not true. Vi can sit on a problem for weeks.

It's her personality. She's a marinater.

"You two are close. If you know something important, it'd be great if you told me, Miller."

I don't think Waters has ever used anything apart from my last name to address me. I wrap the towel around my waist and face him. This is the opportunity I've been looking for. It's perfect. He's stressed over Violet's stress. I'm happy about that. It means he cares. But also, fuck him.

"Like you helped me out with Sunny?"

"You haven't even called her."

"You're right. I haven't. And you have yourself to thank for that."

He frowns. "Wh—"

I cut him off. "Vi left my place today with hives because I asked her about the wedding. They popped up out of nowhere. She's stressed. If I were you, I'd take good care of her right now. Make sure she's okay with what's going on. You don't want to end up swimming in Shit's Creek with me. I remember what you were like the last time she dumped your ass. It wasn't pretty."

I expect some assholey reply, because that's usually what I get, but I'm met with silence. I turn to walk away.

"Miller."

"What?"

"Do you think she's okay? I mean after this shit—" He motions between us. "Should I..."

"Be worried?" I finish for him. "Yeah, man. She may not be my blood, but she's my family. Right now you're fucking things up for more than just me."

34

Puck Waters and His Timing

-MILLER-

The next night I get a call from a number I don't recognize. It's too late for a business call. Still, I don't want to miss something important. I've been fielding a lot of calls for Project Sunshine this week.

"Hello?"

"Hi, is this Miller?"

The female voice is familiar. "Yup. Who's this?"

"It's Lily."

"Oh. Hey." I have a million thoughts, most of them of the *WTF* variety. "Is Sunny okay? Did something happen?"

"She's okay. Well, mostly."

"What do you mean *mostly*?" I'm already throwing off the covers.

"Nothing bad has happened, not apart from you breaking up with her."

That sounds like a dig. I settle against the pillows, the kick in my chest settling. "If she's okay, what's going on?"

I get silence for so long I think she's hung up. Finally she clears her throat. "I wanted to apologize."

Lily doesn't seem like the type to do the apology thing. Not without some difficulty, anyway. Maybe she's different with people she likes more.

"For what?" I ask.

"I was wrong about you. I feel bad about the way I've treated you. I just—I didn't want Sunny to get hurt, and I made some assumptions."

"Oh. Well, thanks, I guess…is that the only reason you called?

"Yes. No." She clears her throat. "So…uh… I don't know if you know this, but my cousin was at Camp Beaver Woods when you were there."

"Randy mentioned something about that."

She makes a weird sound. "Yeah. I guess he would tell you, eh? Uh…anyway, my cousin, Brett, couldn't say enough nice things about you. He and Michael have stayed in touch. What you're doing for him is great."

I'm still processing the apology, so this ups the shock level by a million. Publicity for the charity game went into full swing this morning. Tomorrow we're filming the promo video. "It's not a big deal."

"Yes, it is. You're a really good person. I'm sorry I didn't give you a fair shot." Her voice drops and she mutters, "She'll kill me for doing this. Sunny's a mess over you. Like, really a mess. I've never seen her so, so…sad." She speeds up as she talks. "And I know I'm partly at fault. I kept telling her you weren't good for her."

I want to be good for her, but my fuck ups are abundant when it comes to Sunny. "Maybe you're right."

"I'm not right. I judged you before I knew you. I just don't understand why you haven't reached out."

"It's one thing to mess up my own life, but too many people are affected by my fuck ups." I don't want to do more damage to the people I care about. It might hurt like hell to let her go, but it's better for everyone else.

"When we were on that camping trip you were all she talked about, Miller. She tried to call you every day, but the reception was trash. I know we're all too involved when it comes to her. Me, Alex, even her parents. But having Alex as an older brother was hard for her. She's so sweet and kind. Which you know. And it's obvious you care about her or you wouldn't be putting together a fundraiser with her name on it. She's never been like this over anyone else before. That must mean something."

"It can mean something and still not work out," I say, but even I'm not convinced. Why am I really avoiding talking to her?

What if I try and fail again? What if my mistakes cause more pain? What if I fall even harder than I have and it all ends anyway? How will I manage then?

"She's coming to Chicago next weekend to visit Alex."

"Oh yeah? Thanks for letting me know." I glance at the empty pillow beside me. All I can think about is how much I miss Sunny and I'm sad I don't have a memory of her in my bed. "I appreciate you calling to smooth things over. It means a lot."

"I wish I'd been nicer to you sooner."

"Meh. You were just protecting Sunny. I get it. It makes you a good friend."

"I don't think she'd agree with you right now. Anyway, I thought you should know what was what. I should let you go. Have a good night, Miller."

"Hey, Lily." I catch her before she hangs up.

"Yeah?"

"I don't know what's going on with you and Randy, if anything, but he's been laying low since we got home from Muskoka, and that's not like him. Just figured you should know. Talk to you later."

I let her go before she can answer or ask more questions. I'm not one for interfering, but in this case, maybe a nudge isn't a bad thing.

Looks like for once, we're on the same side.

. . .

The next morning I'm up early for my flight to Toronto. For once, I'm looking forward to the publicity shit. Violet and Amber leave me a million messages apiece, clogging up my phone. It all comes from a good place, though.

Michael's in good form when I get to his place; nervous, but excited. We get through the promo shoot and the interview with hardly any issues, apart from when they insist I wear makeup to cover the bruises from Waters. They've faded to a light yellow-green under my eyes and across the bridge of my nose, but that won't be attractive on camera. It's a pain in the ass to sit through all the powder and crap, but Michael thinks it's hilarious, so I don't put up much of a stink.

I've memorized almost everything, and the few things I haven't I wing, which works out well according to the director. Michael's a natural in front of the camera, and the nerves disappear as soon as they ask him about the camp, his outlook on treatment, and what he wants for his future.

His answer is simple and poignant; he wants to survive, so he can grow up and be like me.

He makes the interviewer cry. I may or may not have had something in my eye. If it means we can help his family stay out of financial trouble, then it's worth maybe crying on national TV. It's a great start to the day, but there's a gray cloud hanging over Michael's head, because this afternoon's chemo treatment won't be fun.

I want to be a distraction for him. I don't particularly like hospitals, since most of my memories of my mom happen to be based there, but I'm willing to deal with that for Michael.

He and I play cards while he's hooked up to all the IV garbage. We're on our sixth game of Crazy Eights, which I apparently suck balls at since I've lost five times so far, when there's a knock on the door.

Another kid I recognize from camp peeks his head in.

"Hey, Brett!" Michael's eyes light up.

It isn't until Lily comes in behind him, followed by Sunny, that I remember why that name is familiar.

Brett and Michael fist bump, and Michael gives Lily a huge, long hug. This feels like a setup.

"Michael, this is my best friend, Sunshine."

"Oh, hey!" His eyes go wide, darting from me to her.

Sunny smiles and returns the greeting, then her gaze shifts to me, and she gives me a shy wave, which I return.

She looks tired, like she hasn't been sleeping all that great, but she's beautiful. I definitely still have a whole shitton of feelings for her based on the way my heart is jumping around in my chest. All I want to do is hug her. Tell her I miss her. That life sucks without her. That I'm so scared to fuck things up again.

Michael glances between us again. "Your name is Sunshine?"

"Mm-hmm." She nods, still smiling. She grips the strap of her purse, her fingers climbing higher until they reach the ends of her hair.

He tilts his head. "Is she the reason for Project Sunshine?"

"Uh..." I rub the back of my neck, not expecting to be called out. "Sunny's who it's named after. But you're the reason for the fundraiser."

"Cool." He nods like he gets it. "You must be super important to Miller."

There's some awkward laughter.

Lily breaks the tension when she asks, "Michael, do you want something to drink? Maybe a ginger ale?"

"Oh! Yes, please."

She looks at me.

"I'm good."

"Are you sure?" Her eyes volley between me and Sunny.

I slap my thighs and stand up. "Actually, I'm thirsty, too. Brett, you want to take over my hand? Michael's kicking my a—my butt."

Brett and I switch places. "Sunshine? You coming?" I ask her.

"Sure. That'd be great." She fingers the ends of her hair, a sure sign she's nervous.

Brett decides he might need a snack, which makes Michael think about it, and in the end, we make a list on Sunny's phone before we head to the cafeteria. Sunny grabs my hand and pulls me into the stairwell. She releases my hand, and leans against the railing.

She gestures to my face. "Your nose looks good. You can't even tell it was broken. Alex has this bump. I don't think it'll ever go away, not without surgery."

It's quite the icebreaker. "Uh. Yeah. It healed well."

"Alex had bruises for, like, forever."

I'm glad I caused him more damage than he did me. "Michael and I had a promo shoot today so they put makeup over the bruises. But they're almost gone." I lean against the wall and cross my arms. "How'd you know I would be here?"

She ducks her head and toes at a black spot on the tile. She's wearing a pair of silvery fabric shoes, fitted jeans and a pale pink t-shirt. I stand there absorbing her, the smell, the sight, the ache in my chest expanding. I almost miss her reply.

"Michael told Lily's cousin you'd be here. Lily thought I should come so I could maybe see you and apologize, but now that I'm here, I'm not sure it was such a good idea. Maybe I'm making things awkward. I should probably go—"

She moves to take a step around me, but I link our pinkies. "Apologize for what?"

"For not standing up for us the way I should have. For letting everyone else make my decisions for me. For not listening to my heart." Sunny's thumb brushes along my wrist.

A door opens somewhere above us, the metallic clang a reminder that we don't have much privacy. This is a much bigger conversation than a few minutes in a stairwell.

"What does your heart say?" I ask.

The door opens across from us halting our conversation. We move aside and awkwardly say hi to the couple as they pass.

Sunny waits until the sound of another steel door opening and closing confirms we're alone again. "That I—"

Another door opens and the sound of male voices filters through the stairwell.

Sunny sighs. "How long are you staying in Toronto? Can we talk after your visit with Michael?

"I have to be back at the airport around six thirty."

"That soon?"

"I have meetings in the morning." I regret already that I didn't plan to stay the night, and that I didn't call her before I came. Like I should have.

"I could drive you to the airport," she offers shyly.

"That could work."

"Only if you want me to, though."

"Sure. That'd be good. Then you can tell me about your heart and what it's saying."

"I would really like that." Sunny bites her lip and steps closer. "Can I hug you?"

"Okay." I open my arms, and she moves into the empty space, clasping her hands behind my back and pressing her cheek against my chest.

She smells like sunshine and mint shampoo. And she feels like she's finally right where she's supposed to be.

Another door opens somewhere below us, and we break apart. Why don't people use the damn elevator?

"We should get the snacks." I open the door and usher Sunny out ahead of me.

We spend the next two hours hanging out with Michael, talking about camp and the upcoming fundraising game. Sunny's quieter than usual, but Lily has all sorts of questions, and she offers to help out however she can, especially since we're holding it in Guelph. My Dad must have used some of Waters' connections to make it happen. It's nice that she and I finally seem to be okay with each other. When I tell her Randy will be playing in the charity game, she gets all blushy and flustered.

Once treatment is finished and Michael's mom takes him home, we all pile into Lily's beat-up Honda Civic.

"Can you take Miller and me to Alex's condo?" Sunny asks.

"Sure." Lily smiles from the front seat.

"You talk to Randy lately?" I ask as we crawl through the streets of Toronto toward the lakeshore.

Her fingers tighten on the steering wheel and a flush creeps up her neck to settle in her cheeks. "He called me a few days ago."

"He did!" Sunny shrieks. "Why didn't you tell me?"

"I missed the call. He left a message."

I keep my mouth shut, but I will be talking to Randy about this. I think he's way more hung up on Lily than he wants to admit. I don't want him to pull his usual crap where he gets involved and then bails. And not just because Sunny and I have enough problems to contend with—that ex of Lily's seems like a big douchey problem. She doesn't need any more.

By the time we make it to Alex's condo, we're running low on talking time, so we say a quick goodbye to Lily and head up to Waters' penthouse. The space is massive, boasting a sweet view of Lake Ontario. It's not a lake anyone wants to swim in, according to Sunny. Apparently pollution means going for a dip could result in additional limbs growing out of funky places.

She lifts a set of car keys from a hook by the door. "I wish you didn't have to leave yet."

"Yeah. Me either."

"You could catch a later flight." She peeks up from under blond lashes.

"Is that what you want?"

She flips the keys over in her hands. "It would give us more time."

We're here now. We need to talk without a time limit. I call Amber. She checks into alternate flights. There are only two options, but at least we can clear the air.

Amber rebooks the flight and adds an alert to my calendar. We take a seat on the couch, Sunny close but not touching. She starts before I can. "I'm sorry for not trusting you."

"I'm sorry for making that difficult. I can't change the past, or who I was before I met you, Sunny. And I can only take ownership of what I say and do—not the context it's taken in, not the way the media wants to skew it." I run a hand through my hair, aware that without the hard conversation, we can't move past this. "It took me a while to see the damage I was doing by not being careful with where I went and who I allowed myself to photographed with. I would never want to repeat your week away with Lily and your ex. I hated how that felt. And I hated even more knowing that's how *you* felt, every single time a picture of me with one of the fans popped up."

"It wasn't intentional."

"I know. But it didn't stop it from hurting. And then when all the shit went down with Alex...which had been brewing for a while, I questioned a lot of things. I don't want to keep making mistakes that will damage the people I care about and their relationships, but part of that is us letting other people dictate the terms of our relationship."

She bites the corner of her lip. "Everyone has always been so protective of me. And growing up with Alex as an older brother...it wasn't always easy. I love him. He's a great brother. And I love my parents too...but he was always the star. He burned so much brighter than I did."

"You're incredible."

"It's all relative, though, isn't it?" She smiles sadly. "I grew up in his shadow. Sometimes guys were only interested in me because of Alex. And then Lily started dating Benji and Kale was always there. It was an easy relationship. He didn't care about Alex's career. He wasn't athletic, or caught up in that stuff. It worked, until it didn't. I had plans for my life and he just...didn't. We weren't destined to be together forever. I knew that even in high school. But when I met you, I realized all the things I'd been missing." She skims the back of my hand, her expression warm and hopeful. "This guy who quietly does all this amazing charity work that no one knows about, who adores his sister and would do anything to protect her. I saw you, Miller, the you that not everyone else got to see. Even with all the noise, and the interference, I never stopped seeing that person in you. I've never been good at standing up for things I want. But I want you. And I know it won't be easy, but the good things never are." She blinks back tears. "I should have trusted my intuition."

"Three months of daily conversation and me coming to visit, even with parental supervision, should've been a dead giveaway that I was pretty invested in you."

"It really should have." Sunny leans her head on my arm. "And then there's the whole Project Sunshine thing." Her nose brushes my skin, and she presses her lips to my bicep.

I wrap a tendril of her hair around my finger, avoiding eye contact. "There is that."

"How long have you been putting that together?"

"A while."

"How long's a while?"

"Does it matter? Will it change anything?" After my first visit to Guelph, I was already a goner. After our first time together, I was trying to figure out how to make the long-distance crap manageable and create a long-term life for us. But I'd like to give us some time to be an actual couple again before I spill that tea.

"No." She skims my jaw with her fingertips. "You're an incredible person."

"Not really."

"Yes, really." Her lips hover close to mine. "Miller."

"I'm right here."

"Will you be my boyfriend?"

I smile. "Yeah. I'll be your boyfriend."

"Good. Because I missed being your girlfriend." She brushes her lips over mine. "I missed talking to you. I missed hearing your voice. I missed everything about you."

"I missed all those things, too."

Sunny strokes the seam of my lips. And just like that, the world rights itself. Like it was all so simple. We talked it out and the world didn't fall apart. She's mine and I'm hers and we're going to try to be us again.

She straddles my lap and slides her hands into my hair.

"What about the distance?" I ask as she peppers kisses along the edge of my jaw.

"We'll manage."

"I'll be traveling a lot soon."

"I'll be done with my courses at the end of December. I'll only have my placement left. I can do that anywhere." Her lips hover over mine.

"Would you move to Chicago?"

"For us, I would." She strokes my cheek. "We can work out the details. One step at a time, right?"

"One step at a time."

I pull her mouth to mine desperate to take advantage of what little time we have left. We're in this together. We kiss and tug at clothing, trying to get closer to each other. To make up for the missed time with no words and lots of uncertainty.

My phone beeps as I pull her shirt over her head. It's the twenty-minute warning.

"Just ignore it," Sunny begs.

"I can't miss my flight."

"We'll be quick." She tugs her shirt and bra over her head. "I need you, Miller. I need this."

Twenty minutes isn't a lot of time, but it's enough. We can have frantic makeup sex and next time take it slow.

We're a flurry of flying clothes as we rush to undress. I pull Sunny into my lap and we grind on each other while we kiss and touch, hands caressing, bodies pressed close. I drop a hand between her legs, skimming her clit before going lower. She sighs, and her eyes close when I slip inside. It doesn't take long for me to find the sweet spot, and Sunny makes soft, needy sounds.

My phone beeps out another alert. I don't have checked baggage. I should make it. Hopefully.

"How much time?" Sunny asks, her voice hoarse.

"Fifteen minutes."

"I need you in me." She pushes my hand away, fists my erection, lines us up and sinks down.

We both groan. Sunny's eyes roll up. "I missed you."

"I missed you, too." I grip her hips. "So damn much."

Using my shoulders as leverage, she rises until just the tip is hugged. Reversing the motion, she drops down slowly, then does it again. "Why does it always feel so good?"

"I could do this every day for the rest of my life and never get enough." I'm wrapped in the smoothest, velvety-est vice.

"Me, too." Sunny cups my face in her hands. "Let's never let anyone mess with us again."

"Never again."

I move her over me, filling her, surrounded by her, memorizing her soft moans and sweet sighs as I push her closer to the edge. Sunny's knees tighten against the outside of my thighs and goosebumps rise along her arms. She rolls her hips hard and fast. The stupid alarm goes off again.

"I'm right th—"

I reach between us a strum her clit, enraptured by the way her mouth drops and her eyes flare. I'm close, but I slow it down so she can recover. Holding her hips, I shift her over me, nice and easy, chasing down my own orgasm.

"I love you, Miller," she whispers, fingers curling around my chin.

"I love you back. More than anything."

I thrust one more time, and the orgasm body checks me. It's damn well magical. I see unicorns prancing behind my eyes instead of stars.

Unfortunately, the awesomeness of the orgasm is destroyed when the front door swings open.

I've about had it with Waters ruining all my best moments.

35

Flashes of Beave

-MILLER-

"Oh, poop," Sunny mutters.

From my spot on the couch, with Sunny straddling me, I have an excellent view of Waters' horrified expression. If it wasn't an interruption to our make-up sex and the love professions, it might be funny. But I'm annoyed more than anything.

Waters turns away. "What the actual fuck is going on?"

"Miller and I are talking things out."

It's pretty clear there's no talking happening here, so I'm not sure why Sunny bothers with the lie, or why Waters asks in the first place.

I lean over and grab my shirt from the floor. Sunny holds out her arms and I pull it over her head so she's not naked anymore. Waters and I have seen enough of each other's bare asses in the locker room.

I help Sunny off my lap. My dick flops onto my leg with a wet smack. Sunny makes a face and gestures to my lap. "That's messy, isn't it?"

"So help me God, Butterson, if you get your bodily fluids all over my couch—"

"Enough! I've had it up to here with the threats, Alex!" Sunny gestures above her head. My shirt lifts.

"Keep your hands down!" He puts one of his own in front of his face.

"Don't tell me what to do!"

I place my hand gently on her back. "You're showing off your cookie, sweets."

"Oh." She drops her hand and props it on her hip instead. "You still don't get to boss me around, Alex."

"What are you two even doing here? Since when have I ever said it was okay to use my condo as a fuck pad?"

"We came here to talk."

"Yeah, well, that sure as hell didn't look like talking to me. Butterson, put some damn clothes on!"

"Don't talk to Miller like that!" Sunny snaps.

"It's my condo. I'll talk to him however I want to. Get dressed, Sunny."

"You want to be belligerent with me, you go right ahead, Waters. But don't use that tone with Sunny." I grab my pants from the floor and jam my legs into them.

"There will be no fighting!" Sunny orders. It's a sexy look on her.

Waters crosses his arms and Sunny streaks over and gets right in his face. She's shaking. "I am so done with this overprotective crap, Alex. I'm not a little girl anymore. I'm an adult. I can make my own decisions, and that includes what I do and who I do it with."

"It doesn't include fucking on my damn couch."

"Are you even serious with this? How much of a hypocrite

can you be? Should I have told you we were coming here? Probably. But you had sex with Miller's sister in your team locker room *during* a game! Everyone walked in on it! Everyone! The whole team talked about it for weeks!" She pauses to breathe. "And we weren't fucking! We were having make-up sex because you keep interfering and messing up my damn life."

Waters looks shocked, whether because of the outburst, Sunny swearing, or her standing up to him I can't be sure, but she's a badass and I'm falling more in love with her with every word out of her beautiful mouth.

"I just don't want you to get hurt."

She props a fist on her hip. "By trying to run my life? By overreacting every time you see a picture of Miller with anyone but me? By breaking my boyfriend's nose? You're not protecting me, Alex, you're being an a-hole. Have you even apologized to Miller for what you did?"

His lips mash into a thin line.

She throws her hands in the air, and we narrowly miss another cookie shot. "Honestly! You promised you'd apologize!"

Waters shoves his hands in his pockets. "I haven't had a chance."

"Well, here he is." She gestures to me. "The opportunity is yours."

Waters stares at a spot above my head. "I'm sorry I broke your face." He doesn't sound like he means it. Not even a little.

Sunny calls him on it. "That's the worst apology ever. Try again."

He heaves a sigh and runs a hand through his hair. This time he looks me in the eye. "I'm sorry for being an asshole."

Sunny motions for him to keep going.

"And for breaking your nose."

When it's clear she expects more, he rolls his head on his

shoulders. "And for interfering. I just want what's best for Sunny. She's my only sister. Up until I met Violet, I wasn't a very good role model. I guess I was trying to make up for it, and I took it too far. I know you care about her, Miller. I can see that. I haven't been very fair. So, yeah. I'm sorry. Can we call a truce?"

He steps forward and holds out his hand. I meet him halfway, then think about where my fingers have been. "Uh, maybe props would be better." I make a fist and hold it up.

His brow furrows, and then he makes this face. He gets what I mean. "I had that coming, didn't I?"

"After the locker room? You sure fucking did."

We bump fists.

"See? That wasn't so bad was it? I mean, you'll be brothers anyway, so you might as well start getting along, right?" Sunny gives Waters a quick hug and then throws her arms around my neck.

"Sunny, I'd appreciate it if you put some clothes on now." Waters is staring at the ceiling.

Her butt is hanging out of the bottom of the shirt.

"Oops!" She drops her arms.

"That elevator takes forever!" Violet comes through the door carrying a bag of takeout. "Oh, hey, guys..." She surveys the scene: Alex is checking the ceiling for spider webs. Sunny's in nothing but my shirt and holding her ass, and I'm in a pair of pants with the rest of our clothes strewn all over the floor.

She shoves the takeout at Alex and rushes over to Sunny. "Oh my God! Are you two back together?"

"Uh-huh."

"Oh, thank fuck! You guys are so stubborn I was worried it would never happen." They jump around and hug each other like they scored backstage passes to a concert. Waters and I stand awkwardly beside each other while they whisper to each other. Sunny's blushing, so I'm sure it's an overshare.

My phone rings from somewhere under the pile of clothes. "Oh shit. What time is it?"

"Seven-thirtyish? You guys want to have dinner with us? Or have you already eaten?" Violet snickers.

Waters rolls his eyes.

"Uh. Thanks for the invite, but I'm supposed to be at the airport, like, now." I was cutting it close already; I'll be lucky to make it at all.

"What time's your flight?" Violet asks.

"Ten."

"Yeah, you won't make that." Waters drops the takeout on the side table and kicks off his shoes. "You might as well reschedule and stay the night. There's a spare room down the hall." He grabs plates from the cupboard.

I reschedule my flight, again, and my dad agrees to attend my morning meetings. Sunny and I spend the night in her brother's spare room having quiet make-up sex.

Sunny drives me to the airport in the morning. I take off my baseball cap and hold it up so we don't offend anyone or attract too much attention when we kiss goodbye. Pictures still end up on the Internet, but I don't mind. Neither does Sunny, apparently. She uses one of them as her profile pic. It's not in your face at all.

36

Defuzzing is Dangerous

-MILLER-

Once I get back to Chicago, I pour my energy into the fundraiser. The promo video went up yesterday and tickets sold out in minutes. I want to do more of this, and I don't want to wait until my hockey career is over. It's had the added benefit of spinning the media attention in a different direction.

Randy's been my right-hand man in both the workout and fundraising-prep departments. Lance rides his ass about not going out more than he does mine, but even he's let up. Last week when we had a home workout at his place, and Lance was on his best behavior with Tash.

Today Sunny's flying in for the weekend. Daily video chats get me by, but being able to hold her again—that's what I'm looking forward to.

Vi stops by to help me prepare. "What's up, brother from another mother?" She's holding a huge box. "And father," she tacks on, then wrinkles her nose. "That wasn't even funny, was it?"

"Uh, no."

She drops the box on the counter. "I think my sense of humor is being affected by this engagement-party-planning shit. I wonder if it's possible to have an allergy to being engaged."

"I have my doubts."

She points a candle at me. "You're not helpful. I can't deal with this ridiculousness. My mom is trying to force her way into my girl's afternoon with Sunny. I said no way. Neither one of us wants blue eyeshadow makeovers." Vi stops her tirade to look around my condo. "Have you done anything to get ready for Sunny?"

"I changed my sheets, and I cleaned off the dining room table." I relocated all the papers to the coffee table so we have somewhere to eat.

"You're such a bachelor."

I unpack the box of stuff while Vi rummages through my cupboards. "This must be yours." I toss her a box with a woman's leg on it. It looks like a shaving product.

She puts her hands up, shielding her face. It hits her in the chest and drops to the floor at her feet. "Ow! Don't throw things at me!"

"I didn't throw it. I tossed it. Underhand. It helps if you don't cower and try to catch it."

She picks it up off the floor and hurls it. I snatch it out of the air before it beans me on the head. Her aim is getting better— either that or it was a lucky shot. "That's for you."

"What is this? Shaving cream?" I turn the box over and scan the back, waiting for her to explain.

"It'll take down your forest of body hair."

I run a hand up my arm. "I don't need this. You can take it home and use it on your mustache." I slide the box across the counter toward her.

Violet puts her hand up to her mouth, then drops it. "I do *not* have a mustache. You, however, should consider grooming your yeti ass. You're having Sunny over to your place for the first time ever. You're going to engage in excessive boning."

"I'm already groomed. I took care of business yesterday. I even shaved my balls."

She makes a gagging noise. "More than I wanted to know. Suit yourself, but it's supposed to be hot tonight. You could manage your arm fur so she doesn't get lost in there." Her phone beeps. "I need to go. I'm picking Sunny up and then we're going to the spa. She and I have a date with my waxer."

"Your waxer?"

"You can thank me later."

"Make sure they leave a landing strip."

"Why? You have a hard time navigating the land of beave without it?"

"No, I like it. And I'm not talking about this with you. Just don't torture my girlfriend."

"Aw, you're so cute with this *girlfriend* stuff. I'm not surprised you lured her back with your yeti magic." She grabs a Vitamin Water from my fridge. Suddenly, loud groaning comes from the wall adjoining my condo. We both freeze. "What the hell is that?"

"My neighbor? Or a cat in heat?" I've only heard her dog before, and never through the walls.

It happens four more times, then stops.

Vi stares at the wall. "Does that happen often?"

"This is a first. She moved in before I left for the camp. Maybe she's getting some morning penance in." It happens again less than a minute later, six groans and then more silence.

I hope there aren't any more of those sounds while Sunny's here. They'd make an embarrassing soundtrack for the evening I have planned.

Vi's phone goes off again. "Okay. Now I need to go. I'll be back in a few hours. You should reconsider using that stuff." She taps the box on the counter and leaves.

I ignore her suggestion and rifle through the contents of the bag. She's gone out of her way for me, and that says a lot. There are nice-smelling candles, massage oil, bath oil, and what I at first assume are a pair of women's panties. Upon closer inspection, they're men's bikini briefs.

At the bottom is a book about the legend of the yeti. I roll my eyes and pull out a comic strip that looks like it was drawn by a six-year-old. In it, I'm a yeti, and Sunny is a sunflower. It's asinine, but it makes me laugh.

I put everything away in its proper place, the candles in the bedroom on my dresser, the massage oil on my nightstand and the bath oils by the tub.

Now that everything's set up, all I can do is wait. I send Sunny a message with speech-to-text:

Miller: *I can't wait to see you tonight.*

Three minutes later I get a message back:

Sunny Sunshine: *Me 2 :) <3*

On my way through the kitchen, I stop to leaf through the yeti book. It's a cute kid's book.

The box with the woman's legs on it sits on the counter where Vi left it. Purely out of curiosity, I pick it up and read the back. Apparently this cream is made of magic. I put it on my arms, leave it for a while, and boom—all the hair disappears. According to the directions, my skin will stay smooth for days, and the hair will be softer when it grows back. It's not the worst.

I've got another hour to kill before Vi gets back...

I strip down and apply it to my arms, then set the timer and get out the video game console. By the thirty-minute mark, my arms feel like they're on fire. I check the instructions again. It's tiny, pain-in-the-ass print. This stuff better work for all the discomfort it causes. Not to mention the horrible chemical odor masked by a fake flowery smell. After a few more minutes I give up. The burning is too intense. I'm en route to the bathroom when the intercom buzzes. I hit the button and call out a greeting.

"I'm back!"

It's Violet. "Can you come back in fifteen?"

"It's eight billion degrees out here. I have underboob sweat from walking to the door from my car. Let me in."

"Can you see it through your shirt? Is it embarrassing?"

"Will you let me in already?"

"I can't. I'm airing out my ball sac. Enjoy the sunshine." This part is true. I haven't put any clothes back on since I applied this crap. I'm at the point where I want to scratch the stuff off, even if my skin comes with it.

"Airing out your berries? Doesn't the yeti fur impede that?" she quips.

"Berries? My balls are the size of grapefruits."

"Only after you've been bitten by a spider. Let me in. I'm not wearing sunscreen. I'll be the color of a tomato in fifteen minutes, and it'll be your fault."

"How is my fault you're a direct descendant of Casper?"

"Screw you, wildebeest. Never mind. Someone's letting me in."

Static follows, along with some muffled conversation between Violet and what sounds like several guys. The door buzzes, and I can't hear her anymore.

Sometimes it takes a few minutes for an elevator to get to this floor. It's the only drawback to the building, but it gives me time to wash the acid cream off my arms.

I turn on the shower; the burning is almost unbearable, and the smell is just as bad. I step under the spray to rinse my whole body since the pain has caused me to sweat.

The cream immediately washes down the drain, along with patches of hair from my forearms. It doesn't take long before the burning feels more like fire ants gnawing at my skin, followed by a hot lava shower.

I might be screaming and it might be high-pitched. I step away from the scalding spray. The arm hair, which should've magically disappeared, is patchy, and my skin is an angry red color. A loud rap tells me Violet is here. Leaving her in the hall is a bad idea at the best of times—she'll talk to anyone, and she can be loud. I wrap a towel around my waist and head for the door.

"Take something! My arms are about to fall off." She's laden with bags.

She unloads everything but one into my arms, which leaves me unable to ensure the security of my towel. It feels loose.

"I think your neighbor might be an adult film star or something." Vi crosses to the kitchen and drops her bag on the counter. Two lemons roll out and bounce to the floor.

"Why do you think that?"

"Three guys were in the elevator with me on the way up. They were all disgustingly buff, and they knocked on your neighbor's door."

"And she answered it naked?"

"No, I didn't see her. I'm surmising based on the sounds we heard this morning. And they were talking about how hard it is to have a four-hour hard-on."

"Really?"

"No. I made up the last part. But it's a possibility, isn't it?"

My neighbor's potential job isn't important, so I change the subject. "How's Sunny? How soon will she be here? Did you make sure the waxer played nice?"

"She's good. Excited and nervous. I didn't ask about the trim job they gave her beaver. I dropped her off at Alex's on my way here. She's getting ready, and then she's getting a ride over. You've got half an hour." She bends down to pick up a fallen lemon.

I'm still holding the bags, and there's something cold inside. It feels nice so I haven't set them down yet. Violet's face is at waist level when my towel unravels and falls to the floor.

"Oh my God!" She gets an eyeful of my man snake. He's dangling out there for the world to see. Well, the world inside my apartment. "What the fuck, Buck?"

She rears up and throws the lemon. It hits me in the cheek, which is surprising. Maybe Alex has been teaching her how to throw. He's braver than I thought.

I move behind the island to hide my junk. "It's your damn fault for handing over all that crap!"

"My fault? You knew I was coming up! Why wouldn't you put on some clothes before you opened the damn door?"

I set everything on the counter and retrieve my towel from the floor. "I was washing that shit off my arms. It didn't work by the way. Look at this!" I hold out my raw, red forearms. Most of the hair is still there, with small irregular patches missing.

Vi stops freaking out and grabs my wrist.

"Ow! Don't do that." I slap her hand, and she lets go.

"That is *not* supposed to happen. Did you have an allergic reaction?"

"Maybe. I couldn't even keep it on the whole time. I don't know what the actual benefit of that crap is. It stinks, and it takes forever. It's like I'm molting."

"Like a yeti in the spring."

"You're a jerk!"

"How long did you have it on for?"

"I made it to the forty-minute mark before it felt like it was eating off my skin." The burning sensation has returned.

"You're only supposed to keep it on for twenty minutes."

"I thought it said fifty. That seemed like a damn long time."

"It's probably a chemical burn." Vi turns the tap on and ushers me over to the sink. "I'm sorry. This was a bad idea."

Cold water eases the burn. She plugs the sink, retrieves an ice cube tray from the freezer, and dumps it in. The cold water stings first, then numbs.

"What can I do? Sunny will be here soon."

"It's not that bad."

I look at my forearms and then at her.

"It could be a lot worse. You can wear long sleeves to cover it up."

"Maybe." It's hot as balls, and I have a feeling anything touching my arms will feel awful. This is worse than the time I went to Cancun and forgot to wear sunscreen. I was the color of a lobster for the entire week.

I slather antibiotic ointment on the worst spots, pop a painkiller and hunt down the numbing spray they gave me the last time I got stitched up during a game. It stings, but once it takes effect, the pain is manageable. By the time we're done treating my chemical burn, it's five minutes to five. Sunny's punctual. I'm only wearing shorts.

Vi cleans up the kitchen and puts all the crap away in the bathroom while I throw on clean clothes, including the briefs from the bag. All my parts barely fit, but it's too late to change.

Vi meets me in the kitchen and cringes at the state of my arms. "Everything's a go. The vegan menu is on the counter with all of Sunny's favorites highlighted. Order one of each, and you'll be golden."

"Okay. Thanks for all your help, except the arm cream."

"I'm so sorry. Does it hurt a lot?"

"It feels like I doused them in acid and threw on some vinegar for good measure."

"I'm sorry. I'll eat ice cream as penance when I get home. Put gauze on it before you go to bed, or you'll stick to your sheets." She hugs me. "I'd wish you luck, but coming from me it's like the kiss of death."

When the buzzer sounds, we head for the front door and I hit the intercom button. "Hello?"

"Miller? It's Sunny."

"Hey! Right on time. I'll buzz you in."

"Okay. See you in a minute."

Vi slips on her blinged-out flip-flops, pats me on the cheek, and leaves. I scan the living room to make sure it looks decent, spray my arms with the numbing solution again, and wait by the door. After a couple minutes there's still nothing, so I peek out into the hallway.

She's out there, except she's standing in front of my neighbor's door. "Hey," I say before she raises her hand to knock.

She stops and looks my way, her confusion turning into a smile. "That would have been embarrassing if I'd gone to the wrong apartment." She's wearing a summery dress. It's off-white with wide straps. She looks beautiful and like everything I've been missing.

"You're good. I caught you." I wink and open the door

wide. "Come on in."

Sunny kicks off her shoes and looks around. "This is nice."

"Thanks. It has an outdoor pool and it's dog friendly." In my head I already have her moving in with me as soon as she's finished school. Andy and Titan, too.

"Really? That's great."

She fiddles with her hair, and I hook my thumb into my pocket—even the backs of my knuckles are burned from that hair-removal crap. "Want me to give you the tour?" I gesture to the open-concept living room-kitchen-dining room combo.

"Can I hug you first?"

"Of course." I hold my arms out. She presses her entire body against mine as I envelop her and drop my face into the crook of her neck. I wish I could turn her smell into an air freshener. "I missed you."

"I missed you, too." Sunny burrows in, her arms tightening around me.

I love this feeling. Being close to her. Having her in my space feels right, like she's the thing that was missing. She tips her head up and I turn my face toward her. Our lips brush and that warmth spreads through me, settling in my chest. Sunny sucks my bottom lip and I open for her, letting her take the lead. All the nervousness I've felt over inviting her here for the first time melts like cotton candy on my tongue. The emotions I couldn't or didn't want to name before we made up in Toronto are clear as we deepen the kiss.

She frames my face with her hands and pulls back so I can see her beautiful face. "This week was long. I like you better in 3D than I do through a computer screen."

"It's way easier to make out, isn't it?" I say cheekily.

She grins. "Definitely."

Our mouths fuse again, and my body responds to the taste

and feel of her, to the soft needy sounds she makes as our tongues tangle.

Sunny runs her hands over my biceps, but I catch her wrists. "Maybe don't do that today."

She glances at my arms. "Oh my Gosh! What happened?"

"I uh... I had an allergic reaction to some cream." It's true.

"Geez. That's terrible."

"It'll be fine in a couple of days." I hope it doesn't scab. I have interviews, and if my arms are a mess, I'll need to wear a long-sleeve shirt. I like golf shirts better; then I don't have to mess around with a tie.

"Is it only on your arms?"

"Yeah."

"I'll have to be extra careful with you then, won't I?"

"Not too careful."

Sunny's expression turns coy as she runs her hands down my chest and slips them under my shirt.

Which is the moment a loud moan filters through the wall I share with the apartment next door. The timing couldn't be worse.

Sunny freezes. "What was that?"

"I think my neighbor's dog's in heat."

The next moan is louder.

"That doesn't sound like a dog."

I'm positive it's not her dog, but I'm hoping it'll stop soon. "I'll turn on some music." I grab the remote from the back of the couch and flip on the TV, but I'm not fast enough.

This time words accompany the groan. "Give it to me one more time!"

"Um—"

"My neighbor moved in while I was away at camp. I haven't had a face-to-face meeting with her yet." It does nothing to explain what's going on over there. Until now, the only thing I ever heard was the occasional thump. Penthouses shouldn't have sound issues.

The noises stop as quickly as they started. I don't trust that this is the last time it'll happen, and I don't want more interruptions of the moaning variety tonight, unless they're coming from Sunny. "I'll be right back."

"Where are you going?"

"To talk to my neighbor."

"But they're having sex. Or something." Sunny's eyes drop to my crotch. I only have a slight semi—nothing obvious, thankfully.

"They can do it less loudly."

Sunny peeks around the jamb while I walk barefoot down the hall. I knock and wait. It takes a minute before someone comes to the door. She's dressed in workout gear and holding a clipboard.

Behind her in the living room are the three buff guys Violet mentioned. They're all fully dressed, in gym attire. One of them is struggling through a bench press while another guy spots him. "Give it to me! Give it to me good!" The spotter shouts.

Guy number three is holding a one-armed plank, sweating his ass off.

I can handle a personal trainer as a neighbor far better than I can an adult film star.

"Can I help you?"

"Uh. Yeah. I'm Miller. I live down the hall." I thumb over my shoulder, and she peeks out as Sunny does the same.

She smiles and waves at Sunny, then extends her hand. "I'm Nina. We're just in the middle of a session." She gestures to the guys in her living room.

"Yeah. About that." I rub the back of my neck. "We can, uh, hear you through the wall."

I glance down the hall as Sunny prances toward us.

"Oh! Really?" She grimaces as the bench presser groans again. Loudly.

Sunny tucks herself under my arm and peeks into the apartment. "Oh! It's a workout! We thought it sounded like something else was going on over here." At Nina's confused expression, she whispers. "It sounded like sex."

"Oh. Shoot. Yeah." She glances over at the bench presser who makes more sex sounds while pumping iron. "That tracks. We're training for a competition. Normally we go to Igor's but he's having his place painted this week."

"We're having date night!" Sunny smiles widely.

"Oh! I'm so sorry. This must be distracting! I'll take the guys down to the gym."

"Great. Thanks. We really appreciate it!" Sunny says. "And if we get too loud, and you can hear us through the walls, let us know!"

"Okay. Will do," Nina says through a slightly confused smile.

Sunny laces her fingers through mine. "Come on, Miller."

Sunny puts extra sway in her hips as I follow her down the hallway. She waits until the door is closed before she whispers, "I'm really glad your neighbor is a personal trainer and not an adult film star."

"That makes both of us. I would have had to consider putting an offer in on the house next door to your brother. I'm sure he'd love to have me for a neighbor."

Sunny rolls her eyes.

"You don't think I'd do it? You know you have me wrapped around your finger."

She smirks. "I do, don't I?"

"Mmm... don't look so happy about it." I brush my lips over hers. "Maybe you have some parts you'd like to wrap around me, to make it fair?"

Sunny's laugh is as warm as her name. We get back to kissing. "You should take me on that tour now," she says with her lips still attached to mine.

"My condo is pretty boring. I was liking the making out thing we had going on here."

"Me too, but it might be nicer if we could do it lying down and naked."

"You have the best ideas." I lead her down the hall, still half-kissing while I point out rooms. There aren't many, so it's a quick tour.

I open the bedroom door and realize we haven't even had dinner. "Wait. This is a date. We're supposed to eat food."

"We can do that later."

"But—"

Sunny pulls her dress over her head. She's not wearing a bra. She twirls around. She's wearing a thong. "You don't see anything you want to eat?"

"Eat? No." I give my head a slow shake. "Devour? Definitely."

Goose bumps rise along her arms. She backs up until she hits the mattress and sits on the edge. Tucking her feet under her, she rises to her knees, motioning me closer.

Every part of me wants to tackle her and do exactly what I said, *devour*. But that implies quick and dirty. It's been a week. I want slow and long right from the start. I sweep her hair over her shoulders and skim the length of her arm.

Starting at her shoulder, I kiss a path along her collarbones and brush over her peaked nipple with my thumb. Sunny moans softly and runs her fingers through my hair.

"I missed that sound." I circle her nipple, pleased when it elicits the same sound. Sunny grabs the hem of my shirt and tugs it upwards. "Easy, sweets."

"Oh, right. Your arms."

I take care of removing my shirt. It doesn't feel particularly good. My arms are red and sensitive.

Sunny smooths her hands down my chest, the tip of her tongue caught between her teeth as she reaches the waistband. She flicks open the button and drags the zipper down, exposing the red underwear. The head of my cock is playing peek-a-boo. "Looks like someone's excited to see me."

"We sure are."

She strokes the tip with her finger. "What's with the underwear?"

"Tryin' something new."

"Hmm. They're a little inadequate, don't you think?"

"You want to get a better look? Give me your assessment?" She sits back on her knees. "Go for it."

I drop my shorts. "I think they do a good job of highlighting my business."

"They're way too small. You should take them off."

"Maybe you should do that with your teeth." I gently tackle her to the bed, and she dissolves in a fit of giggles. I smile down at her, skimming her cheek with my fingers. "I love that sound."

"I love you," she whispers.

"I love you back." I circle her waist and army-crawl us to the pillows. The comforter feels like sandpaper on the chemical burns, but everywhere else it's soft skin against mine, so I'll live. I kiss her chin before I take her lips again. We make out like that, neither of us in a hurry as our hands roam and our tongues tangle. Eventually I kiss my way down her body, giving her nipples some attention before I go lower. I can't get enough of her hands in my hair, or the hitch in her breath when I kiss below her navel.

I fold back on my knees and tug the thong over her hips. "Are these new?"

She nods. "I wanted to try something new, too. It feels like a permanent wedgie, though."

"I vote no underwear forever and only dresses; then I can have cookie snacks whenever I want."

"Best idea ever, except in the winter or on a windy day."

"Hmm. Good point. Maybe you should just live in my shirts when we're home alone, then." I spread her thighs and lower my head, licking up the length of her on a low groan. "I missed the way you taste."

"I missed everything about you," she whispers.

I take my time, bringing her orgasm with my mouth before I settle between her thighs and sink into her. We have slow, intimate sex, and I feel our connection in more than just the physical. She's in my heart and soul, too.

Later, when I've wrung several orgasms out of Sunny, we shower and order takeout. I wear boxers and she wears my shirt. We eat dinner at the dining room table and snuggle on the couch and watch a movie together. I could get used to this. Having her here, filling up the space with her sweetness.

I kiss the top of her head. "I know you have a semester left, but maybe when you have that internship you could do it out here, in Chicago."

She tips her head up and settles her chin on my chest. "You want me to move out here?"

"Yeah. I do." I stroke her cheek. "I have all the space and it feels more like home when you're here to share it with me. When you're ready, the right side of my bed is yours."

"I would love that." Her smile makes my heart swell. "Speaking of bed, I'd like to go there now."

"So I can love you?"

She presses her lips to mine. "So we can love each other."

Epilogue
Walking on Sunshine

-MILLER-

THREE WEEKS LATER

I scan the packed arena, satisfaction and pride make me feel invincible. We're up two-one against Waters' team. He's pissed. It's awesome. The game is for charity, but you can't pit a bunch of professional hockey players against each other and expect us to ignore our competitive edge. With only three minutes left, it's unlikely Waters' team will make a comeback. Unlikely, but not impossible.

Waters and Randy face off against each other. He's giving Waters a run for his money this season. He's fast and aggressive on the ice. But Waters has experience and all his years of figure skating.

Michael's on the bench beside me, bouncing with excitement. There's a check for fifty thousand dollars ready to be handed over at the end of the game. Things are looking up for him. Chemo and radiation, while shitty, are proving to be effective.

If progress continues, he'll go for surgery before the holidays. The prognosis is positive, which is good, because I've gotten attached to that kid, and so has Sunny.

She stands behind me with her hands on my shoulders. The contact is welcome even if it's distracting. She's been fantastic these past few weeks, helping execute the event and spending time with Michael when I can't. She's way more organized than I can ever hope to be. We make a good team. A great one, even. I love her more every damn day. It's terrifyingly awesome.

My dad stands beside her, his arms crossed, a small, smug grin tugging the corner of his mouth. The puck drops, and Balls snatches it from Waters, shoulder-checking him out of the way as he flies down the ice.

Training starts next week and I'm ready for this season. I'm ready for a lot of things.

I'll be on the ice in thirty seconds. I turn to Sunny. She's wearing a jersey, her cheeks and nose are red from the cold, and her eyes are bright with the same excitement that makes the crowd buzz. I tap my lips with my glove. "I need some luck, Sunny Sunshine."

Her smile is soft as she plants a chaste one on my lips. "Kick my brother's ass. But not literally."

I give Michael props and skate out onto the ice, replacing Lance. We knock gloves as we pass, and I zip down the rink toward our goalie.

I deflect a goal, and Randy scoops up the puck again, shooting off down the ice toward the opposing net. The seconds count down. With less than a minute to go, Waters' team gets control of the puck.

Waters is on it, barreling down the ice with the grace and speed that helped us win the Cup last year. I get into position, ready to protect the goalie. The turn Waters makes is too tight as he aims the puck behind me. He's coming in fast, and the hit is inevitable.

A second later, I'm slammed into the boards by two hundred and twenty pounds of Waters. We both scramble, grabbing each others' jerseys to keep from going down. There's a whole lot of noise from the crowd. I drop and take Waters with me. My head hits the ice; thankfully the helmet does its job, but the impact still stuns me. I try pushing him off, but he's heavy, and I don't have much leverage, ice being slippery and all. He rolls off and gets to his knees.

"Miller?" Waters drops his glove. For a second I think he plans to hit me. But he snaps his fingers in my face. "You all right, man?"

I give my head a shake. "I'm fine. Just don't punch me in the face again."

I grab his jersey instead of his hand, and he loses his balance again. A whistle blows, and the buzzer sounds.

"Stop trying to make out with me and give me your hand, Butterson."

I drop a glove and manage to take his outstretched hand this time. "Stop trying to hump me on the ice."

He grunts as he pulls me to my feet. Then he laughs and keeps a solid hold on my jersey until I have my balance. "You were supposed to get out of the way so I could score."

"Fuck that." I butt my head against his. "I want to win more than I want you to like me."

He raises my arm in the air, boxer style. "Nice save. Next time you won't be so lucky."

It's then that I realize stopping the goal won us the game.

It's a whirlwind of excitement as players flood the ice. I skate over to the bench and get Michael out on the ice. We carry him around on our shoulders like he's the Cup. In a way he is. He's the reason we came together for this—and the reason things keep getting better between me and Sunny.

She's waiting for me when I step off the ice, looking adorable in her too-big jersey. There's local media waiting to interview me. I haven't prepared a damn thing, and Amber wanted it that way. They can wait, though, because Sunny's more important. She's my best everything.

As soon as I drop my gloves and helmet, she takes my face in her hands. Her nose scrunches. "You're sweaty."

"I'm going to kiss you anyway."

She laughs when I wrap my around the waist and cover her beautiful, perfect mouth with mine. Cheesy music about walking on sunshine blasts through the speakers. The flash of cameras doesn't ruin the moment. Not for me.

"What is this?" she asks against my mouth.

"It's our song now. I thought it was appropriate and way less depressing than You Are My Sunshine. Waters isn't the only one who can pull off cheesy moves."

Her smile is all the best sunrises put together. "I love you."

"I love you back."

There are no refunds and no exchanges with love. It comes with flaws and imperfections. It's raw, unfiltered, and sometimes it isn't easy. But I've found the best things in this life are the ones I've had to work hardest for. Especially Sunny.

Exclusive

Bonus

Content

The First Kiss

-Sunny-

I'm not opposed to watching my brother play hockey, but the sight of blood makes me faint, so I'm always a little on edge when we attend his live games. When I watch them on TV, I can leave the room or put my head between my knees. Neither is easy in an arena.

Which is why I chugged an amaretto sour the moment we arrived at the bar and am now drinking a second one. Also, bars are not my favorite. They're loud with too many people, and I get overwhelmed. And say things I shouldn't. I've just been introduced to Alex's new girlfriend, Violet, and accidentally called them out in front of my mom for their dueling tongue viral picture, when a godlike, fairy-tale prince of a man joins the group.

I'm grateful for the interruption for so many reasons. It means no one is focused on the silly things that just came out of my mouth. And honestly, this huge man might just be my knight in a really nice blue suit that complements his ocean eyes.

He hugs Violet, and he and my brother exchange hellos. And then he turns his megawatt smile my way. The moment our eyes meet, I experience a full-body tingle. It starts in my toes and works its way up my legs. It reminds me of when the fairy godmother in *Cinderella* performs her spell and transforms Cinderella's dress from shreds to a magnificent gown. The feeling pings around my stomach, continuing its upward trajectory until it reaches my head. My scalp prickles pleasantly.

And then I'm being introduced to this stunningly handsome man.

His huge hand curves around mine, making unexpected parts tingle even more.

A wide, bright smile tugs his full lips skyward. "My teammates call me Buck, but you can call me Miller."

"I'm Sunshine, but you can call me Sunny." I'm so grateful a normal statement leaves my lips.

"Yeah, you are." His smile widens and turns my insides to marshmallow as he says hi to my mom. "You two could be sisters." And then he kisses the back of my hand.

I melt.

My mom giggles like a schoolgirl. I can't blame her. Inside, I'm doing cartwheels.

"Can I get you something to drink?" Miller asks.

"Okay. Sure. Yes, please." I don't know anything about him, other than that he's my brother's teammate and apparently Alex's girlfriend's brother, but getting a drink with him will give me an opportunity to learn more.

"You two have fun!" Mom gives me an approving smile.

Miller guides me toward the bar, his hand pressed gently against my lower back. I feel that single point of contact everywhere.

When we reach the bar, Miller puts a protective arm around me. His side is pressed against my side. He smells like mint and deodorant. I tip my head up and take in his angular jaw, full lips, and blue eyes framed with thick light-brown lashes. He really does look like a prince out of a fairy tale. Miller orders us drinks and finds us a private table, away from the crowds and the rest of the team. He moves his chair so he's beside me instead of across from me.

He unbuttons his suit jacket and rests his elbows on the table.

"I feel underdressed," I admit, a little self-conscious about my jeans-and-T-shirt ensemble.

"You're perfect."

I cross my legs and accidentally brush his shin. He glances at my foot, and a ridiculously pretty grin lights up his face again. "Toe socks and Birkenstocks?"

I shrug and blush. They're rainbow striped and my favorite. "They're comfy and I can wear thong sandals with them."

"Yeah, you can. You're pretty darn cute." He runs a hand through his thick blond hair, blue eyes twinkling. "Tell me about yourself, Sunny Sunshine."

Butterflies flit around in my stomach. "What do you want to know?"

"Anything. Everything. What's your favorite flower?"

"Buttercups and daisies."

"Not sunflowers?" His fingertips brush mine, and it sends an electric jolt through my body that settles low in my belly.

"They're up there but not quite at the top."

"Fair. Delicate suits you, anyway. If you could only eat one food for the rest of your life, what would it be?"

"Hmm." I tap my lips. "Cinnamon rolls are my number one."

"I like that."

"What about you? What's your favorite food?"

"Cookies. Any kind. I'm an equal-opportunity cookie enthusiast." His grin makes my stomach flip.

"Chewy or crunchy?" I ask.

"Oooh. Either. Both."

"What if you could only pick one flavor and type?"

He blows out a breath. "That's tough. I would go with chewy—oatmeal raisin."

"Those are my favorite, too." I press my hand to my heart. We're cookie twins. "What else is your favorite?"

"You. You're my new favorite."

I roll my eyes. "That's a line."

"It's not a line if it's the truth." He bites his thumbnail.

"Another line!"

He ducks his head and peeks up at me. "Seriously, Sunny Sunshine. You ever see someone and feel like your whole world would be better if they were in it?"

"You're too smooth for your own good." I gulp my drink. But wasn't that the feeling I had when our eyes met? Like I'd just stumbled across something special.

"Do you want to get out of here? Go get some chewy oatmeal raisin cookies and find a quiet place to talk?" Miller chews his bottom lip like he's worried I'll say no.

"I'd really like that." I'm a little wobbly when I slide off my chair, so we stop at the bar so I can chug a glass of water before I find my parents. My mom seems happy about my sudden date with Miller, and my dad seems like...well...my dad. I'm pretty sure he's been eating weed cookies all night.

We leave the busy bar, hop in an Uber, and end up at an all-night diner. They even have warm oatmeal raisin cookies with ice cream. Miller orders an unreal amount of food to share. I sip an herbal tea while he drinks a chocolate milkshake. He takes off his suit jacket and unbuttons his cuffs, rolling his sleeves up to expose muscular forearms.

"How old were you when you knew you wanted to be a hockey player?" I drag a bite of warm cookie through the melting ice cream.

"Hmm." He taps his chin. "I could skate almost as soon as I could walk. But I think I was three when my dad built our first backyard rink."

"We always had one, too." I smile at the memory of my brother doing pirouettes while aiming shots on net. He figure skated before he played hockey. "Did Violet play hockey with you?"

Miller laughs, and it's a musical sound. "Violet can barely walk across a flat surface without hurting herself. I don't think she's ever put on a pair of skates. Not willingly, anyway. Vi's my stepsister. Her mom and my dad met when we were teenagers."

"Oh, I didn't realize that."

"We get along great. Most of the time. What about you? Did you play hockey with Alex?"

"Mostly I liked skating just to skate."

"What else do you like to do, Sunny Sunshine?"

"I like the outdoors, swimming, hiking. Being in nature grounds me. I have two dogs, so I take them to the park a lot. And I teach yoga. Oh, and I like to bake! I also volunteer a lot. I'm in college for nonprofit management." I roll my eyes. "I sound like I'm reciting my resume."

"It's an impressive resume. Where do you volunteer?"

"An animal shelter, and I help run a subsidized after-school program a couple of days a week."

His smile is soft and warm. "You're pretty amazing."

I point my spoon at him, more of those butterflies loose in

my stomach. "Is that another line?"

"Nope. It's still the truth." He tips his head. "Do you believe in things like fate?"

I throw the question back at him. "Do you?"

"Until tonight, no."

I give him a look.

"Seriously." He laces our fingers together. It sends another warm jolt through me. "Do you feel that?"

"Feel what?"

"I don't know how to explain it. It's like someone just poured warm chocolate sauce all over my feelings. And like... there's this energy that makes me want to be close to you. I probably sound like a loon."

"No you don't." I squeeze his hand. "And yes, I believe in fate."

"Good. Me, too. As of the moment I met you." He kisses the back of my hand. "Tell me what it was like to grow up with a brother like Alex."

"He was always destined for greatness. His presence filled the room. He's also the biggest nerd in the universe. He used to challenge me to Scrabble tournaments all the time, which was the worst because I'm a terrible speller."

"I feel this on a soul-deep level. My spelling is atrocious. I rely heavily on autocorrect, and it often does me dirty."

"This!" I agree. "But having Alex as a brother has always taught me to reach for the stars, and that it's okay if mine isn't as flashy as his. I just want to do good things and help people who need it."

"Yeah, you do." His smile is full of warmth that makes my heart flutter.

"Do you know what you want to do after hockey?" I ask.

"I sure do. I volunteer at hockey camp every summer, and

one day I want to run my own program. But I want to make sure that kids who come from families with financial struggles can play, too."

"Hockey is expensive."

"It is."

We talk for hours. About everything from my dogs, Titan and Andy, to our favorite vacation destinations and our favorite movies. I feel like I've known Miller my entire life.

At the end of the night, we exchange numbers.

He laces our fingers. "What are you doing tomorrow?"

"I don't have plans."

"Can I see you again?"

"I'd like that."

"I'll call you in the morning." He closes one eye. "Or later in the morning. Much later. At least eight and a half hours from now."

I grin. "That sounds great."

"Would it be okay if I kissed you?"

"I would like that very much."

He lifts his hand and strokes my cheek. It makes every nerve ending in my body come alive. I tip my chin up, and he drops his head, lips brushing over mine. The next press is soft and sweet. I curve a hand around the back of his neck, and he wraps one around my waist. We angle our heads at the same time, lips parting. He tastes like chocolate and mint. Warmth floods my body as our tongues meet.

Miller's arm tightens around me, and his other hand slides into my hair, gently cupping the back of my head. I press closer as I sink into the kiss, into the way he holds me like I'm precious, into the glorious warmth humming beneath my skin. It's the sweetest, most incredible kiss of my entire life. I never want it to end. But eventually Miller pulls back. And then comes in for another long, bone-melting kiss.

He rests his forehead against mine. "Why does breathing have to be so necessary?"

I laugh. "We can do more of that tomorrow."

"A hundred percent yes. We can and we definitely should." He presses his lips to mine one last time, then takes my hands and peppers those with kisses, too, before he lets them go and steps back. "I can't wait to see you again, Sunny Sunshine. I hope you have the sweetest dreams. I know I will."

Tomorrow can't come soon enough.

Author's Note

I decided to add this note because of a conversation I had with a small group of readers at Book Bonanza in Dallas of 2019. We were talking about the Pucked Series and the conversation shifted to this book, and Miller and Sunny's story. If you've read *Pucked* then you'll know that Miller has a bit of a reputation and that Sunny is Alex Waters' younger sister, who he happens to be highly protective of (as a good older brother is).

While we were discussing Sunny and Miller's relationship I mentioned that both Sunny and Miller have learning exceptionalities (or learning disabilities, but I prefer the term exceptionality as it's more widely used in education) which received an "ooooooh" reaction. It hadn't occurred to me that readers might not realize this, but once I explained what I meant, suddenly all the puzzle pieces fell into place. So I felt this author's note might help frame Sunny and Miller's very sweet connection.

I grew up with a sibling with a learning exceptionality, and my first career was working with individuals with unique learning profiles, so it's always been part of my life.

Speech-to-text and audio messaging (and audiobooks, which I'm eternally grateful for) have come a long way since I wrote this book nearly a decade ago. While these exceptionalities are not the focus of the story, I thought it might help frame some of Sunny and Miller's interactions and how they handle situations.

~Helena

Acknowledgments

Husband of mine, you really are the best. I couldn't do any of this without you. Thank you for giving me a chance to do this thing. I love you.

Debra, you're the pepper to my salt. Even the hardest parts are easier with you around.

Kimberly, you are made of awesome. I'm so glad you had lunch with Nina and the stars aligned. This has been an incredible journey so far, thank you for being a source of encouragement, for the feedback, for the brainstorming and for making this roller coaster so much fun to ride.

Nina, I don't know how you do it, but I'm grateful that you do. Thank you for years of friendship and putting up with my neurotic squirreliness.

Shalu, you have so much talent. I can't wait to see you shine. Thank you for making the outsides reflect the insides.

Jessica, I always know I'm in good hands with you. Thank you for all your patience, even when I kept on changing things at the end. Marla, thank you for cleaning up the crumbs and the typos. Mayhem, so many texts in this one! You make amazing innards!

To the originals who have been with me from the beginning, I'm here because of you.

*Don't miss the exciting new books
Entangled has to offer.*

Follow us!

@EntangledPublishing

@Entangled_Publishing

@EntangledPub

AMARA
an imprint of Entangled Publishing LLC